THE
SIXTH
MAN

ALSO BY JOHN FEINSTEIN

THE TRIPLE THREAT

The Walk On
The Sixth Man
The DH

THE SPORTS BEAT

Last Shot: Mystery at the Final Four
Vanishing Act: Mystery at the U.S. Open
Cover-Up: Mystery at the Super Bowl
Change-Up: Mystery at the World Series
The Rivalry: Mystery at the Army-Navy Game
Rush for the Gold: Mystery at the Olympics

Foul Trouble

THE SIXTH MAN

THE TRIPLE THREAT • BOOK 2

JOHN FEINSTEIN

A YEARLING BOOK

Text copyright © 2015 by John Feinstein
Cover photograph copyright © 2015 by Shutterstock
Photograph of basketball copyright © 2015 by Shutterstock

All rights reserved. Published in the United States by Yearling, an imprint of Random House Children's Books, a division of Penguin Random House LLC, New York. Originally published in hardcover in the United States by Alfred A. Knopf, an imprint of Random House Children's Books, New York, in 2015.

Yearling and the jumping horse design are registered trademarks of Penguin Random House LLC.

Visit us on the Web! randomhousekids.com

Educators and librarians, for a variety of teaching tools, visit us at RHTeachersLibrarians.com

The Library of Congress has cataloged the hardcover edition of this work as follows:
Feinstein, John.
The sixth man / John Feinstein. — First edition.
p.   cm. — (The triple threat ; book 2)
Summary: New kid Max Bellotti has the talent to lead the Lions basketball team straight to victory, but Max also has a secret that could disrupt their winning streak once it's exposed.
ISBN 978-0-385-75350-0 (trade) — ISBN 978-0-385-75351-7 (lib. bdg.) — ISBN 978-0-385-75352-4 (ebook)
[1. Basketball—Fiction. 2. Coaches—Fiction. 3. Secrets—Fiction. 4. High schools—Fiction. 5. Schools—Fiction.] I. Title.
PZ7.F3343Six 2015
[Fic]—dc23
2014045357

ISBN 978-0-385-75353-1 (pbk.)

Printed in the United States of America
10 9 8 7 6 5
First Yearling Edition 2016

THIS IS FOR NEIL OXMAN—
UNDERRATED AS A BAG TOTER,
NEVER UNDERRATED AS A FRIEND

THE SIXTH MAN

PROLOGUE

Alex Myers couldn't believe how cold the ground was. He hadn't noticed it all night, but now, as the finality hit him, he felt himself shivering in the frigid November air.

"Hey, man, great game."

Alex looked up from his prone position and saw one of Beaver Falls High School's massive defensive linemen leaning down, hand outstretched to help him up. He hadn't seen where his last pass of the season had gone, but he knew it hadn't connected. He could see the Beaver Falls players celebrating and his teammates standing around the field, staring into space or kneeling on the turf, hoping the scoreboard would change if they avoided looking at it.

But Alex looked, taking in the reality that Chester Heights High School's dream of a state football championship had just died.

BEAVER FALLS: 28, CHESTER HGHTS: 24.

Alex and his teammates had come through in every do-or-die situation all season.

True to form, in the final minutes of this game they had driven the ball down the field, reaching the 13-yard line with four seconds left, giving them time for one more play.

There was complete calm in the huddle as Alex's best friend, Jonas Ellington—who was also the Lions' best wide receiver—brought in the play from the bench. It was exactly the play Alex would have called: all-stop.

There would be four receivers in the pattern. All would run straight into the end zone, strung out as far apart as possible, and then curl back to the goal line. Alex's job was to find the first open target and get the ball to him.

"I gotta have time, guys," Alex had said as he called the play.

"You'll have it, Goldie," center Steve Allison said, calling Alex by his nickname—as in "Golden Arm."

"On three," Alex said, and they came to the line. Alex had a vague sense that all thirty-five thousand people inside Heinz Field—the home of the Pittsburgh Steelers—were screaming, but he felt as if he were playing inside a cone of silence.

"Blue!" he barked. It didn't matter what he said; his teammates knew the ball would be snapped on the third word he uttered. "Gold!" He paused a split second and then yelled, "Omaha!" It was his personal tribute to Peyton Manning, who had adopted the name of the Nebraska city as his signature snap call.

The ball had come back into his hands, delivered right where he wanted it from Allison's shotgun snap. He retreated quickly, looking at all four receivers, but focused on Jonas, who was always a beat quicker than everyone else getting downfield. Sure enough, he saw him plant his foot about three yards into the end zone and spin back in the direction of the goal line.

Alex knew—*knew*—at that moment that they were going to make the play. But as he stepped up to throw, he sensed someone bearing down on him from the left side. He had to take a quick step to his right to avoid the rusher, and as the ball came out of his hands, he realized he hadn't gotten everything behind the throw because of it. The Beaver Falls lineman piled into him just as he released the ball, and they went down in a heap together.

The season was over. And it didn't have a happy ending.

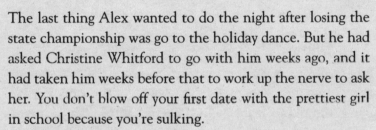

The last thing Alex wanted to do the night after losing the state championship was go to the holiday dance. But he had asked Christine Whitford to go with him weeks ago, and it had taken him weeks before that to work up the nerve to ask her. You don't blow off your first date with the prettiest girl in school because you're sulking.

"It'll be good for you," his mom insisted when he came downstairs, feeling goofy in the blue blazer, white shirt, red tie, and khaki pants she had laid out for him. "You look very handsome."

If being with Christine didn't take his mind off the game, nothing would. She had texted him that afternoon to make sure he still wanted to go. *Of course!* he'd texted back, even though moping had become his favorite sport at that point.

Christine was waiting for him in the lobby just outside the gym, where the dance was being held. They had agreed to meet at school—the better, Alex thought, to avoid awkward parental hovering. Life would be much simpler in two years when he had a driver's license.

She looked spectacular in a black dress and low black heels. She smiled when he walked in—the smile he'd seen the first day of school in French class. Entire rooms, entire *towns*, lit up when Christine Whitford smiled.

"You clean up very nicely," she said. "I'm impressed."

"You mean surprised," he answered.

"That too," she said, taking his arm.

He realized as they walked in that he had forgotten to compliment her.

"Um, you look really good too," he said. "I mean, better than good . . . Just, um, wow."

Oh God, if only this were as easy as football.

She laughed. "Thanks, Alex—I get it."

He took a deep breath. He appreciated the fact that she was trying to make it easy for him—and that she hadn't brought up the game. Since she worked for the school newspaper, the *Weekly Roar*, she had been in Pittsburgh the night before too. He was about to ask her how the trip home had gone when, as the police would say, the trouble began.

"Hey, Myers, nice try. Too bad," came one voice.

Then another: "Don't feel bad, Alex; there's always next year!"

And: "What happened on the last play? Sooo close."

They were surrounded before Alex could even ask Christine if she wanted something to drink. Earlier in the year, when he was the new kid in school and surgically attached to the bench as the third-string quarterback, he would have adored the attention. Now he wanted to run and hide.

He looked up and thought he saw the cavalry coming in the form of Matt Gordon—who had been the starting quarterback and team captain until he had admitted to taking steroids just prior to the championship game. He'd been a good friend to Alex, though. A mentor and a supporter even though they both wanted the same spot on the team.

Now here he was, coming to Alex's rescue as he had done so often in the past.

"Hey, Goldie," he said. "You look busy. Mind if I dance with your date so she doesn't get bored?"

Maybe, Alex thought, he was joking. Or maybe Christine would say no thanks.

No such luck.

"Do you mind, Alex?" she said. She leaned up and whispered in his ear, "I'll be back by the time you get rid of all your fans."

She was gone an instant later, leaving Alex with all his fans. He'd never felt more alone in his life.

■ ■ ■

It wasn't until Sunday morning that Alex saw what had happened on the last play on Friday night. He was up early after a semi-sleepless night. He'd gotten to dance with Christine exactly *once*. As soon as other guys saw her with Matt, they had practically lined up to dance with her. She hadn't seemed to mind the attention.

Alex fast-forwarded through the recording of the game

until he reached the final minute and heard the breathless voice of the play-by-play announcer:

"The Pennsylvania state championship comes down to one final play! Myers is in the shotgun. He drops—Nichols almost has him! He dodges right and throws . . . ! There's Ellington in the end zone . . . ! No—no! Knocked away by Kendrick Martin for Beaver Falls! It looked like the pass was there, but Martin got his hand on it at the last possible second!

"Beaver Falls wins! Beaver Falls is the state champion!"

Alex hit the mute button. He couldn't bear to hear another word, although he did watch the Beaver Falls players celebrating. There was a brief shot of the lineman helping him up and his teammates coming to console him.

They showed a replay, and Alex could see that he'd thrown a good pass—pretty close to perfect—but the Beaver Falls defender had made a great diving play to get his hand on the ball. They had missed being state champions by about two inches.

He clicked the TV off just as his mother walked into the room.

"You watched it?" she said.

"Twice," Alex said. "I needed to throw the ball about two inches more to the left."

"But you couldn't have known that. . . ."

Alex held up his hand. "I know, Mom. I'm not beating myself up. It was a tough play and I just didn't quite pull it off."

"Next year," his mom said.

Alex smiled. He'd heard that at least a hundred times the

previous night. Next year was a long way off, and the team would be in upheaval. Several key seniors were graduating, and he wondered if Matt Gordon would be allowed to play after the steroid thing. Plus, there would be a new coaching staff. Matt's father, who had been the head coach, was forced to resign after trying to cover up his son's use of steroids by making it seem like *Alex* was the one using PEDs. It had been a mess. It would continue to be a mess.

"We'll see," Alex finally said in response to his mother. "Things will be a lot different."

"They'll be better," his mom said, putting her hands on her hips in her *I'm right, don't argue with me* pose. "At least you can rest a little bit now."

Alex shook his head. "Not exactly," he said. "I start basketball tomorrow."

Basketball practice had started during the football playoffs, so Alex and Jonas were two weeks behind. But Tom Hillier, the interim head football coach, had pled their case with the basketball coach and had set up a meeting for them at the hideous time of 7:00 a.m. Monday morning.

Alex dragged into the gym, at 6:55. There were still remnants from the dance—extra chairs, strings of lights, and the podium where the band had been. Alex shuddered, and not just because of the cold, dark December morning.

The basketball offices were located right off the gym floor. Unlike the football offices, which were new and spacious, the basketball offices were dingy and cramped. There were two of them: one that said HEAD COACH and one across the narrow hallway that said ASSISTANTS.

Alex found Jonas standing in the hallway—there was no

place to sit—leaning against the wall. Apparently Coach Archer hadn't arrived yet.

"Thought you were going to be late, Goldie," Jonas said sleepily. "It's 6:59."

"So I'm a minute early," Alex said. "No coach?"

Jonas yawned and shook his head.

Jonas was a little taller than Alex, about six two, and had the wiry build of a wide receiver, which was what he had been all fall. Alex had played enough pickup basketball with him to know he was a very good shooter. Those long arms would serve him well.

Alex wasn't the natural in basketball that he was in football. His "golden arm" wouldn't do him much good on a basketball court. But his junior high coach back in Massachusetts had said he had a lot of court sense as a point guard, and Alex was hoping to move up to varsity here. Chester Heights had won only seven basketball games last year—clearly they could use some help.

He and Jonas waited in silence. Alex kept checking his watch. First period was seven-thirty and they still had to go to their lockers and make their way through the crowded hallways to get to class. If Coach Archer didn't arrive soon, there wouldn't be very much time to talk.

Evan Archer was new at Chester Heights. According to what Alex had read, he was thirty-six years old and had been hired from Bishop O'Connell High School in Arlington, Virginia, where he'd been an assistant coach for seven years.

The school's website described Archer this way: "A fiery competitor throughout his playing days at Virginia Tech, he led the Hokies to postseason play in both his junior and senior years."

Alex had looked up Archer's college statistics. Apparently he had "led" the Hokies from the bench, because he had averaged four minutes per game as a senior and had scored a total of twenty-nine points in thirty-three games. Still, Alex thought playing for a coach who had gone to school in the ACC, one of *the* college basketball conferences, would be cool.

Jonas moved away from the wall he had been leaning on. There was a window that looked out on the gym floor, so he must have seen someone coming.

"About time," Jonas mumbled, a moment before the door opened.

If Coach Archer felt any guilt about being late, he didn't show it.

"Come on in here," he said, unlocking the door to his office without so much as a hello, a good morning, or a thanks for coming in early.

Two chairs sat opposite Coach Archer's desk. He gestured for Alex and Jonas to sit down.

"This won't take long," he said. "I know you guys have to get to class."

Good, Alex thought, he's at least aware of the fact that we're expected to go to school.

"So. We've been practicing for two weeks and our first game, as you probably know, is Friday night," he said. "I'm not inclined to disrupt the progress we've made by bringing two new guys in a few days before the opener.

"I know you couldn't make tryouts or practice because

you were playing football. And I know you were both team stars, but basketball's a different game. So, here's what I can do. I'll put you with the JVs, who don't start practice until tomorrow. That way we'll get to see what you can or can't do and you won't interfere with our game prep for Wilmington North."

Alex glanced quickly at Jonas to see his reaction to this. His face gave away nothing.

"You guys okay with that?" Coach Archer asked when neither Alex nor Jonas said anything. "If not, you can just be football heroes all winter and we'll call it no harm, no foul."

"I'm okay with the JVs, Coach," Jonas said. "As long as we'll get a chance to prove we can help the team."

Coach Archer raised an eyebrow, then leaned forward and pointed a finger at Jonas. "*Anyone* who gives us a chance to win will be given a chance, Ellington. Including football heroes."

Clearly, he had some kind of thing against football players. Alex was beginning to wonder if all high school coaches in all sports had to prove they were the boss by making it clear you had no power whatsoever.

"Coach, I'm fine with it too," he said, becoming aware that both Jonas and Coach Archer were waiting for him to say something.

"Good," Coach Archer said, standing up to indicate the meeting was over. "The JVs practice at 6:00 a.m. because both the boys' and girls' varsity teams have the court after school. Be here at 5:45 tomorrow and report to Coach Birdy. He'll be expecting you."

Alex's head was spinning. To get here at 5:45 he'd have

to be up by 5:00 and out of the house on his bike—in the cold—by 5:20. He couldn't ask his mom to get up that early to drive him. If Jonas was thinking the same thing, he didn't show it.

"We'll be here, Coach," Jonas said, suddenly becoming the spokesman for both of them. "Thanks for the opportunity."

They shook hands and turned to go, Jonas practically pushing Alex through the door. Once they were away from the gym and heading to their lockers, Alex exploded.

"What is his problem?! The JVs—at 6:00 a.m.? Football heroes?! He's worse than Coach Gordon, and I didn't think that was possible!"

"Easy there, big fella," Jonas said, smiling—which made Alex even angrier. "We won't be on the JVs very long. The guy wants to win, right? You've played pickup with Gormley and Holder, right?"

"So?"

"They're the two best players on varsity. They better than us?"

"Not Gormley. Holder's good. But he's not a guard."

"Exactly. Coach's gonna need us, and he knows it. He's just trying to be a tough guy. I'll bet you our next trip to Stark's that we both play Friday night."

"Deal," Alex said. "But if you're wrong, I'm ordering a second burger—*and* fries."

■ ■ ■

At lunch that day, Alex began to think he might lose his bet to Jonas.

He and Jonas were sitting at their usual table with Christine. Christine had sent him a text Sunday night saying she'd had a good time on Saturday. Alex resisted the urge to ask if she'd sent the same text to all the guys she'd danced with. He simply replied *Me too*—and then wanted to kick himself the minute he'd hit send. Was that the best he could do?

Alex and Jonas were filling Christine in on their meeting with Coach Archer when Matt Gordon, carrying a vanilla milk shake, walked over and sat down.

"When did you start drinking milk shakes?" Alex asked.

"I'm not an athlete anymore," Matt said. "Might as well enjoy myself."

Matt had been suspended by the Pennsylvania High School Athletic Association from participating in any varsity sports for the rest of the school year.

"You'll be an athlete again; you know that," Alex said. "Come on."

Gordon grinned. He was one of those guys who was impossible not to like. He was funny, self-deprecating, and a natural leader. Alex thought of the line he'd heard his dad use to describe Patriots quarterback Tom Brady: "Girls want to be with him; guys want to be like him."

And then he couldn't help but think of Matt dancing with Christine. . . .

"For now, I'm happy to be a non-athlete," Matt said. "If I never see a weight room again, it'll be fine by me."

They were quiet for a moment. Matt changed the subject. "So, you guys ready to start hoops practice this afternoon?"

"Ha," Alex laughed. "Not exactly."

He filled Matt in on their meeting with Coach Archer.

Matt was shaking his head and laughing by the time he was finished.

"I give it a day for you to get with the varsity," he said. "Two, because he's new and still trying to prove he's in charge."

"You sure?" Alex said. Jonas was grinning like a cat that had just swallowed a canary.

"Have you *seen* who's on our team?" Matt said. "Goldie, I've never played with either of you guys, but I *know* you're better than what we've got. We won seven games last year. The good news is that nobody on the team graduated."

He paused. "That's also the bad news."

They all laughed.

"So you think we'll play Friday night?" Alex asked.

"Bet on it," Matt said.

Alex shrugged. "I already did," he said, glancing at Jonas, who had apparently just swallowed a second canary.

At first Alex thought he was dreaming that his alarm was going off. After all, he'd only been in bed for a few minutes, so he must have been dreaming.

But the buzzing sound persisted, so he opened his eyes and looked at the clock next to the bed. It read 5:00 a.m. Then it came back to him. He had to get to JV basketball practice.

He groaned, pulled himself up in bed, and wondered if he had time for a shower. Nope. He groaned again and got up. Twenty-five minutes later, having had a quick bowl of cereal and a hot chocolate, he was on his bike and on his way to school.

It was still pitch-dark, and he was wearing a glow-in-the-dark orange jacket and a white helmet. Alex had checked on his computer before leaving and had learned that the current Philadelphia temperature was seventeen degrees but that it felt like six degrees with the windchill. Whichever, it was unbelievably cold.

It was 5:42 when he chained his bike outside the back entrance to the gym. As he did, a car pulled up, and Jonas jumped out with a big smile on his face.

"You got a ride from your mom?" Alex said. "Cushy."

"She insisted," Jonas said, shrugging. "She has to be at work at seven, so she's usually up by five-thirty anyway."

Alex's mom was working part-time as a substitute teacher but usually in the junior high, which didn't start until quarter after eight.

They walked in the back door and headed for the basketball offices. They found a young African American man, maybe twenty-five or thirty, waiting for them.

"Right on time," he said, smiling. "I told Coach Archer that any player who shows up on time for a 5:45 meeting is someone we want on our team. I don't think I've met either of you, but I know who you are. I'm Alan Birdy. I work in the counseling office, but I'm also helping out Coach Archer this season since I've got some basketball experience."

"Where'd you play?" Jonas asked.

Coach Birdy grimaced. "I played high school ball across town at Chester, but please don't hold that against me. Then I played a little at Drexel."

Alex wondered if Coach Birdy had "led" Drexel the way Coach Archer had led Virginia Tech.

"I like Bruiser Flint," Alex said, thinking of the always-wound-up Drexel coach. "But I think he might be a little bit crazy."

Coach Birdy smiled. "Oh no, he's not a little bit crazy. He's a *lot* crazy. But I loved playing for him."

They all laughed. Alex liked Coach Birdy right away—almost as much as he had disliked Coach Archer.

"Follow me," Coach Birdy said. "Let's get you some practice gear."

The door opened and several kids Alex recognized from pickup games came in.

"You got twelve minutes, guys," Coach Birdy yelled at them. "Most of the others are already in the locker room. You better hustle."

Alex and Jonas followed Coach Birdy, who had now picked up his own pace, in the direction of the locker room.

■ ■ ■

As it turned out, there wasn't that much to be briefed on.

"We had three days of tryouts," Coach Birdy said. "We worked on defense, the two-three zone. Offense is just as basic: pick-and-roll stuff. Big guys come out to set screens, and little guys shoot off the screens or look to pass inside. You two know how to do that?"

They nodded as he was handing them red shorts and red practice shirts that said CHESTER HEIGHTS on the front and WINNING IS AN ATTITUDE on the back, right above the number.

"What does 'winning is an attitude' mean?" Jonas asked.

"That was John Chaney's slogan when he coached at Temple, and I always liked it. Big Temple fan."

"But you went to Drexel," Alex said.

Coach Birdy shrugged. "They offered me a scholarship," he said. "Temple didn't."

Alex and Jonas changed and walked onto the court just before six, where they found twelve other players warming up. Alex recognized most of them—all freshmen and sophomores. He guessed there wasn't much point sticking around if you were still on the JV team as a junior. Alex grabbed a ball and managed about a half-dozen warm-up shots before the whistle blew and they all moved to the center-court circle to meet Coach Birdy.

"Okay, fellas, thanks for showing up so early," he said. "To be honest, this is the only time we can get the gym, so if you want to play, you'll have to get used to it."

Everyone nodded—sleepily, Alex thought.

"We have two guys here who didn't participate in tryouts. I'm sure most of you know Myers and Ellington." He pointed first at Alex and then at Jonas. "They have a semi-legitimate excuse for missing tryouts—they were trying to win a state championship in football."

There were a few laughs at that. Coach Birdy continued: "Okay, so we'll start with some stretching, then we'll run, and then do some five on five. I'll work the new guys in along the way."

Twenty minutes later, Alex and Jonas stood and watched as Coach Birdy told five guys to turn their T-shirts inside out so they would be white, while five other guys continued to wear red.

"You guys both put on white," he said quietly as he lined the players up to begin a five-on-five drill.

Coach Birdy matched the two biggest guys—Richie Corman, who was about six eight, and Trey Coleman, who was a couple inches shorter—against one another. Neither could catch a pass, much less score. Alex focused on the two guys playing point guard: Ricky Lorenz and Frank West. Lorenz seemed to have a decent jump shot. West handled the ball well and had some quickness, but he didn't look to shoot the ball at all.

Ten minutes in, Coach Birdy turned to Alex and Jonas. "Myers, go get Lorenz. Ellington, you get Thompson."

Alex wasn't sure who Thompson was, but a reed-thin kid jogged off the court as Alex and Jonas came in.

"Red ball," Coach Birdy said.

The red team had a new point guard whom Alex didn't know. Coach Birdy handed him the ball, and he took a few dribbles toward the top of the key, glanced to his left—where Jonas was in the passing lane—and then glanced right, in Alex's direction. Alex stayed back, giving him room. As soon as the point guard turned to pass to the wing, Alex jumped into the passing lane and intercepted the ball. Before the point guard had a chance to stop him, he was gone, down the court for an easy layup.

As he banked the ball in, Alex remembered a quote he had once read from the great coach Bob Knight: "The best play in basketball is one on zero. If you have two on zero, someone might be tempted to pass and mess the whole thing up."

The whistle blew. Coach Birdy, hands on hips, was walking in the direction of the point guard.

"T. J., you just learned lesson one of playing the point," he said.

Coach Birdy turned and looked at everyone else. "What is lesson one of playing the point?"

There was a second of silence and then Jonas answered: "Don't telegraph your pass."

"Exactly," Coach Birdy said. "You have to look off the defender. It's like a quarterback in football—right, Myers? You never just throw the ball to someone. You look one way, then throw the other. Got it?

"Good play, Myers," he added. "White ball."

He flipped the ball to Alex. A couple seconds later, after making a ball fake as if to pass to Jonas, Alex slipped between two noticeably slow defenders for another easy layup.

Coach Birdy blew the whistle again for another lecture on basics: stop the basketball first and foremost. The defenders had let Alex's fake take their focus away from stopping him en route to the basket.

On the next play, Alex passed to Jonas, who swished a quick three-pointer.

Lorenz came back in to play point for the red team soon after that, and its offense ran better. There were no more easy steals, and the reds' defense picked up. Still, Alex felt as if he and Jonas were the two best players on the court.

With the digital clock in the corner of the gym showing 6:53, Coach Birdy said, "Okay, guys, we're going to play full court for five minutes, running clock. Winners shower, losers run. Start with the ten on the court; I'll sub you other four in."

He flipped the ball to Alex. "White ball. You can inbound from midcourt."

Alex did as instructed. Richie Corman, who had been

able to make a couple of baskets in the half-court drill off passes from Alex, took the inbounds and gave the ball back to Alex. They moved into their offense. Alex found Jonas in the corner. Jonas shot-faked, got around his man, and had an open lane to the basket. But as one of the outside defenders tried to drop down to stop him, he flipped the ball to Alex wide-open at the three-point line.

Alex stepped right into his shooting motion, the same one he had practiced with his dad in the driveway in Boston hundreds of times. The ball swished, and Alex began to backpedal on defense. Seeing that T. J. wasn't paying much attention as he inbounded, Alex stopped, sprinted forward, and easily stole the pass for a quick layup and a 5–0 lead.

"Wake up, Johnstone!" Coach Birdy barked. T. J. came out again, replaced by West. With West and Lorenz playing together for the reds, they were able to make the mini-game competitive.

With the whites up 12–7, Alex dropped back on defense and saw the clock was under a minute. As Alex set up in his spot in the zone, he noticed someone standing at the far end of the court, leaning against the wall with his arms crossed.

Coach Archer.

"Nice of you to come," he murmured, and got into position, looking for his next chance to make a play.

■ ■ ■

The final score of the mini-game was 17–11. Alex had eight of the white team's points, and Jonas had six. As Coach Birdy gathered everyone at the center jump circle, Alex noticed that Coach Archer was gone.

"Good first day, guys," he said. "You all worked hard. Whites, hit the showers. Reds, you've got some suicides to do with me before you go. See you all here at six tomorrow. Myers, Ellington, hang on one second before you go."

He told the reds to run two suicides. The seven kids lined up. Coach Birdy blew his whistle and they took off. No one was running that hard. If Coach Birdy minded, he didn't show it.

He turned to Alex and Jonas.

"You two are clearly playing a level above these other guys," he said. "Coach Archer was here for a while, so I'm sure he knows already, but I'm going to recommend you both be at varsity practice this afternoon. You think you can handle a second practice in one day?"

"Yes sir!" they both said.

"I'll send you a text to make it official," he said. "So sneak a look at your phones in between classes. Now hit the showers."

They did, both grinning from ear to ear.

"That wasn't so bad after all," Jonas said as they quickly dressed to make first period on time.

"Coach Birdy seems like a good guy," Alex said as they hustled out the door.

"Just think—if the other assistant is a good guy too, we'll have a majority," Jonas said. "Two good guys, one bad guy."

"Let's give Coach Archer a chance," Alex said. "Maybe we judged him too quickly."

He felt energized as he headed to class. It was, he knew, the adrenaline of success.

Alex, Jonas, Christine, and Matt were halfway through lunch when Alex's and Jonas's phones began buzzing at the same moment.

Alex was just starting to read his when he heard Jonas say, "You gotta be kidding."

The text was from Coach Birdy: *Sorry, guys. I spoke too soon. Coach wants to keep things as they are for now. See you tomorrow morning.*

"What is it?" Christine asked.

In response, they each showed her their phones.

"I'm *not* playing JV," Alex said. "For one thing, there's no one, and I mean *no one*, on that team who can play."

"The two guards aren't bad," Jonas said.

"And Jonas is pretty good too, right?" Christine said helpfully, causing Alex to give her a look.

"Take it easy, Goldie," Matt said. "I talked to Steve Holder in math class. He says he thinks Archer wants to give the older guys a shot to play. He thinks we should win pretty easily on Friday, since Wilmington North is pretty bad. It will give them some confidence."

"Wilmington North is worse than us?" Christine asked.

"We're not *that* bad," Matt said. "But we'll lose to Mercer next week without some help."

Alex had played against Mercer in the opening game of the football season. Sort of. He had come in to kneel down on the final two plays of the game, with the score 77–0, and been knocked cold by a Mercer player who was angry that Coach Gordon had run up the score. The kid had called the next day to apologize and mentioned that Mercer was considerably better in basketball than it was in football.

"Well, if you don't get switched, I'll be doing a story on it for the *Weekly Roar*," Christine said.

"You might be accused of bias on that one, Christine," Matt teased.

Christine actually reddened a little, which Alex took as a good sign. "Why, because I went to one dance with Alex?" she said. "Anyway, do you think I'd have much trouble getting players on the varsity *and* the JV to tell me Alex and Jonas should be on the varsity if that's the truth?"

Alex was pretty sure Christine could get any boy in the school to tell her almost anything. Partly because she was beautiful. But also because she was a really good reporter. Her father was a newspaper editor and had been a reporter for a long time. Christine wanted to follow in his footsteps, and she seemed well on her way.

"I'd hold your fire, Christine," Matt said, finishing off what Alex assumed was his now-daily milk shake. "Coach Archer will probably make them get up at sunrise for the rest of the week and then put them on varsity next week when he really needs them."

"Up at sunrise?" Jonas said. "Matty, we were *in* the gym before sunrise. Heck, we were done practicing before sunrise!"

"You get my point," Matt said.

"Did Holder say anything about what Archer's been like in practice so far?" Alex asked. "Do the guys like him?"

"Did the guys like my father?" Matt said.

"Not so much," Jonas said.

"It isn't a coach's job to be everybody's friend. Give him a chance."

"Okay," Alex said. "He's got one chance left. Three strikes and he's out."

■ ■ ■

Alex wasn't sure what was worse, getting up at 5:00 a.m. or doing so to go to a practice where neither he nor Jonas felt terribly challenged. Coach Birdy did his best to keep things interesting, putting them on opposite teams a lot of the time to even things up, but that was kind of self-defeating because when the games began Alex and Jonas would be playing together.

Each morning, Coach Archer would walk into the gym at about 6:45 carrying his coffee and pause to watch for a few minutes. Then he would disappear into his office. He never said anything to Alex or Jonas. Coach Birdy could tell they were frustrated. After practice on Thursday he asked them to stay a minute.

"I just want you to know that Coach Archer is fully aware of what you guys can do for the varsity," he said. "He's seen it in here, and I've told him. I think he just wants the guys who have been at practice since day one to get a crack at the first game before he adds you guys. I actually think he's trying to help you out by putting you through this right now."

"Help us out?" Alex said. "How is he helping us out?"

Coach Birdy laughed. "The football coaches told me how feisty you are, Myers," he said. "It's about football. If you guys finish football season on Friday, waltz into practice on Monday, having missed the first couple weeks, and then get serious playing time in the opener—which I'm sure you would—some guys will think you're getting star treatment.

"This way," he added, "the guys know you've been coming to JV practice at 6:00 a.m. all week. No special treatment. It'll make your life easier next week."

Alex looked at Jonas to see if he was buying this.

"But will we be on the varsity next week?" Jonas asked.

"I certainly hope so," Coach Birdy said. "I certainly hope so."

■ ■ ■

The JV game started at five o'clock on Friday. There was almost no one in the gym when Alex and Jonas and the other three starters for Chester Heights walked out to begin the game against the JVs from Wilmington North. The first thing Alex noticed was that the kid jumping center for Wilmington was no taller than he was. And the kid he was lining up next to outside the jump circle was about five six. Maybe, Alex thought, he's quick and athletic.

As it turned out, neither the Wilmington point guard nor anyone else on their team was quick *or* athletic. Richie Corman was Kareem Abdul-Jabbar compared to their center, and Alex was Magic Johnson. At halftime the score was 46–8, and Alex felt a little embarrassed. He and Jonas each had eighteen points.

"Honestly, I'm not sure how they scored eight on you," Coach Birdy said at halftime. "Myers, Ellington, I'm going to let you play another couple minutes, but that'll be it. No need to humiliate these kids."

Alex was fine with that. It was 56–8 when he and Jonas came out. They had all heeded Coach Birdy and actually clamped down a little more on defense. Wilmington North had trouble completing a pass, much less making a shot. The final score, after Coach Birdy ordered the guys playing in the fourth quarter not to shoot until they had passed the ball at least six times, was 70–19. It could have been much worse.

After walking through the handshake line, Alex and Jonas were headed for the locker room when they saw Coach Archer standing just outside the door. He was dressed in a jacket and tie for the varsity game.

"Good playing, you two," he said.

Alex waited. That was it. Nothing about being at varsity practice on Monday.

"Thanks, Coach," he said, and headed inside.

He was tempted to not stick around for the varsity game, but Jonas talked him out of it. "Don't give him an excuse," he said. "Play this his way and let's see what happens."

Alex sighed—but agreed. They joined the other JV players and sat behind the bench as they had been told to do. Alex would have much preferred sitting on the other side of the gym with Christine and Matt—who, he noted, were laughing most of the game.

Matt's scouting report on Wilmington North proved accurate—not that big a surprise given how awful their JVs had been. Chester Heights won easily, though the game wasn't a rout. The final was 64–52. The lead was comfortable most of the game, but there was no doubt in Alex's mind that he and Jonas would have made a difference.

As the teams went through the postgame handshakes, Alex heard Coach Birdy calling to him and Jonas. He waved them down on the court.

"Coach wants you guys to come downstairs to the locker room," he said.

"When?" Alex asked.

"Now," Coach Birdy said. "Follow me."

Unlike the football team, which had its own locker room, the basketball players changed in the massive general locker room. There was one privilege of being a varsity basketball player, though: you got your own locker with a nameplate on it. For everyone else it was first come, first served, with signs all over the place about locks left on overnight being cut off.

Alex and Jonas followed Coach Birdy to the varsity corner, and they stood off to the side while the players sat in front of their lockers and Coach Archer stood in front of them.

"Okay, guys, let me say this: any win is a good win," he said. "You don't throw them back. But I think you all know that's probably the worst team we're going to play all season, and we didn't exactly blow them away. Mercer has four starters back from a team that won fourteen games last season— one of those against us. We won't start Sunday practices until we're playing two games a week. But we have a lot of work to do on Monday, so enjoy the weekend."

They all started to stand, but he held up a hand to indicate he wasn't finished. "I think you all know Myers and Ellington from the football team. They spent the week practicing with the JVs and played in their game tonight. I've watched them all week, and I think they've earned a place on varsity."

He turned to Alex and Jonas. "Myers, Ellington—welcome."

Alex wasn't sure if they were supposed to say or do anything other than nod, but Coach Archer answered the question for him. He turned back to the rest of the team and said, "Okay, fellas, let's get it in. Beat Mercer on three."

The players stood up and came together between the rows of lockers. Steve Holder, the captain, was in the middle. Each put a hand up and leaned in.

"Hang on," Holder said. "Myers, Ellington—get in here. You're part of the team now."

Alex and Jonas walked to the outer edges of the circle and put their hands in.

"On three," Holder said.

"One, two, three," they all said. "Beat Mercer!"

As they broke the huddle, everyone clapped Alex and Jonas on the back or offered handshakes.

Alex turned to find Coach Archer so he could thank him for the promotion.

He was nowhere in sight.

When Alex and Jonas came back up the steps to the gym floor, there were quite a few people milling around—mostly family and friends waiting for the varsity players.

Christine was there too, notebook in hand.

"So, what happened down there?" she asked, getting right to the point as she always did.

"Down where?" Alex said innocently.

She gave him a look—the one where she raised her eyebrow at him in disgust. It almost made him laugh, because it meant she was angry, frustrated, and impatient all at once.

"In the locker room," she finally said, her teeth nearly clenched.

"Oh that," he said. "We're on the team, starting Monday."

"So Matt was right."

Alex felt a twinge. He liked Matt, looked up to him even.

But Matt could date almost any girl in the school. And he chose to sit with Christine. . . .

"Yeah, Matt was right," Alex said finally. "Did it take a genius to figure it out?"

This time the look she gave him was a lot sharper. "What's with you?" she said.

"Nothing," he said. "Are you going to the party at Janie Jasper's house?"

"After I get through talking to the players," she said. "I have to write the game story for next week's paper. Everyone else is *still* writing about football."

"There *was* a lot to write about," he said.

Out of the corner of his eye he saw Coach Archer emerging from the locker room. He went to stand against a wall while a handful of reporters—maybe a quarter of the number that had come out for a football game—went to talk to him.

"Gotta go," Christine said. "I'll see you there."

"But . . . how are you getting—"

"I've got a ride," she said—and was gone, off to talk to the coach of the undefeated Chester Heights Lions.

Fine, he thought. Not going to worry about it.

Jonas walked over. "You look worried about something," he said.

"Me?" Alex said. "What would I be worried about?"

■ ■ ■

Alex and his mom had a deal on Friday nights: he could go to a party until midnight. "I know you're a big football star," she'd said when he had pleaded for an extra hour. "But you're still only fourteen."

Alex's respect for his mom had grown considerably during the crisis involving his "failed" drug test. She had more or less taken control of the situation in a way he would have thought only his father could. His father, meanwhile, had been MIA since he and his mom and his sister, Molly, had moved in late July. Alex knew his mom had his back when it counted, which didn't make the curfew less annoying, but it did keep him from giving her too much grief about it.

Happily Christine had the same midnight curfew, so they ended up walking out of the party together. Alex hadn't seen Matt all night—which was a relief.

"How about Stark's for lunch tomorrow?" she said.

"You only ask me to Stark's when you're working on a story," he said.

"Guilty," she said, giving him the smile he could never resist. "I'm going to do a sidebar on you and Jonas being called up to the varsity. I talked to Coach Archer about it."

"What'd he say?"

"I'll tell you tomorrow," she said as her mom's car pulled up. "See you at noon."

He sighed. As usual, she had the last word.

■ ■ ■

Christine was already sitting in the back booth when Alex walked into Stark's at 11:55 the next morning. Any small notion Alex might have had to try to make this their second date disappeared when he saw Jonas sitting across from her.

"You should be happy to see me," Jonas said, reading Alex's face as he sat down. "I do owe you a hamburger."

"Two," Alex said.

"Why does Jonas owe you a hamburger?" Christine asked.

"We had a bet on whether we'd play in the opening varsity game," Alex answered.

"When did you make that bet?"

"Monday, after our first meeting with Archer."

"You better get used to calling him *Coach* Archer," she said.

Alex rolled his eyes. Jonas laughed.

"She's right," he said. "And so are you. I owe you two hamburgers."

Christine had her notebook out. "You two guys ready to be the saviors again?"

"What do you mean?" Alex asked.

"You watched the varsity game Friday night, right?"

"So?" Alex wasn't ready to bite anything but a hamburger at the moment. The waitress interrupted and they ordered— Alex opting for one burger, for now.

"So was there anyone playing for us who is as good as you or Jonas?" Christine continued.

"Steve Holder's good. And Patton Gormley isn't bad either."

"Steve's an inside player. Patton's okay; you're right. But that's it. That means Archer's going to have to start you and Jonas—if not right away, pretty soon."

"You say that like it's a bad thing," Jonas said.

"Not at all. I just don't think Coach Archer wants to make that move yet."

"What makes you say that?"

"I asked him if he thought you guys would start next week against Mercer."

"What'd he say?"

"He just raised an eyebrow. So I told him I'd watched the JV game and the varsity game, and I didn't think either Wakefield or Early was nearly as good as you or Jonas."

Zane Wakefield and Tony Early were the starting guards on varsity—both seniors.

"And?"

Christine flushed. "He had the nerve to say, 'Didn't you go to the holiday dance with Myers?'"

"Busted," Jonas laughed at the same time that Alex blurted, "How did he know that?"

"He was a chaperone, remember? All the senior girls were trying to get him to dance."

Alex did remember, now that she mentioned it. Coach Archer was apparently much admired by the girls in school. He doubted the boys who played on his basketball team felt quite the same way.

"So what did you say to that?" he asked.

"I told him that had nothing to do with my ability to judge your athletic skill, and that I suspected he was trying to avoid a legitimate question."

"Hah." Jonas shook his head. "No back-off in you, is there, Christine?"

"Nope." She grinned.

"But what did he say?" asked Alex.

"He said, 'Time will tell.' Then he relented and said something that made more sense."

"Yeah?" Jonas asked.

"He said, 'If the thought even crossed my mind to sit

down a senior—any senior—in favor of a freshman, do you think I'd tell a reporter first or the players first?' "

Jonas smiled. "He's right about that."

"I know," Christine said. She looked at Alex. "Then he asked me if I thought you were a good dancer."

"What?!"

"I think he was testing my ability to be impartial where you are concerned. . . ."

Jonas started cracking up. "Oh man, that's harsh."

Alex shoved him. "Shut up, Jonas. I can dance."

"Uh-huh," he said, trying to suppress a grin. "What'd you say, Christine?"

"I told him," she said, "that Alex has a very good French accent."

"What does that have to do with my dancing?" Alex fumed, while Jonas practically fell out of his chair laughing.

Christine shook her head, trying not to laugh too.

Luckily the food arrived just then. And Alex comforted himself by thinking of the extra burger he'd be ordering so that Jonas would pay. . . .

■ ■ ■

The good news for Alex and Jonas when they arrived for practice on Monday afternoon was that they already had lockers with their names on them—the two nearest the shower room, directly across from one another. That, however, was pretty much the end of the good news.

No one except Steve Holder, the team captain, looked up or even said hello when Alex and Jonas walked in.

"Glad to have you guys," he said. "Just so you know, the last freshman who played on the varsity was me—two years ago." He smiled.

"We just hope we can help," Alex said.

Zane Wakefield, the starting point guard—the player Alex was most likely to displace if Coach Archer changed the lineup—turned around at that moment.

"You'll help us by getting your butts into your practice gear and being on court at three-thirty. Anybody's late, we all run."

"Easy, Zane," Holder said. "It's their first day."

"You think Coach cares if it's their first day?"

"Probably not," Holder conceded. "We should all hustle."

Watching the team play Friday night, Alex had identified Zane Wakefield and Tony Early as the weakest of the five starters. Neither appeared to be a true point guard: someone capable of handling the ball in traffic, setting up the offense, and making sure the plays the coach called were being run properly. In fact, he hadn't seen anyone on the floor who looked to be point guard material. Early was a decent shooter, but he needed to be set up with an open shot—he couldn't create his own shot off the dribble. At times, Holder, who was the team's best inside player, had brought the ball up-court.

Alex and Jonas opened their lockers and were relieved to find practice gear hanging inside. There was no doubt in Alex's mind that Wakefield was right about Coach Archer not caring that it was their first day.

He and Jonas were the last two out of the locker room,

just in time to hear a sharp whistle blow. Everyone else instantly raced to the jump circle, where Coach Archer was standing. Alex and Jonas glanced at one another and then sprinted as fast as they could to join the others.

"Okay, fellas, the easy part of the season ended Friday," Coach Archer said. "I think all of you know I'm not exaggerating when I say that. Mercer's not only good, but I have a feeling they're also going to show up in a bad mood because of the way you guys"—he nodded at Alex and Jonas—"ran up the score on them in football."

Everyone snickered a little. Alex wanted to point out that if anyone had reason to be upset about Coach Gordon running up the score that night it was him, since he was the one who had been knocked cold as a result.

"Myers, Ellington, we run a lot of the same plays as the JVs, so you shouldn't have much trouble fitting in today. Watch the starters and the second team for a while and then we'll fit you in when we get a chance.

"Okay, let's stretch."

They went through their stretching with the team's other assistant coach, Scott Swanson—who was also one of the football strength coaches. Then they got into layup lines and did shell drills (running offensive sets with no defense) before moving on to more complicated offensive drills and then working on their defense—mostly zone but with some man-to-man mixed in. Neither Alex nor Jonas had seen the floor when Coach Archer blew his whistle and said, "Okay, fellas, get some water, then shoot some free throws."

Alex's throat was dry—perhaps from frustration. He

jogged in the direction of the two watercoolers and was about to pour himself some water when he heard Zane Wakefield's voice.

"Hey, Myers, what do you think you're doing?"

"Getting water?" Alex answered, a bit baffled.

"Not yet," Wakefield answered. "We get water by class. Freshmen go last."

He pushed Alex out of the way, sending his cup flying. Alex was about to say something when he heard the whistle again.

"Myers, out of the way!" Coach Archer said sharply. "You get water when I say 'freshmen,' not before then!"

"Juniors!" he yelled.

Alex stepped out of the way while Wakefield, cup of water in hand, smirked at him.

"Welcome to the varsity," Jonas whispered.

Things finally got better after Coach Archer had blown his whistle—for about the ten thousandth time, Alex thought—to end the water break.

"Ellington, Myers, take the guard spots with the whites," he said. "Red on offense. Run regular offense against man-to-man."

The red team was, most of the time, made up of the starters. The white team mostly consisted of the bench players.

"Take the point, Myers," Coach Archer said.

With pleasure, Alex thought. That meant he'd be going head to head with Zane Wakefield.

They were playing half-court with the reds on offense all the time. This was a routine drill designed to work on the first-team offense more than the second-team defense, but Alex was happy just to see the floor and have a chance.

"Mercer's going to start the game in man-to-man," Coach

Archer said, tossing a ball to Wakefield on one bounce. "We've got to be very sharp against it."

"Okay, let's go."

Wakefield took several dribbles right at Alex, then veered to his left. Seeing Alex come up to challenge him, he tried to drive past him. His dribble was too high, though, and Alex was able to slap the ball loose. Before Wakefield could turn to try to get it back, Alex tipped it toward midcourt, sprinted after it, and picked it up with nothing—and no one—between him and the basket at the far end. He took one dribble and heard the whistle—that incessant whistle. He stopped. Coach Archer was walking in his direction, hands out so Alex could toss him the ball. Which he did.

"Good play, Myers," he said. "I know you can make a layup; that's why I blew the whistle."

He turned in the direction of the other players. "Wakefield, what'd you do wrong there?"

"Get fouled?" Wakefield asked.

Coach Archer glared at him a moment. "You didn't get fouled. First, you tried to dribble past a defender rather than looking to pass to start the offense. Second, you had the ball practically on your hip, which made it easy for Myers to slap it loose. Third, you did *not* get fouled. Fourth, you gave me a wise-guy answer when you made the mistake, so you can go put on a white shirt. And, when practice is over, you owe me three suicides."

One suicide was tiring. Two were exhausting. Three were, well, suicide. Alex was hoping he wasn't smirking when he heard Coach Archer speaking to him. "Myers, take the point with the reds."

Alex was stunned. In thirty seconds Coach Archer had complimented him, climbed all over one of his starters, albeit justifiably, and had made him the starting point guard—at least for one possession.

He turned his shirt inside out so he would be wearing red instead of white and took the ball from Coach Archer when he flipped it to him.

"Just run regular," Coach Archer said. "You know the calls. Same as the JVs." And then, more softly: "You don't have to prove how good you are in one possession. Just run the offense."

Alex nodded. He wished Coach Archer had also put Jonas in red, but he figured he couldn't get everything he wanted all in the same minute.

"Screen one," he called, holding up a finger to indicate he wanted Steve Holder to come out to set a screen at the top of the key. It would then be up to the point guard—Alex—to decide what to do once he used the screen to clear some space.

Holder came out to a spot just to the right of the key. Alex dribbled patiently behind him, waiting to see what Wakefield, now playing point for the white team, would do. If Wakefield tried to get around Holder, Alex would pass the ball. If he didn't, he would shoot.

Wakefield hedged, almost lunging at Alex. For a split second, Alex was tempted to dribble past him, but he saw Holder rolling away toward the basket. Pete Taylor, the backup center, had come up on him when he set the screen, and Holder was past him in an instant. Alex picked up his dribble and found Holder, who laid the ball in just as Taylor—trying to recover too late—crashed into him.

Another whistle.

"Wakefield, how good a shooter is Myers?" Coach Archer asked.

"I have no idea, Coach. I've never seen him play."

Coach Archer nodded. "If you don't know if a guy can make a jump shot, why not make him try one?"

Alex loved the fact that Wakefield was getting lectured *again*.

"Okay, run it one more time."

They ran the exact same play. This time, Wakefield didn't go over the screen, staying behind Holder, leaving Alex open at the three-point line. Wide open, Alex took the shot and nailed it. He could almost hear Wakefield thinking, *Okay, Coach, now that I know he can shoot, what should I do* next?

Neither Wakefield nor Coach Archer commented on Alex's play. Instead, Coach Archer just said, "Okay, let's run double-high." That was a play where both inside players came to the high post and the shooting guard, Tony Early, came off a screen and made a curl cut to get open. Alex found Early, who passed up an open shot and drove the lane. This time, though, Taylor recovered and poked the ball loose from Early. It went right to Wakefield.

The ever-present whistle blew.

"Early, why do you pass up an open shot to dribble into the teeth of the defense?"

"Coach, the lane looked open."

"Was it open?"

Early hung his head.

"Guys, you have to anticipate to play basketball. You have to always see the play in front of you as a moving picture, not as a freeze-frame."

He paused. "Okay, Ellington, put on red. Early, white."

Alex's heart almost skipped a beat. He and Jonas were not only together; they were also together on the first team.

Of course that didn't mean they wouldn't have to wait their turn at the next water break.

■ ■ ■

Coach Archer spent the rest of the practice moving players around from red to white and back, using different combinations to see who worked well together. One thing was apparent to Alex: the team had four pretty good players, two not named Myers or Ellington. One was Holder, the other Patton Gormley, a forward who, Alex guessed, was about six four. Gormley was a good shooter and was quicker than anyone else playing up front—although, being honest, that was a low bar.

Jonas's presence on the red team opened things up for the offense. If Alex got the ball inside to Holder and the whites tried to double-team, Holder would pitch the ball outside to Jonas, who had a quick release when he caught the ball and a silky-smooth jump shot. If Jonas wasn't open when he caught the ball on the perimeter, he put the ball on the floor and used his quickness to get to the basket.

On one play, when Early came out to challenge him, Jonas slipped the ball to Holder, who was so wide open that he dunked the ball with such force that Alex thought it might go through the floor.

"*That's* the way to run an offense," Coach Archer said, *not* blowing his whistle for a change. "Good vision, Ellington."

Just before five-thirty, with members of the girls' team ringing the court to start their practice, Coach Archer instructed the managers to put five minutes on the scoreboard clock. He then told Alex, Jonas, Holder, Gormley, and Jameer Wilson to put on red.

The scrimmage was one-sided. The reds were better at every position than the whites. Wakefield and Early simply couldn't guard Alex and Jonas, and no one could stop Holder inside. When the clock hit one minute with the reds leading 16–2, Coach Archer blew his whistle and called everyone to the center jump circle.

"Good work today, fellas," he said. "We're still a work in progress, but today we definitely moved forward." He paused. "Myers, Ellington—good job fitting in. Wakefield, Early— these two guys are going to make you better players. Keep your heads up, because we're going to need you.

"This is a good week, guys, because we're only playing one game. Once we get into playing Tuesdays and Fridays, we won't have as much practice time. So let's get better every day.

"Okay, Steve, bring 'em in," he added.

"On three," Holder said. "Beat Mercer!"

Alex looked at Jonas as they walked to the locker room.

"Think we can?" he asked.

"If their guards are as good as Wakefield and Early, we'll be fine," Jones said, grinning.

Alex laughed.

He felt good. He and Jonas had come a long way in a week.

■ ■ ■

Practice the next few days was pretty much the same. Coach Archer kept moving Alex and Jonas back and forth between the red and the white, even though it was apparent to everyone that Wakefield and Early couldn't compete with the two freshmen.

The other players remained cool to Alex and Jonas, though less so on the court than off. It was something of a surprise when Steve Holder walked over to their table during lunch on Thursday.

"Mind if I join you guys for a minute?" he asked.

"Have a seat," Matt Gordon said. He had become a regular at the table, which was fine with Alex—sort of. He still felt uncomfortable with the way Christine looked at him—or the way Alex *thought* she was looking at him.

"Listen," Holder said as he sat down. "I think you guys ought to know what the deal is with Coach Archer."

"What deal?" Jonas asked.

"The deal with you two guys," Holder answered.

"How do *you* know what the deal is with us?" Alex asked.

Holder shrugged and picked up a handful of French fries. "Look, I've spent time with him during the fall. Remember, Coach Birdy is new too, so Archer kind of reached out to me as team captain from the beginning of the school year. We've talked a lot, actually, and he's not as bad a guy as you probably think he is. He just doesn't want you guys—or more importantly, the seniors—to think he's just handing you playing time."

"You don't think we deserve playing time?" Jonas asked.

Holder smiled. "Of course you do, and you'll get it. Coach isn't dumb—and he really wants to win."

"Every coach wants to win," Alex said dismissively.

Holder shook his head. "Wanting to win and *wanting to win*

are two different things, Myers. Our last coach was basically a teacher making some extra money on the side by coaching. We weren't very good, and he was okay with that. Coach Archer will *not* be okay with that. You haven't seen him go off yet—I mean really go off, but he did before you joined us. Not for a mistake, but when he thought someone wasn't giving a hundred percent. He's a pretty intense competitor.

"So I think he'll play you both plenty but not right away," Holder added. "He kind of has a thing about football."

"What does football have to do with anything?" Christine asked.

Holder held up a hand, but Christine continued: "He already made them spend a week with the JVs because they missed practice to finish football season. Isn't that enough? Especially since you guys *need* them."

"It isn't about missing practice; it goes beyond that."

"To what?" Jonas said. "The guy hasn't spoken twenty words to us since we met him in his office and he told us we had to try out with the JV team."

"I don't know," Alex said. "If you count all the times he's said 'Myers, put on white' or 'Ellington, put on red,' it could be closer to a hundred words."

Holder shook his head. "He just doesn't like football or football players. In fact, if there was any way he thought we could beat anyone without you two guys, you might not be on the team at all."

"What in the world does he have against football players?" Christine asked almost at the same time that Alex said, "That's the dumbest thing I've ever heard. . . ."

"Let him talk," Matt said. "What's the deal, Steve?"

"The deal is, Coach Archer played at Virginia Tech—"

"More like watched at Virginia Tech," Alex said, causing Jonas, Matt, and Christine to say almost in unison, "Alex, shut up!"

Holder continued. "Virginia Tech is a football school. I mean, a *football* school."

Alex was about to say something about the fact that, to him, Virginia Tech was a wannabe football school. Good enough to beat up on weak teams in the Atlantic Coast Conference but never good enough to compete with the real powers in college football. He stifled all that, though, because he didn't want to be told to shut up again.

Holder seemed to read his mind. "I know they're never *great*, but they win eight or nine games just about every year, go to bowl games—all that. And they sell out their stadium all the time. According to Coach Archer, about the only time the basketball arena was full when he played there was when they played Duke or North Carolina."

"That's true in a lot of places," Christine said.

"More so at Virginia Tech, apparently," Holder said. "Seth Greenberg, the guy on ESPN now, was coaching back then, and it burned him up that almost nothing his team did got anyone's attention down there. Coach Archer also went to a high school that's a lot like ours: football's king. So the idea that he *needs* two guys who were stars on the football team really bugs him."

"So we're screwed," said Jonas.

"You're going to play because he wants to win games. But he'd rather have twelve guys who *just* play basketball and love the game like he does."

"That's just dumb," Matt said. "You can love more than one sport. It'd be one thing if Alex and Jonas came in with some kind of attitude like, 'We're more important than you other guys because we almost won the state title in football.' But that's not who they are."

"I *know* that," Holder said. "I've talked to Coach about it all fall. I asked him yesterday if you guys had done anything at all to show you thought you deserved special treatment because you played football. But he just said, 'Not so far.'"

Alex shook his head and then looked at Jonas and then at Christine and Matt.

"Any thoughts?" he asked.

It was Matt who answered. "Yeah," he said, smiling in spite of himself. "By the end of basketball season, you may wish you were still playing for my dad."

Everyone laughed—except Holder.

"I understand why you might feel that way, but give Coach a chance. He's new to this job, and kinda stubborn. But he really knows basketball, and he's not a bad guy."

"Why are you telling us all this?" Jonas asked. "What are we supposed to do?"

Holder paused. "I feel like I should be the link between the coach and the rest of the team. I wanted you to know what was going on. And that I've got your backs. And I need you to play it cool if you don't start tomorrow. The more humble you are, the more playing time you'll get." He paused and took a deep breath.

"And we aren't going to win a lot of games if that doesn't happen."

The bus ride to Mercer took about two hours. Steve Holder had told Alex and Jonas that in the past, the cheerleaders and the dance team had ridden on the same bus as the team, but Coach Archer had banned them.

"I heard he told the principal, 'No wonder you've only won nineteen games the last three seasons. You think riding on a bus with cheerleaders helps you get ready to play a game?'"

Alex kind of agreed with Coach Archer on that one. He'd seen the cheerleaders and the dance team, and they were definitely a distraction.

"You think maybe they only won nineteen games because they were just bad?" Jonas asked.

Whatever the reason, no one was distracted as the bus rumbled toward central Pennsylvania. In fact, it was completely silent, almost everyone listening to something on headphones. Alex put his head back and tried to sleep. It was pretty much impossible. Coach Archer hadn't given him or Jonas any indication about how much they could expect to play. He felt sure they wouldn't start—that would be too much of an admission that they were among the best players on the team—but he figured they would get in the game pretty quickly, especially if the Lions got behind.

Mercer had the look of a small college campus. The bus rolled by all the various playing fields: every sport seemed to have its own separate facility. There was a football stadium, a baseball park, a soccer and lacrosse field. All had different names on them—wealthy donors, Alex assumed, who had given the school money.

They finally pulled up to the entrance of the David Felkoff Basketball Arena. It practically gleamed, even in the darkness of a December night.

The Lions walked through a glass doorway and were led onto the court en route to the locker room. The man who was escorting them was telling Coach Archer about the building in a voice loud enough for everyone to hear.

"We opened it two years ago," he said. "It seats three thousand six hundred, and for conference play, we often sell out."

"How much did it cost?" Coach Archer asked.

"About twelve million," the man said. "Mr. Felkoff is a graduate. He's very generous."

It was Alex's favorite teammate, Zane Wakefield, who asked what Alex was wondering.

"Who's Mr. Felkoff?"

The man braked to a halt as if he'd been asked who's Abraham Lincoln.

"Mr. Felkoff is one of the most distinguished and important sports agents in the country," he said.

"I didn't think there was such a thing as a distinguished sports agent," Coach Archer said.

At that moment Alex heard a sound he had never heard before around Coach Archer: laughter.

■ ■ ■

Alex was standing near midcourt doing some stretching exercises when he heard someone calling his name. He turned around and saw a big kid, probably about six four and at least 220 pounds, approaching him wearing a Mercer uniform.

The kid must have seen the confused look on his face because he grinned as he walked up and said, "Dave Krenchek. Remember? I'm the guy who tried to kill you."

Alex remembered—he'd never actually met Krenchek, unless you counted being knocked cold by someone as meeting them. In the opening game of the football season, when he was still the last-string quarterback, Alex had been sent into the football game against Mercer to kneel down for the final two plays and run out the clock. Chester Heights was leading 77–0 when Alex came in, and Krenchek—like most of his teammates—was upset about Coach Gordon running up the score.

He had called Alex the next day to apologize and to make sure he was okay. Alex remembered now that Krenchek had mentioned he played basketball.

Alex shook the extended hand but put up his left hand protectively. "You aren't going to hit me, are you?" he said.

Krenchek laughed. "Not unless you guys are up 77–0."

"Not likely," Alex said. He looked around and lowered his voice. "We're a little rocky."

"Not according to our coach," Krenchek said. "He says you guys are the Spurs and the Thunder rolled into one."

"Yeah sure," Alex said. "I'm Duncan and here comes Durant."

Jonas had walked up. "I remember you," he said. "You're the guy who tried to kill my buddy."

"Guilty," Krenchek said.

"You went after the wrong guy," Jonas said.

"Yeah, I know. I should have gone after your coach. But I guess you don't need to worry about him anymore, do you?"

Alex was about to give Krenchek some of the backstory when he heard a sharp whistle. He looked up and saw—surprise—Coach Archer with his hands on his hips.

"Myers, Ellington, get over here!" he said.

"Gotta go," Alex said. "Maybe we can talk after the game."

Krenchek nodded, and Alex and Jonas jogged over to Coach Archer.

"What do you think, we're here for a party or something?" he said. "You want to socialize, you can sit in the stands and talk to anyone you want."

"Coach, it was the guy who slammed me in football season and—"

"Myers, I don't care if it was your long-lost brother. And I really don't care about anything that happened during football season. Are you here to play basketball or have a good time?"

"Play basketball."

"Good. Go warm up."

Clearly, the Evan Archer comedy minute was now over.

Just as clearly, Holder hadn't been kidding about the coach's disdain for football. Alex was kicking himself that he'd even mentioned the word. . . .

■ ■ ■

There was nothing funny about the game. Krenchek had been right: Mercer was a lot better in basketball than it was in football. One of the reasons was Krenchek, who, despite his lineman's body, was very agile in the low post and quickly got Steve Holder into foul trouble. Coach Archer, as Alex had expected, started Tony Early and Zane Wakefield at the guard spots, and they were overmatched from the start. Six minutes in, Mercer led 21–7.

"That's a football score," Jonas murmured to Alex. "Except we aren't playing football."

"Watch yourself. We're not allowed to use the f-word," Alex murmured back.

At that moment, Wakefield was stripped by Mercer's point guard, who went in for a layup to make it 23–7. So much for the football score. Coach Archer called time-out. He turned to Alex and Jonas and pointed in the direction of the scorer's table.

"Go for Wakefield and Early," he said.

Alex and Jonas jogged to the scorer's table to report into the game.

"We're in for twelve and twenty," Alex said to the scorer, who nodded. They jogged back to the huddle. Alex could see that Wakefield was glaring daggers at him. He looked right back at him, wanting to say, *Not my fault we're down twenty-three to seven.*

Coach Archer was kneeling in front of them. The five players in the game sat on the bench, while the rest of the team huddled behind the coach.

"There are no sixteen-point plays in basketball, fellas," Coach Archer said. "We aren't going to catch them by trying to be spectacular. Let's go back to two-three zone for a while on defense, see if we can make them shoot from outside on occasion. You two guys are out front," he said, pointing to Alex and Jonas.

He looked directly at Alex and said, "I need you to double on your pal Krenchek when he gets the ball in the post. He's just too big and strong for one guy to guard. Can you handle that?"

Alex nodded. He had never been asked to double-team a big guy inside, but this wasn't middle school basketball anymore.

"Yes sir," he said.

The horn went, sending them back onto the court. As they broke the huddle, Coach Archer took his arm. "I meant what I said about sixteen-point plays," he said. "Just play."

Alex looked at him and saw that he wasn't giving him his icy stare. It was more of a pleading look. Alex nodded.

Mercer's coach had seen Alex and Jonas report in and figured this was as good a time as any to press full-court. As soon as Alex took the inbounds pass, two Mercer players were in his face, pushing him toward the corner. He tried to dribble, but a hand was reaching in. He picked up his dribble in order to keep from being stripped. That was a mistake.

The two Mercer players had him completely surrounded.

He leaned back and tried to throw a pass crosscourt to Jonas. That was a worse idea than picking up his dribble. With surprising quickness, Krenchek darted into the passing lane and reached up with his left hand to intercept the ball. In one quick motion, he switched the ball to his right hand and dunked.

Alex put his hands on his hips in disgust as the gym, which was close to full, exploded. Jonas was trying to get the ball inbounds again. This time, Alex came right to the ball, so he'd be in the center of the floor. And before Mercer could trap him again, he turned and went straight upcourt.

He was able to get it across half-court just in time to see a Mercer player charging at him as if he intended to run right through him. The guy was even bigger than Krenchek and was acting as if he was rushing the passer, not a point guard. Over his shoulder Alex could see Holder with his arms up, waving for the ball. He got the pass off just as the big guy, who was out of control, piled into him. They went down in a heap and Alex heard the whistle.

"What the—" Alex yelled as they untangled. Krenchek came running up and stepped between Alex and his tackler.

"Joey, cool it," he said.

Joey was shaking his head. "I'm sorry, man. I'm still thinking about football, I guess."

"He plays football too?" Alex said. Krenchek nodded—sheepishly.

From behind him, Alex could hear Coach Archer screaming—he presumed at him.

He was wrong. He was yelling at the official.

"You've got to call that intentional *and* count the basket!" he was saying as one of the refs walked in his direction, holding his hand up as if to say calm down.

"The foul was before the basket, Coach. It's your ball, side out-of-bounds."

"How can you not call that intentional?!"

"He was going for the ball."

"He practically put my guy through the floor! You're penalizing my team, taking away a layup because their guy was trying to *kill* my guy?!"

"Coach, that's enough," the ref said. He was walking to the sideline with the ball, indicating to Alex that he should come over and inbound since it was a nonshooting foul.

"Enough?!" Coach Archer screamed. "What is this, your first game? Have you ever *watched* basketball? Do you know anything about the concept of not taking away advantage? That kid should be ejected for a play like that! My kid could have been seriously hurt!"

Alex didn't disagree. In fact, the shoulder he'd landed on—his throwing shoulder—was a little sore and so was his elbow, which he noticed was turning bright red.

This time, the ref didn't answer. He put his whistle in his mouth, blew it, pointed at Coach Archer, and formed a *T* with his hands to indicate he had just given Coach Archer a technical foul.

Coach Archer tore his sports coat off and threw it on the ground. "That's total b——!" he screamed, using a word that Alex *knew* was going to get him thrown out of the game.

Sure enough, the official gave another *T* signal and then put his arm up in the *you're out of here* signal.

At that point, Archer actually charged at the ref. Alex reacted instinctively, jumping in Coach Archer's path to keep him from getting to the official. Coach Birdy was right there too, trying to get ahold of his boss from behind. Jonas jumped in, and between the three of them, they managed to keep Coach Archer away from the official, who was glaring, hands on hips.

"One more step in my direction and you won't coach for a month!" the ref yelled. Alex noticed that the gym was now in complete bedlam, the fans on their feet, directing invective at Coach Archer.

"I'm going to make sure you don't ref *ever*!" Coach Archer yelled back, even as Alex, Jonas, and Coach Birdy were pulling him backward. Coach Archer was right to be angry—but at that moment right and wrong had become irrelevant.

BOOM. The ref gave the *T* sign again.

"Keep it up, Coach," he said. "You're out of the game, but until you leave the floor, I'll just keep giving them to you."

"Come on, Evan, let's get away from this guy," Coach Birdy said. "Nothing left to be done here."

Coach Archer finally seemed to understand that the whistle gave the ref absolute power. He slumped and said to his assistant and his two players, "You can let go; I'm done."

They did. Two yellow-jacketed security guards had come out to escort Coach Archer to the locker room. He saw them coming and pointed a finger in their direction. "Don't even think about touching me," he said.

One put his hands up defensively. "Just here to do our job, Coach. We want to make sure you get off the floor safely."

Coach Archer turned to Coach Birdy. "Play the two kids,"

he said softly, but loudly enough for Alex to hear. "And play man-to-man—"

He was interrupted by the officious referee, who really seemed to be enjoying the whole thing.

"Time's up, Coach. Leave now or I'll have to tee you up again."

"*Have* to tee me up?" Coach Archer said. "You're loving every second of this."

He turned to go before the ref could, in fact, tee him up again. Alex agreed with him. There had been no reason for the ref to walk over. He had clearly done it to get in one last shot.

As he watched Coach Archer leave to a chorus of boos from the Mercer fans, he heard Coach Birdy's voice behind him. "Come on, Myers, let's huddle up. We've still got a game to play."

Alex glanced at the scoreboard. It was 25–7 with nineteen seconds left in the first quarter, and if his math was right, Mercer was about to shoot six free throws—two for each technical foul. If someone was going to run up the score this time, it would be Mercer—not Chester Heights.

After Chuck Swenson, Mercer's point guard, made five of the six free throws brought on by the technicals, the first quarter ended with Mercer leading 30–7. By halftime, even though the Camels' coach only pressed on occasion, it was 53–18.

Alex was surprised when they got into the locker room to find that Coach Archer was nowhere in sight. He had figured Coach would be waiting for them. As if reading Alex's (and no doubt everyone else's) mind, Coach Birdy explained that, by rule, any coach who had been ejected had to leave the building.

"He can come back in when the game's over," Coach Birdy said. "For now, he's waiting on the bus."

Alex hoped the bus driver had turned on the engine. Otherwise, it would be pretty cold sitting out there for two more quarters.

The Lions played better in the second half, in part because Mercer's intensity clearly lapsed with such a huge lead, and in part because Mercer's coach—unlike Coach Gordon in the football game back in September—played his subs liberally, especially in the fourth quarter.

After his shaky start, Alex played better, ending up with twelve points and three assists—along with three turnovers. Jonas was the team's best player, with fourteen points and six rebounds. Steve Holder did very little until Krenchek came out of the game, and then he finished with ten points. The final was 86–56, and Alex knew it could have been much worse.

As they went through the handshake line, Krenchek introduced him to Joey Cohen—whose tackle had led to Coach Archer's ejection.

"I'm really sorry, man," he said. "I'd tell you my linebacker mentality came out there, except I'm not a very good linebacker."

Alex just nodded. His shoulder and elbow were both still a little sore, and to be honest, he was a little tired of getting beaten up for no reason by kids from Mercer.

Krenchek jumped in to try to lighten the mood. "Wouldn't have been so bad if the ref had gotten the call right," he said. "Your coach was right. It should have been an intentional foul."

Cohen didn't argue.

Krenchek batted Alex on the head. "Good luck," he said. "You guys will get better—especially if your coach realizes he needs to play you and Ellington and not those two stiffs who started at guard."

Alex liked the fact that Krenchek recognized how much better he and Jonas were than Wakefield and Early. He'd been a little disappointed when Coach Birdy, despite Coach Archer telling him to "play the kids," had split time pretty equally among the four guards in the second half.

Coach Archer was waiting for them when they walked into the locker room—apparently he'd been allowed back inside once the final buzzer sounded. He stood in front of them for a long moment, as if trying to decide what to say.

"First of all, fellas, I apologize," he said finally. "There's no excuse for me losing it the way I did. I embarrassed myself, I embarrassed you, and I embarrassed Chester Heights." He paused, then smiled briefly. "Giving them six free throws at that point in the game didn't exactly help our cause either, did it?"

He paced back and forth for a moment, then stopped. "Tonight's a good lesson for all of us. That's a very good team, but it's not a great team. It isn't ranked in the USA Today Top Twenty-Five. It's the kind of team we have to find a way to beat when we get to conference play. Clearly, we're a long way from that. We have to keep working and try to get a little better in practice every day."

He pointed a finger at Holder. "Steve, you're the captain. Do you think we have the talent in this room to do that?"

"Yes sir, I do."

"So do I. And you guys should know, if I didn't feel that way, I'd say so. I'd say, 'Let's try to improve and win whenever we can.' But I honestly think we're a lot better than that—or can be a lot better than that."

He nodded at Holder, who stood up in the middle of the

room with his right arm raised. The players formed a circle around him, each with an arm in the air, pushing up against one another to make the circle tighter.

"On three," Holder said. "Good enough to win!"

Alex wasn't completely sure if he thought that was true, but he did know one thing: Evan Archer was a lot better coach than he had given him credit for before tonight.

■ ■ ■

"He's going to get suspended. They have to suspend him. *Three* technicals?"

Christine hadn't gone to the game. Only Steve Garland, the sports editor of the *Weekly Roar*, had made the trip. She hadn't needed to be at the game to know what had happened, though, since some fan had recorded the entire confrontation between Coach Archer and the referee and put it up on YouTube, where it was quickly becoming a sensation under the heading HIGH SCHOOL COACH LOSES HIS MIND.

Now Christine, Jonas, and Alex were back at Stark's, eating Saturday lunch, and Christine was trashing Coach Archer.

"He got the three techs because the ref was looking for a fight," Alex said. "The ref should have walked away, especially after he called the first one. Instead, he kept walking in Coach's direction. He wanted the confrontation."

Christine was shaking her head, the ponytail that her long black hair was tied in wagging behind her.

"Doesn't work that way and you know it. And anyway, when did you become president of the Evan Archer fan club?"

Jonas snorted at that one. "Yeah, when did you guys get tight?"

"Do you think he should be suspended?" Alex asked Jonas.

"Actually, yes," Jonas said. "But you're right about the ref. Guy was a jerk."

"Then why should he be suspended?" Alex asked.

Jonas sighed. "The ref got the call right. You got fouled way before Holder made the layup, before he even caught the ball. It may seem unfair, but that's the rule."

"Shouldn't it have been an intentional foul?" Christine asked.

"Yes, it should have been," Alex said. "But Jonas might be right that the basket shouldn't have counted."

"Which means Coach shouldn't have gone *that* nuts," Jonas said. "And charging the ref . . . that was over the top."

"Yeah, maybe," Alex said. "But it felt pretty good that he stood up for me when I got clocked that way. He got ejected. That's enough of a penalty."

Their hamburgers arrived. Alex was so hungry the thought of ordering a second one crossed his mind even before he took a bite of the first.

"Well, for what it's worth, our favorite coach's son thinks he should be suspended," Christine said.

"Matt?" Alex said.

She nodded, putting a French fry into her mouth as she did.

"How do you know that?" Alex asked, hoping he didn't sound accusatory. He suspected he did.

"He texted me this morning after he saw it on YouTube."

Alex managed not to ask her how often the two of them

texted. He had been so busy since the start of basketball season—especially with first semester finals coming up next week—that he hadn't found a time to ask Christine out again. Classes ended on Tuesday, and then exams ran until the end of the week. The holiday break came afterward.

"I guess the good news is we should still win on Friday with or without him," Jonas said. "Saint Pius is supposed to be awful."

"How do you know they're awful?" Alex asked.

Jonas looked a little embarrassed. "Christine told me," he said.

Alex didn't need to ask how Christine knew. He had nicknamed her Hermione long ago, in part because she was petite, dark-haired, and very pretty, much like the *Harry Potter* character. And, like Hermione, Christine seemed to know everything about everything.

"They won two games last year, and they were one of our seven wins," Christine said, authoritative as usual. "They may be worse this year—if that's possible."

"So, fine, we don't need Coach Archer on Friday. But we probably will need him when we go out to play Main Line after break, right?"

"You'll need all the help you can get against Main Line," all-knowing Christine/Hermione said. "They have two players being recruited by Division I colleges. They're probably as good as or better than Mercer."

"Great," Jonas said, draining his milk shake. His hamburger was gone. So was Alex's. Christine had eaten about three bites. Alex was still starving. "At least we've got a couple weeks to practice before that game."

"There is one downside to Coach Archer not being there Friday if they suspend him," Christine said.

"What's that?" they both asked.

"Fewer spectators at the game," she said with a big smile. Seeing the confused look on both their faces, she went on. "Most of the girls think he's easily the hottest teacher or coach in the school."

"Really?" Jonas asked.

She picked up her hamburger and took a bite, swallowed, and said, "Uh-huh."

"So girls come to the games to watch the *coach?*" Alex asked.

"Absolutely," she said.

"But he's old," Jonas said.

She shrugged. "He's thirty-six. Cute is cute," she said.

Alex just shook his head, and decided to order another hamburger.

"One game," Christine said as they walked into French class on Monday. Naturally Christine had found out about Coach Archer's suspension before Alex did. "He'll miss the game Friday but can come back for the nonconference games after Christmas break."

"Too bad for all you girls," Alex said.

She gave him a withering look and walked into the classroom. Alex had resolved to ask Christine on a date this coming weekend—a real date—but, seeing her look after his wisecrack, he decided this wasn't the time.

He was vaguely aware of the fact that a lot of people around him were speaking in French, but he wasn't really listening when he heard Mademoiselle Schiff, his French teacher, saying, *"Monsieur Myers, écoutez, s'il vous plaît."*

Even though she was saying it politely—listen, please— the sharpness in her voice told him that she had been trying to get his attention for a while. The giggling in the room confirmed it.

"*Pardonnez-moi,*" he said. "*Je suis un peu malade.*"

She looked at him suspiciously. Claiming he was a little sick had probably not been his best idea.

She switched to English, which she almost never did. "Alex, if you're sick you should go see the nurse," she said.

"*Non, non,*" he said. "*Je suis fatigué, mais je suis ça va maintenant.*"

"*Vous allez très bien,*" she said, correcting him because he had said "I'm tired, but I'm fine now" incorrectly.

Fortunately, she decided not to press the issue further.

Alex saw Christine staring at him from across the room. He buried his head in the vocabulary book they were working from and prayed that class would end without him being caught daydreaming again.

Maybe Mademoiselle Schiff understood he was a lost cause that day, because she left him alone.

As they left the classroom, Alex caught up with Christine.

"*Vous êtes malade?*" she said, grinning.

"Yeah, yeah, what else should I have said?"

"I don't know. How do you say 'I was acting like a jerk walking into class with Christine' in French?"

"Okay, fine," he said. "I'm sorry."

"Jealous?" she said, her dark eyes dancing as they walked down the crowded hallway.

He saw an opening. "Yeah," he said. "Well, no, not really. It's not like I think you're going to go out with Coach Archer or anything."

"Duh," she said. "I think Ryan Gosling is good-looking too, but I'm not going to go out with him."

"Right," he said. "But maybe you'll go to a movie Saturday with me?"

She kept walking for a moment, saying nothing.

"Okay," she said finally. "Maybe after Stark's?"

"In the afternoon?"

"Something wrong with that?"

"No, not really, but—"

"Gotta go," she said. They had reached the turn in the hallway where he headed in the direction of the gym and the locker room and she headed for the office where the student newspaper was located.

"I'll pick the movie," she said, starting to walk away.

"Nothing with Ryan Gosling," he called after her.

She turned back for a split second and gave him a devilish grin. "We'll see," she said, and then she was gone.

Alex pumped his fist and said "Yes!" under his breath.

Then he headed for practice.

■ ■ ■

Steve Holder told everyone in the locker room that the suspension didn't include practice. "He can't be in the building on Friday night until the game's over," he said. "That's it."

After that, Alex wasn't surprised to see both coaches—Archer and Birdy—standing at midcourt while the team warmed up. The surprise came when, instead of using his whistle to get their attention, Coach Archer just said, "Hey, fellas, gather round here for a minute."

When they all raced over the way they would have if he had blown his whistle, he smiled.

"Good hustle," he said softly. "Look, I'm sure you've all heard that I'm suspended for Friday night's game. I think you also know that Coach Birdy is more than capable of filling in."

He paused for a second, as if deciding what to say next. "I've had a long weekend to think about the kind of coach I want to be. I've been pretty hard on everyone since we started practice. This is my first head-coach job and there may be times when I've tried too hard. Friday was an example. I'm not saying we would have won the game if I hadn't gotten tossed, but we would have had a lot better chance."

He glanced at Alex. "Fact is, the whole thing happened because Myers made a great play. I got frustrated because the ref was wiping that play out. For the record, he had the call at least half right—which makes me feel worse.

"So I'm going to try to do a better job going forward, especially with my temper—even more so when we're on the practice court. That doesn't mean I won't get on you for mistakes, and I *will* get on you if I think you aren't giving a hundred percent, but I'm going to try to be more patient."

He paused again, clearly deciding if there was anything more he needed to say. Apparently there wasn't.

"Okay, then," he said. "Let's run five-man shells. Reds at the north end, whites at the south."

Alex and Jonas had walked onto the court wearing white because they had started practice every day with the second team. Alex had wondered if that might change after Friday.

It didn't.

He and Jonas glanced at each other, then headed to the south end of the court.

They stopped when they heard Coach Archer calling their names. "Myers, Ellington, sorry," he said. "You guys are in red."

He turned to Zane Wakefield and Tony Early, who were headed in the other direction. "Wakefield, Early, my mistake. I need you in white."

He walked to the side of the court and stood next to Coach Birdy with his arms crossed. As Alex passed Wakefield and Early heading to the south end, he could almost feel the anger coming off of them. He said nothing, but inside his head he was repeating the same words over and over: deal with it, boys, deal with it.

■ ■ ■

Coach Archer had players switching from red to white throughout practice. Even Holder spent some time in white. It was almost as if he was trying to make the point that there were *no* starters—or that there were ten starters. Alex didn't mind. All he knew was that he was on the court throughout the practice and that if there had been any doubt about who the team's best guards were, they should be gone by now.

On several occasions Coach Archer paired Alex and Jonas in the red team's backcourt but put the rest of the starters with Wakefield and Early on the white team. The reds consistently held their own during those periods because Wakefield and Early couldn't guard Alex or Jonas. Alex could almost feel Wakefield's frustration—which finally bubbled over during the last scrimmage of the day.

Wakefield was bringing the ball upcourt, with Alex guarding him. Steve Holder came to the top of the key to set a screen and try to set up a pick-and-roll. But Wakefield gave the play away by dribbling almost directly to his right instead of dribbling diagonally around the screen toward the basket. Alex read the move, and instead of staying behind the screener, which he normally would have done, he darted around him—a mistake, technically, since it meant he was now behind the man he was guarding. Except that Wakefield's dribble was right in front of him and he was able to easily swipe the ball away.

He chased the ball down and headed in the other direction, aware that Wakefield was trying to run him down from behind. As he went up for a layup, Wakefield piled into him. Alex didn't see exactly what Wakefield had done, but it was clear—and Jonas confirmed later—that Wakefield had made no play for the ball. He had just jumped on Alex's back and pushed him to the floor.

Alex managed to break his fall with his hands, but pain shot through his right arm as he fell with Wakefield on top of him. Wakefield still had his arms locked around him in a wrestling hold, but Alex finally freed his left arm and was trying to push Wakefield away from him when he felt several pairs of hands pulling them apart.

"Get off me, Ellington!" Wakefield screamed. "What do you think you're doing?"

Alex couldn't hear Jonas's answer. He had rolled over and was pushing himself up with his left arm, ready to charge Wakefield—who he had decided to kill—as the pain continued to scream through his right arm. But he saw that

Coach Birdy had placed himself in front of him, blocking his path to Wakefield. Even though he knew he wouldn't get to Wakefield, he charged toward Coach Birdy, screaming, "Did you see what he did?" He pointed at Wakefield. "You dirty little— You ever do that again, I'll kill you!"

"Come and get me," Wakefield, still being held back by both Jonas and Steve Holder, sneered.

Alex tried to take a step around Coach Birdy, but it was futile.

"Hang on, Myers," he said. "Let Coach Archer handle this."

At that point, Alex remembered how much his arm hurt and grabbed his wrist.

Coach Archer came up behind Coach Birdy and pointed at the hand.

"You okay?" he asked.

"I don't know," Alex said, being honest. "It hurts."

Coach Archer turned and waved at J. J. Crowder, the team trainer. "J. J., get over here and take a look at Myers."

Alex was now bent over in pain.

Coach Archer turned to Wakefield. "Wakefield, you're off the hook tonight because the women have the court now and I can't make you run suicides until you drop. You be in my office tomorrow morning at 6:00 a.m. . . ."

"But, Coach, I was just trying to make a play, and—"

"NO, you weren't," Coach Archer said. "You were trying to hurt him and it looks like you may have succeeded. Bad enough to pull something like that in a game against an opponent. But to a teammate? I don't want to hear another word. Everyone hit the showers. I'll see you at practice tomorrow. Except for you, Wakefield. I'll see *you* at six. We'll be running some steps."

He turned his back on the rest of the team and walked over to where J. J. Crowder was poking gently at Alex's hand, wrist, and arm. Jonas and Holder lingered, and Coach Archer didn't shoo them away.

"How's it look, J. J.?" he said softly.

J. J. had been applying pressure to various places on Alex's arm, saying "Hurt?" each time. So far, the pain had been minimal.

"Can't tell yet," J. J. answered.

Then he put his thumb on a spot on the inside of Alex's wrist about an inch above his palm.

Alex screamed in pain, his knees buckling.

J. J. nodded. "It's a tendon," he said to Coach Archer. "Judging by his reaction, he probably tore something in there. It could just be stretched, but I'm guessing it's a tear. We need to get it X-rayed to see how bad it is."

"Where do we take him?" Coach Archer said.

"Sinai General," J. J. said. "It's a couple miles from here. I'll call Dr. Taylor and ask him to meet us there so Alex won't have to wait too long in the emergency room."

"I'll take him," Coach Archer said. "Give me the address and call the doctor. Come on, Alex."

He put his hand gently under Alex's arm to support it and led him out of the gym.

Coach Archer tossed Alex's bicycle into the back of his Jeep Cherokee, and as they climbed into the car, he suggested that Alex call his mom.

Alex downplayed the injury, but it didn't work.

"You're going to the hospital?" she said. "Is something broken?"

"The trainer doesn't think so," Alex said. "It might just be a stretched ligament. Coach wants me to get an X-ray to be sure."

"What hospital?" his mom said. "I'll meet you there."

"You stay home with Molly. I promise to call as soon as we know what the problem is."

His mom was replying, but Coach Archer asked for the phone.

"Mrs. Myers, this is Evan Archer," he said. "I'm Alex's basketball coach. I understand your concern, but Alex tells me he has a sister at home, and it's pretty close to dinner-time. I promise I'll call you and tell you exactly what we're dealing with, and then I'll bring him home."

Alex couldn't hear what his mom was saying, but he figured it out when Coach Archer answered. "Actually, Alex made a terrific play right at the end of practice," he said. "Took a fall while he was being fouled and broke the fall with his hands. Very smart of him, really. I don't think anything's broken, but as he said, we need to be sure."

He listened again. "The father of one of our players is a doctor who practices at Sinai General, so we're hoping he can expedite things when we get there."

Alex saw him shake his head. "I understand. No thanks; I'm fine, but thanks for offering."

He said goodbye and hung up just as Alex spotted a sign for the hospital.

He gave Alex a smile. "I tried, but she's coming anyway," he said.

"What about Molly and dinner?" Alex asked.

"She said she was going to stop at McDonald's and get something for Molly and you too. She even offered to bring me something, but I said no."

Alex didn't mind the thought of getting something to eat sooner rather than later, but he wasn't thrilled at the thought of his mother *and* sister coming to the hospital.

Someone was standing on the sidewalk waving at them as they pulled up to the emergency room entrance.

Coach Archer rolled down his window. "Are you Dr. Taylor?" he asked.

"That's right. Nice to meet you, Coach. I can take Alex in while you park."

Alex got out gingerly, using his left arm to cushion the right one.

"Alex, I'm Dean Taylor, Pete's dad," the doctor said. Pete was a backup big guy who played rarely. "Under the circumstances, I won't shake your hand. Let's get you inside. I've got an X-ray room set up already. We can worry about the paperwork once we take the pictures."

Dr. Taylor walked Alex straight through the emergency room waiting area into an empty room. A nurse walked in a minute later, and Dr. Taylor carefully took Alex's right arm and placed it on a table that appeared to have a camera inside it.

"I'm going to move your arm a few times so we can get several angles," he said. "I'll try my best not to hurt you. If what J. J. told me on the phone is accurate, we should be able to tell pretty quickly what's going on here."

They took about six pictures, and then Dr. Taylor told the nurse to tell Coach Archer it was okay to come in. He must have been waiting outside the door, because he walked in seconds later.

"Give me about ten minutes," Dr. Taylor said.

Ten minutes felt like an hour to Alex. Coach Archer asked him how the pain was, and he said it was fine—as long as he could rest his arm on the table and not move it. Dr. Taylor finally came back with two X-rays. He put them up on the wall and told Alex and Coach Archer to come and take a look. Before they could start to look at the pictures, the phone on the wall rang. Dr. Taylor picked it up. "Send them on back here," he said.

He turned to Alex. "Your mom and sister just arrived," he said.

A moment later they were there, and after a cautious hug from his mom and introductions all around, they turned to the X-rays.

"Perfect timing, Mrs. Myers," Dr. Taylor said. "I was just about to explain to Alex what's going on."

"Is it very serious?" Alex's mom asked—the question Alex had been wanting to ask all along.

"Not very, no—it could have been much worse," the doctor said. "Here, let me show you.

"See the white spot right here?" he added, pointing to one of the pictures. "That's a tear—J. J. was right. When he touched you on that spot, it hurt because that's where the bad tear is."

"The bad tear?" Coach Archer said.

Dr. Taylor nodded. "Look at this other X-ray," he said. "See that small white spot and that other one up in the corner? Those are small tears. Alex tore the tendon in three places, but only the big one right near his hand is significant."

"How significant?" Alex, his mom, and Coach Archer asked together.

"Well, I'm going to put you in a soft cast," Dr. Taylor said. "Two weeks from today, you'll come back and we'll take another look. But I think you'll need more like three weeks for it to heal completely."

"And basketball?" Alex asked.

"We'll see once the cast is off," Dr. Taylor said. "Your arm is going to atrophy some while it's in the cast, so you'll need time to get your strength back. I think we can have you back on the court in about four weeks. Maybe a little less."

"We start conference play January ninth," Coach Archer said.

"What is it now? The fifteenth? That'll be tight," Dr. Taylor said. "He should be healed by then, but I don't know what kind of basketball shape he'll be in. That'll be your call."

Alex's mom had been listening intently. Now she looked at Coach Archer. "I'm sure you want him back as soon as possible, Coach Archer," she said.

"Evan," he said.

She smiled. "Evan. But I don't want to rush him back if there's a chance he'll reinjure his wrist."

Dr. Taylor smiled. "That's a very understandable fear. But I'm not going to okay him to play until he's fully healed. As I'm sure Coach Archer would agree."

"You've got my word, Mrs. Myers," Coach Archer said.

"Linda," she said.

■ ■ ■

Dr. Taylor put Alex in a soft cast, which was a relief. He had broken an ankle in the fourth grade, and the hard cast he'd been in for a month had made him miserable.

With the soft cast, he could still use his hand, which meant that he could write and use a computer—albeit clumsily. He could also shower, which had been impossible in the hard cast.

Coach Archer stayed with them until they were ready to go, and he insisted on transferring Alex's bike from his car to the Myerses' car himself.

"Thanks for bringing him to the hospital," Alex's mom said.

"Not a problem," Coach Archer said. "I'm really sorry this happened. One of the other guys on the team isn't handling the fact that your son is a better player than he is very well. I'll deal with him tomorrow. The good news is kids heal quickly, and I have a feeling Alex will be an even quicker healer than most."

"What makes you say that?" Alex's mom said skeptically.

"Just knowing him for a couple of weeks now," Coach Archer said with a smile.

For a moment, there was an awkward silence. Alex was starting to shiver.

"Listen," Coach Archer said, now holding the door open for Alex's mom to get into the car. "Alex isn't going to be able to ride his bike to school very comfortably while he's got that cast on. I could pick him up in the mornings the rest of the week. That way you'd only have to pick him up after school."

"Oh, you don't have to do that . . . ," his mom said.

"But I'd *like* to do it," Coach Archer said. "And it's really not a problem. I can't do it tomorrow because young Mr. Wakefield is going to be running at 6:00 a.m. But after that, I'm happy to do it."

Alex's mom looked at Alex. A week ago, the thought of riding to school every morning with Coach Archer would have been somewhat sickening. Now Alex thought it'd be okay. He nodded slightly to let his mom know.

"If you really think it isn't too inconvenient, that would be terrific," she said. "It should only be this week, with the holidays coming up."

"Exactly," Coach Archer said.

Alex was already in the car and digging into the McDonald's bag he'd found on the passenger seat. The French fries were cold, but he didn't care. He was starving. "I'm sorry about the circumstances," Alex's mom said as Coach Archer was—finally—closing the driver's-side door. "But it's nice to meet you."

"You too." Coach Archer leaned down and gave Alex a wave. "Come see me during lunch tomorrow, Alex," he said. "We'll work out a schedule."

He stuck his hands into his coat pockets and headed back to his car.

Alex's mom pulled out of the parking space and glanced at him. "Food cold?" she asked.

"Yes, but it's fine," he answered.

"So, didn't you tell me Coach Archer was kind of a jerk?" his mom asked as he dug into the bag for a second hamburger. His mom always got him two.

"Starting out, he was a jerk," Alex said. "He's gotten better. Tonight, he was really nice."

He saw her smile in the darkness. "You also didn't tell me he was so good-looking."

Alex groaned. First Christine, now his mom? Seriously, his *mom*?

"*Very* handsome," Molly piped up from the backseat. It was the first thing she'd said all night.

Alex decided to keep his mouth shut—except to put food in it.

As soon as he walked in his house, it occurred to Alex that he hadn't looked at his phone—which had been buzzing repeatedly in his pocket—in a long time.

Sure enough, there were texts from teammates, both football and basketball, asking him what had happened at the hospital. Jonas had texted six times, the last one saying, *Unless you died in that hospital you better have a good explanation why you aren't answering me!*

Christine, he noticed, had sent just one text, saying, simply, *Call when you can.*

Clearly, she was in an absolute panic about his injury.

Alex called Jonas first—since he seemed more concerned, and he figured it couldn't hurt to make Christine wait.

"Coach sent us all a text," Jonas said. "He said you're probably out for about a month."

"Yeah, sounds like it," Alex said, feeling a surge of anger

directed at Zane Wakefield. "It better not be any longer than that, or I may kill Wakefield. Come to think of it, I may kill him anyway."

Jonas laughed. "Coach Archer may beat you to it. You probably didn't see the look he gave him while J. J. was checking you out."

"Well, I guess I'll have more time to study before finals," he said. It had just occurred to him that he would be going home right after classes on Tuesday, something he hadn't done since the start of school.

"You could always come and watch practice."

"Oh sure, that'd be great. Sit there and watch Wakefield play while I can't."

"Yeah, I hear you. But *I'll* miss you at practice. No one else talks to me."

"Wanna trade places?"

"Yeah—no, good point," Jonas said. "See you at school tomorrow, and we'll figure out how to deal with Wakefield."

Alex called Christine next.

"I hear you're out for a month," she said. "I'm so sorry."

"Thanks," he said.

"How did it happen?" she said.

It suddenly occurred to Alex that she might not be calling as a friend but as a reporter for the *Weekly Roar*.

"Is this on the record?" he asked, having learned newspaper talk from her during the football season.

"Is there any reason for it not to be on the record?" she said.

Alex thought about that for a moment. Heck with it, he

decided; if Zane Wakefield didn't like what he had to say, what did he care?

So he told her.

"And Wakefield's going to be running at 6:00 a.m. tomorrow?" she said.

"That's what Coach Archer said. You going to get up and check it out?"

"Well, I can't make deadline for this week. And finals start on Wednesday. But it might be worth it just to see how much he actually makes Zane run."

She said *Zane* in a way that made Alex ask, "Do you know Wakefield? I mean, other than him being on the basketball team?"

"He asked me out once," she said matter-of-factly.

Now Alex *really* wanted to kill Wakefield.

"What did you say?" He was almost afraid to hear the answer.

"I said no," she replied, sounding insulted. "Please."

It occurred to Alex that Christine probably got asked out a lot. And then he wondered just how often "a lot" was. . . .

"Right, sorry," he said. "Are we still going to a movie on Saturday?"

"If you stop asking dumb questions, we are," she said. He could hear the smile in her voice as she said it.

"Okay, okay," he said. "If you do go watch Wakefield run tomorrow, I want to hear all about it."

"You don't want to meet me there?"

"At 6:00 a.m.? No thanks. Been there, done that."

"How's your wrist?" she asked. "Does it hurt a lot?"

"It's not awful if I don't move it," he said. "The doctor gave me something in case it gets bad during the night."

"You just seem to find trouble one way or the other, don't you?" she said.

"Actually, I don't," Alex said. "But it *does* seem to find me."

■ ■ ■

On Tuesday, Alex was just sitting down to eat a quick lunch before going to see Coach Archer, juggling his tray since he only had partial use of his right hand, when he saw Zane Wakefield walking toward their table. He steeled himself for trouble.

"How's the wrist?" Wakefield asked, not bothering to say hello but managing not to sound quite as hostile as he normally did.

"Hurt," Alex said. "Thanks to you."

He had absolutely no desire to make nice on any level with Wakefield.

"I know," Zane said. "It was my fault. I'm sorry."

Wakefield didn't put out a hand—perhaps because he knew a handshake wasn't a good idea for Alex at that moment.

Alex stared at him for a second.

"Apology accepted," he said finally, hearing Jonas making a choking sound behind him. "But do me a favor."

"What?"

"Don't ever speak to me again."

"I thought you said you accepted my apology?"

"I do. But I still think you're a jerk."

Christine had just walked up to the table, tray in hand.

Wakefield turned and pointed at her. "You're a witness; I did what I was told."

He stalked away.

"What was that about?" Alex said as Christine sat down.

"Coach Archer told him if he didn't apologize to you he wouldn't play again until you could," she said. "Either way, he has to run at six for the rest of the week."

"So it wasn't a real apology, then," Jonas said.

"It was real," Alex said. "He did say I'm sorry. He just didn't mean it."

"He's sorry he got in trouble," Christine said. "You should have come this morning, Alex. You would have enjoyed it. I honestly thought Zane was going to pass out."

"So you went?" Alex said. "You really are a good reporter. Seriously. The day before exams start and you got up for that? How many times did he run the steps?"

"I think it was ten, but that wasn't what was so hard. Coach Archer ran with him, and he told him if he fell more than five steps behind him on any trip up and down, it didn't count. Zane was running so hard to keep up he actually got sick at one point. Coach Archer is in *shape*."

Alex didn't really want to hear anything about Coach Archer being in shape—especially after his mother's comment from the previous night. But he had to admit the vision of Wakefield bent over getting sick didn't bother him in the least. He wondered if that made him a bad guy. Jonas cleared that up for him quickly.

"Too bad he didn't throw up twice," he said.

■ ■ ■

Alex finished eating and excused himself to go see Coach Archer. He found him in his office watching what looked like a recording of the Mercer game on a small TV set up in the corner.

"This is my version of running at 6:00 a.m.," he said, freezing the on-screen image. "I coached badly that night, so I'm making myself watch the tape again."

He gestured to Alex to take a seat. "How's the wrist feel?" he asked.

"Got through the night without the painkillers," Alex said. "It hurts now, though."

"What about taking finals?" Coach Archer asked. "We could probably get you excused until you're out of the soft cast."

Alex had actually discussed that with his mother on the way to school. "I'd like to at least try to get through them," he said. "To be honest, I'd rather get them over with."

Coach Archer nodded. Then, to Alex's surprise, he changed the subject completely. "How long have your parents been divorced?" he asked.

"They're not divorced," he said, caught a little off guard. "They separated this summer. My dad is still in Boston."

"And you guys came here?"

"Yeah, my mom has family here."

"So the new kid in town had to compete with the coach's son for playing time in football."

Alex smiled. "Actually, there wasn't any competition," he said. "Matt was the quarterback and I was third string until he got hurt."

"And started taking steroids."

Alex grimaced a little. "That came later."

Coach Archer leaned back in his chair. "So let me see if I've got the story straight: your parents split in the summer, you move, come to a new school with no friends, you get your head bashed in the opening game because the coach is running up the score, you're wrongly accused of taking steroids, clear your name in time to play in the state championship, lose by a whisker, and then the basketball coach decides to give you a hard time the minute you walk in the door."

Alex held up his arm. "You forgot this," he said.

Coach Archer smiled. "You're a tough kid, Alex. Tell your mom she should be proud of you."

■ ■ ■

Alex didn't know what to do with himself when he got home that afternoon. The smart thing to do was start studying for his first final—math, which was the next day. English and history would come Thursday and then earth science and the one he *really* needed to study for—French—on Friday.

But he couldn't get started. First he had a snack. Then he texted with a few people—starting out answering people who had inquired about his wrist, then getting into a couple of back-and-forths with friends. Then he went on the Internet and got caught up on the sports websites. He watched an episode of *Monk*, the show he and his dad had watched together all the time.

His mom came into the room and found him sitting on the bed.

"How's the studying going?" she asked, sitting on the edge of the bed.

He smiled. He never bothered to try lying to his mother. She said he had a "tell" when he was lying—that his mouth twitched just a little.

"It's not," he answered. "I got distracted by some stuff. I'll start right after dinner like I usually do."

She nodded. "That's fine. You're entitled to some down-time. And I'm guessing you're ready for your tests . . . ?" She paused and smiled. "Except maybe French, right? Three more days and then it'll be Christmas break, and by the time it's over, you'll have the cast off."

"You think so?"

"I do. Doctors tend to give patients the worst-case scenario so they don't get upset. I think you'll have the cast off by New Year's."

She nodded in the direction of his computer. "What're you watching?"

"*Monk.*"

She smiled. "Makes you think about your dad, doesn't it?" she said. "Did you talk to him last night?"

He shook his head. "I left him a message. Then he sent a text this morning, saying he was catching an early flight to LA but would try to call tonight."

"He *did* have an early flight," she said.

"Mom, you don't have to make excuses for him."

"I'm not," she said. "I've told him he needs to work harder on making time for you and Molly. He gets it . . . I think."

"Well, he *did* make the state championship game, at least. I guess that was progress."

She nodded. "Different subject. I have a question to ask you."

"Yeah?"

She paused for a moment, which made him nervous.

"Okay," she said finally. "Let me put it this way. How would you feel if I went on a date?"

Alex involuntarily shivered. He had known this moment was going to come at some point. He knew his dad was seeing someone in Boston, and that bugged him—if he was being honest. But the thought of his mom on a "date" was somehow worse. He wanted her to be happy, but this was all moving so fast.

She and his dad had talked about their separation as an "experiment" in the summer. But they had already filed divorce papers, and now it was just a matter of time before it was final.

He realized he had spaced out when he heard his mom say, "Alex, are you okay?"

"Sure, Mom, sorry," he said, snapping back to reality. "Of course you should go on a date. Dad's doing it; why shouldn't you?"

She smiled. "I didn't know you knew about your dad seeing someone. Did he tell you?"

Alex nodded. It was one of the few conversations he'd had with his dad that had lasted more than two minutes.

"Good, then," his mom said. "Let me ask you another question. How would you feel if I went on a date with Evan Archer?"

Alex felt his entire body go stiff. His hands started tingling the way they did when something frightened him. He thought, I should have seen that one coming. But he hadn't.

"Isn't he a lot younger than you?" he said.

She laughed. "Actually, I thought that too. I told him I was thirty-nine and probably a little too old for him. Turns out he's thirty-six. He just looks younger."

His mom, he knew, looked younger than thirty-nine.

"So . . . you want to go out with him?"

She shrugged. "I didn't really feel like seeing anyone for a long time. . . . But I think I'm ready to give it a try now, and he seems like a nice guy."

"And he's good-looking."

"Doesn't hurt." She smiled. "But if it's going to bother you, I'll tell him no. I didn't give him an answer yet."

"Did you tell him you were going to talk to me about it?"

She shook her head. "No. I didn't want to put you in an awkward position if I ended up saying no and he thought it was because of you. I said I hadn't dated anyone yet and that I needed to think about it."

Thank God for small favors, Alex thought.

"You want to go, though, don't you?" he said.

She looked him directly in the eye. "Not if it'll bother you," she said. "But yes. I think it's time."

Alex sighed. "You should do it."

"Sure?"

"Sure."

She leaned forward and kissed him on the cheek as she stood up. Alex couldn't remember the last time he had seen her look so happy.

12

"So they're going to dinner tonight?"

"Yup. I think he's taking her to the Oyster House downtown."

Christine nodded. "Oh yeah, I've heard of it. Supposed to be the best seafood in Philadelphia. It's really nice."

Alex and Christine's date wasn't nearly so fancy. They'd decided to ride their bikes to the mall and get pizza. The day was surprisingly mild for December, and Alex had found that riding his bike wasn't that difficult since his fingers were free. Christine's mom had volunteered to pick them up at the mall after the movie.

"So how are you feeling about this?" Christine asked.

Alex realized he had been holding a slice of pizza in his good hand and staring into space for several seconds.

"I guess I have to be okay with it, don't I?" he said. "I just wish it had been anybody but my basketball coach."

She nodded. "I get that."

He looked at her. "How did you feel when your parents started seeing other people?" Christine's parents had been divorced for a while.

"Honestly, I was too young to understand it," she said. "Now my mom has been going out with the same guy for a long time, and he's nice. I don't think I've ever met anyone my dad goes out with. Which is fine with me. I don't think there's anyone serious."

Alex nodded. "Well, who knows. Maybe they won't like each other."

"What if they do?"

"I'll deal with it when I have to."

"Did Coach Archer say anything about it when he picked you up for school the last few mornings?"

He shook his head. "No. I guess he figured I'd bring it up if I wanted to talk about it. Can we talk about something else?"

"You *did* bring it up with me. . . ."

"I know. But I'm done now."

■ ■ ■

The best part of the day, as far as Alex was concerned, was walking through the mall and seeing the way the other guys looked at Christine. She wasn't dressed up—jeans, sneakers, and a red-and-gold Lions hoodie—but she was still hard to miss. Her long black hair wasn't tied back the way it usually was for school. Alex wished he could wear a sign that said, Yes, She's with Me.

He also liked the fact that she was so easy to talk to. She

was smart and funny, and—perhaps most important—she knew at least as much about sports as he did. And a lot more about dealing with divorced parents.

Alex didn't really see much of the movie. His mind was on other things. Finals, which he thought he'd squeaked through okay. Friday night's game, which Chester Heights had won easily. And his mom's date, which he kind of hoped wouldn't go so well.

He also spent a good amount of time wondering if he should put his arm around Christine. He was on her right, so his good arm, the left one, was available. But then he remembered his dad warning him about putting your arm around a date at the movies.

"Once you put your arm there you can *not* remove it," he had said. "If you remove it, your date will think you don't like her, and there will be hell to pay when the movie is over. So you have to leave it there. And, after a while, your arm is going to go to sleep. Then you are going to feel pain like no pain you have ever felt. You will *wish* you were in a dentist's office having your teeth drilled."

Alex knew his dad had probably been exaggerating, but still. He kept his hands in his lap—and thought about how he really missed doing things with his dad.

After the movie, Alex was hungry again, so they found an ice cream shop and ordered cones.

"What's your favorite sport?" Christine asked as he was trying to keep his cone from dripping all over his hand. They were sitting at a table in the food court.

"To play or to watch?" he asked once he had the cone under control.

"Play," she said.

He hadn't really ever thought about that. He knew that a lot of guys his age had been focused on one sport for years. His best friend in Boston, Buzz Capra, had gone to live at a tennis academy when he was eleven. He heard occasionally from Buzz by email and knew two things: he was now ranked number twelve in the nation among fourteen-and-under tennis players, and he was miserable.

"Probably baseball," he answered finally. "I love to pitch and I love to hit. Basketball's a lot of fun too, but I'd say I like baseball the most."

She looked surprised.

"What about football?" she said. "You're a very good quarterback, in case you hadn't noticed."

He smiled. "Thanks," he said. "I like football. But it beats you up. The practices are hard. It might be my *best* sport, but I enjoy baseball and basketball more."

She nodded.

"When you go to college, you'll have to choose," she said.

"I know," he said. "But I'm not worried about that yet. I'm only a freshman. Right now I'm just worried about getting my wrist healthy."

"So you can punch Zane Wakefield in the nose?" she said.

"There's a thought," he said, smiling. "Definitely a thought."

■ ■ ■

It occurred to Alex as they went to get their bikes and meet Christine's mom that once they were in the car he really wouldn't have a chance to kiss her goodbye. Which, maybe, was a little bit of a relief. He had no idea if she wanted him to kiss her or not.

But as they wheeled their bikes to where they were supposed to be picked up, he decided to venture out onto a different limb.

"So," he said. "I had fun."

"Me too," she said. "I think I've seen about eight versions of that same movie, but I liked it anyway."

That wasn't very helpful. Had she had a good time because she liked the movie or because she had gone to the movie with him?

He decided to take the plunge.

"So maybe we can do something after Christmas, then?" he said. "Before school starts?" He knew she'd be visiting relatives for a while, then back before New Year's.

She looked at him and smiled that smile that made his knees feel weak.

"Are you asking me out on another date?" she said.

Why did girls—at least this girl—have to make life so difficult?

He squared his shoulders.

"Yes, I am," he said.

"Okay, then, sure," she said, and then waved at her mother, whose car was pulling up.

Alex let out a deep breath. He'd have time to reconsider that kiss soon.

■ ■ ■

Alex hadn't seen his mom dressed up for a long time. He was sitting on the couch in the family room, eating Chinese food, when she came downstairs. Molly had gone to sleep over at their cousins' house, so he would have the place to himself for the evening.

Alex knew that his mom was pretty. His friends had told him that for as long as he could remember. Now, seeing her in a fancy dress and wearing high heels, Alex had to admit they were right.

"Mom, you look fantastic," he said. He had decided it was important to be a good sport about all this—no matter how queasy it made him feel.

"Thanks," she said. "You really think so?"

On cue, the doorbell rang. Alex answered it. Coach Archer, dressed in tan pants, a blue blazer, a white shirt, and a pale blue tie, stood there, looking nervous.

"How's the wrist, Alex?" he asked as he walked inside.

"Better," he said. "No real pain anymore."

Coach Archer walked over to his date. "Wow, Linda, you look great," he said.

He turned back to Alex. "I promise to bring her home early," he said with a smile.

This was a very different Coach Archer than the one Alex saw at school. He was smiling and clearly trying to make a good impression—on everyone.

"I'll be waiting up for you, young lady," Alex said jokingly to his mom. "Check in every hour."

They both laughed, and Alex's mom grabbed her coat.

"Call or text if you need me," she said in the doorway.

"I'll be fine, Mom. Lots of hoops to watch. You go have fun," he said, silently adding, but not *too* much fun.

The door closed. Alex turned on the television. Villanova

was playing Saint Joseph's. He knew the game was a big deal in Philadelphia since both schools were part of the Big Five. He tried to focus but wasn't doing a very good job. The phone rang.

It was his dad.

"Hey, Alex, I was hoping you'd be home," he said.

Alex had learned to be skeptical about almost everything his dad said. There had been a lot of promises to come visit that hadn't been kept. If his dad really wanted to talk to him, why hadn't he called his cell phone, which was sitting right in front of him?

"Just watching a basketball game," Alex said. "What's up?"

"Nothing, really," his dad said. "Back from LA. I was going to check with your mom to see how you and Molly were doing. Talk about your coming up here . . ."

"Molly's spending the night at Aunt Joan's," he said. "Mom's out. . . ." He paused. "With a friend."

If his dad wanted to know more about the friend or where his mom had gone, Alex couldn't tell. In fact, he quickly changed the subject.

"How's the wrist," he said. "Still hurting?"

"Not as much," Alex said. "It throbbed a lot the first couple days, but now, as long as I don't let the cast hit anything, it's fine."

"That means it's healing," his dad said. "That's good."

"Yeah, I guess so. We don't play again until the twenty-ninth. I probably won't be back by then. But conference starts on the ninth, so I hope I'll be ready for that."

"So you'll only miss a few games—that's not too bad."

"Four," Alex said. "We played last night."

"How'd they do without you?"

Alex almost smiled. "Won pretty easily. Bad team."

Alex heard someone talking in the background. His dad broke in. "Alex, I gotta go. Tell your mom I'll try to call tomorrow."

"Dad, she's out on a date."

The words came out of Alex's mouth before he had even finished wondering if he should say something about it. The voice in the background had been female. For a moment, there was silence on the other end of the phone.

Then his dad spoke slowly. "Well, good . . . That's good. . . . Who . . . is . . . it?"

Alex was deciding whether he should tell his father anything more when he heard the voice again. This time the words were clear. "Dave, we've got to go."

His dad had turned away from the phone, but Alex could still hear him clearly. "I'll be there in a minute—"

"Look, if you'd rather talk to your ex-wife—"

"I'm talking to my *son*."

Alex heard a spark of anger in his father's voice that made him smile.

"I'll be in the car," the voice said.

"Alex, I'm sorry," his dad said, coming back on the line.

"It's okay, Dad," Alex said. "You have to go."

"I'll call tomorrow. I—"

"Don't say you promise, Dad," Alex said. "Just call if you can."

"I love you, Alex."

Alex hesitated. His dad hadn't said that to him in a long, long time.

"I love you too, Dad."

13

Alex tried to wait up for his mother but failed. He was sleeping on the couch when he heard her come in. He glanced at his cell phone—almost 1:00 a.m.—and pulled himself into a sitting position.

"Alex, why aren't you upstairs?"

He pointed at the TV and reached for the remote to turn it off. "Fell asleep watching a game."

She sat down next to him and smiled. "Waiting up to make sure I didn't stay out too late?"

"Sort of. Did you have fun?"

She nodded. "Yes. He's a nice guy. He's really upset about what happened to you."

"Where did you go after dinner?"

"You mean, 'Why were you out so late, young lady?' We went to a club downtown. To tell you the truth, it was much too loud for me. Even when I was young I didn't like places like that. Now I'm a middle-aged mom. It's not for me for sure."

"Mom, you're only thirty-nine."

"Which means I'm almost forty. Come on, let's go to bed. It's way past both our bedtimes."

That sounded good to Alex. He decided against asking her if she thought she and Coach Archer would go out again. He had a feeling he knew the answer.

■ ■ ■

Lighting Hanukkah candles on Sunday night felt very strange to Alex without his father.

Alex and Molly had grown accustomed to celebrating both Hanukkah and Christmas. Dave Myers was Jewish; Linda Myers—the former Linda Reilly—was Catholic. Neither practiced their religion very much, so Alex and Molly hadn't gotten any formal religious training. But their mom insisted that holidays—both Christian and Jewish—be celebrated so the kids would know something about their heritage on both sides. Which was why their home always had a menorah and a Christmas tree. Their mom sang Christmas carols, and their dad knew enough Hebrew to recite a prayer each night of Hanukkah while they lit the evening's candles.

Both his parents loved to tell the story of Alex's first Hanukkah prayer, which had taken place when he was six. Alex's own memory of it was vague, but he knew the story by heart because it had been told so many times.

Apparently, when Alex's mom had asked him if he wanted to say a prayer as they lit the menorah, Alex had eagerly replied, "Oh yes, I'd really like to."

"Then go ahead," his mom had said.

"Oh, God," Alex said as he lit the candle, "thank you for inventing *Christmas*!"

When his dad told the story, he would always finish it by saying, "Let's face it, Christmas *is* more fun."

Alex had always enjoyed Hanukkah too—even though his parents had never accepted their kids' contention that there should be eight presents for eight nights. There were usually two—one on the first night and one on the last night.

Molly got two new apps for her cell phone, and Alex got a new Patriots sweatshirt with a hoodie, à la Bill Belichick. His mom had done her best with the candle-lighting prayer, but it still felt strange without his dad.

"You haven't got the accent," Molly said.

"I know," Linda Myers said, looking a little sad.

"Yeah, but it was still pretty good," Alex said, seeing the look on her face. "Better than I could have done."

She smiled. "Thanks, Alex."

He and Molly were taking a train to Boston on Monday morning to spend three days with their dad—their first visit since the move to Philadelphia. They would be back on Christmas Eve, but their mom would be alone for three days. So, after the candle lighting, when they sat down to dinner, Alex asked his mom if she had any plans for when he and Molly were gone.

"Mostly I plan to do nothing," she said. "I'll finish my Christmas shopping, try to get the house clean—unpack some boxes we've never opened—and relax. I'll miss you both, but a few days of no pickups or drop-offs or cooking won't be a terrible thing."

Alex decided not to ask her if she had any social plans.

After dinner, Alex volunteered to help with the dishes, while Molly headed off to try out her new apps.

"By the way," his mom said as he was loading the dishwasher. "Evan's visiting family this week, so you don't have to worry about me out on another date while you're gone."

He wouldn't have said he was *worried*, exactly, but it was kind of a relief.

"What about when he comes back?" Alex asked.

"Oh, we'll see," she said.

The upbeat tone in her voice—even in just three words—answered his question. If he had said a Hanukkah prayer at that moment, it would have had very little to do with thanking God for Christmas.

■ ■ ■

The next morning, their mom drove Alex and Molly to Thirtieth Street Station to catch the Acela Express to Boston. Alex saw no need for their mom to escort them into the station, but she insisted.

It occurred to Alex as they walked into the huge lobby of the station that he had never traveled by train before. The family had always traveled by car or, for a big trip, by plane. And all the teams he had played on had traveled by bus.

"Wow, this place is gigantic," Molly said.

"That's why I wanted to come in with you," Linda Myers said.

They found the train listed on a big board in the middle of the lobby. En route to the gate, they stopped so Alex could pick up a copy of the *New York Times*. He knew his dad read the *Times* and the *Boston Globe* every morning. Since his mom only subscribed to the *Inquirer* at home, he couldn't access the *Times* online and he missed some of the sportswriters.

They found the gate and their mom hugged them both. Alex thought he saw a tear or two in her eyes.

"You okay, Mom?" he asked. "We'll be back on Wednesday."

"I know," she said. "But this is the first time you two have traveled alone. . . ."

"We'll be fine," he said.

"I *know* you will," she said. "It's just that you're both so . . . grown up. I mean, look at the two of you!"

Alex was now six one, meaning he was about six inches taller than his mom. Even Molly was closing in, no more than an inch or two shorter than she was.

Alex couldn't think of anything comforting to say at that moment. He and Molly weren't going to get shorter—or younger—anytime soon.

"Mom, you're the most beautiful mom I know," Molly blurted.

It was the perfect thing to say. Their mom lit up.

"Let me know as soon as you get there," she said.

A voice called "All aboard." Alex gave his mom one more quick hug, and then he and Molly headed for the train.

■ ■ ■

The visit started out well. Much to Alex's relief, their dad was waiting for them when they came up the escalator at North Station in Boston. He had texted them that he might be a few minutes late, but he wasn't late—a good start.

His dad had moved into an apartment in the north end of town that had a nice view of Boston Harbor. They went to dinner that night at Legal Sea Foods, and Alex and Molly caught him up on what was going on in their lives. Alex kept waiting for his dad to ask about his mom's date, but he said nothing.

The next night, they all went to see the Celtics play the Knicks. Alex and his dad had often gone to games, but this was different: Dave Myers's law firm had apparently purchased four of the TD Garden's front-row seats—right on the court.

Spike Lee seats! The great film director had made the seats famous in Madison Square Garden by taunting opposing players from only a few feet away when they were playing against the Knicks. Lee's antics had become so well known that his verbal duels with Reggie Miller, the former Indiana Pacers star, had become the subject of a documentary.

An usher escorted them to their seats, and Alex was stunned to see Carmelo Anthony, the Knicks superstar, practicing his jump shot a few feet away.

"This is why I wanted to get here early," his dad said. "I thought you'd like to watch how the pros warm up."

It wasn't all that different from the way the Chester Heights Lions warmed up, except that the Knicks and Celtics casually took shots from much farther out than Alex would have dreamed of shooting and *made* quite a few of them. Alex was transfixed watching Anthony when he noticed that someone was walking right toward them with a security guard trailing in his wake. He looked more closely and saw it was Brad Stevens, the coach of the Celtics.

"Is this our injured player, Dave?" Stevens said, shaking hands with Alex's dad as if they were old friends.

"This is Alex," his dad said. "And his sister, Molly."

"The soccer player," Stevens said, smiling. He shook hands with both of them and then pointed at Alex's cast.

"How much longer?" he asked.

Alex was stumped by the question. Not because it was difficult—somewhere in the back of his brain he knew the answer was another week to ten days—but because he was staring at Stevens in disbelief.

"He's hoping to get it off before New Year's," his dad said, recognizing the stunned look on his son's face. "With luck he'll be ready to go when conference play starts next month."

Stevens smiled and looked at Alex. "Your dad said you tore a tendon. I did the same thing in college. I came back and was as good a shooter as I'd ever been." He smiled again. "Of course, I wasn't that good to begin with."

That brought Alex back to planet Earth. He laughed.

"Coach, it's really good to see you guys playing so much better this season," he said, happy to learn he still had a voice.

"Well, we couldn't be much worse than last year, could we?" Stevens said. He put out his left hand again. "It's nice to meet you both. Good luck with the wrist, Alex—it'll be fine, I promise."

Alex and Molly shook hands with him, as did their dad, who said, "Thanks for this, Brad. I really appreciate it."

"Have a great holiday, Dave," Stevens said, and turned to go back to work.

Alex was staring at his dad in amazement.

"His best friend from college is a partner in the firm now," his dad said. "When I knew I was going to bring you guys tonight, I asked Ted if there was any way Brad might come over and say hello. I know what a big Butler fan you were."

Alex had become a big fan of Butler when Stevens had coached them to back-to-back national championship games in 2010 and 2011. He tried to model a lot of his game on the way Gordon Hayward, the Butler star, played. He'd been excited when Stevens had taken the Celtics job. Now he felt even more connected to the team.

The Celtics won the game, thanks to a Marcus Smart three-pointer in the final seconds that he took from right in front of the Myers family, and Alex walked out of the arena feeling as happy and relaxed as he had felt at any point since the move to Philadelphia.

He'd thought it might be weird staying with his dad in a new place, but the trip was going great. It'd been nice to just hang out with his father again. And he had met Brad Stevens!

That feeling lasted about twelve hours.

Their train home on Wednesday didn't leave until late afternoon, so they had most of the day to be together.

"You guys can sleep in. Then we'll go have lunch up at the club," his dad said. "We'll eat in the grill room and sit by the fire like we used to."

His dad was a very good golfer and had joined the Country Club in Brookline, one of the most famous golf clubs in the country, a few years earlier. Alex had been wondering if he could find a course in Philadelphia. He'd made real progress the previous summer but hadn't played at all after the move from Boston.

The club was just as warm as he remembered, and they got a table almost right in front of the fireplace. Alex and Molly were ordering hot chocolate when Alex saw his dad's face light up. He followed his gaze and saw a tall, fashionably dressed woman with shoulder-length dark hair heading in their direction. Alex's dad stood up and greeted her with a kiss on the cheek.

"Sorry I'm late," she said. "When I pulled up, the valet was nowhere in sight. You should talk to someone about that."

Alex almost snickered. His dad had always laughed about the "club snobs," who valet-parked their cars instead of just finding a spot themselves. He noticed Molly was staring at the woman and had a fierce look on her face. She looked exactly like their mom when she was angry.

"Alex, Molly, I want you to meet someone," his dad was saying. "This is Megan Wheeler." He paused for a moment, and Alex had the sense that Megan Wheeler was waiting for him to add something to the introduction.

Alex was right.

"Megan," he added, "is my fiancée."

Things went downhill quickly from there.

Later, Alex wondered exactly what his dad could have been thinking to deliver the news that he was engaged at the same moment he was introducing his new girlfriend to his kids for the first time. But in that moment, he was just stunned.

Molly's instantaneous shriek was greeted by a glare from Megan Wheeler. But it snapped Alex out of his stupor long enough for him to stand up and say, "I'm Alex." He considered adding *Nice to meet you*, and then passed on the idea.

"And this is Molly," his dad said, stating the obvious. Molly managed to put her hand out but recoiled at the same time.

"Dad, how can you be engaged to someone?" Molly said. "You're still married to Mom."

"Legally, that's true," Dave Myers said, pulling a chair out for Megan to sit down. "But your mom and I have worked everything out. Obviously, Megan and I won't be getting married until the divorce is final. After all, I wouldn't want to be accused of bigamy."

If that was supposed to be funny, no one at the table saw the humor in it. Alex had given up on the notion months ago that his parents might get back together. But he was still worried about how his mom would take the news.

"Does Mom know?" he asked.

"Of course," his dad said as if the question were insulting. "But really, this just happened over the weekend."

A waiter came up to see if Megan Wheeler wanted something to drink. She asked for a glass of chardonnay. Alex glanced at his watch. It was 12:08. He wasn't sure he'd ever seen someone drink wine this early in the day.

"You know, Alex, Molly, I hope we're going to be very good friends," she said. "I understand your surprise at all this. It *did* happen rather fast."

Alex studied her. He guessed she was about the same age as his parents. She was *not* as pretty as his mother. She wore a lot of makeup, a good deal of jewelry, and what looked like expensive clothes.

"So where do you work?" he asked, desperate for a neutral topic of conversation.

"I'm a party planner," she said. "That's how I met your dad. I was in charge of putting together his office Christmas party, and—"

"Wait a minute," Molly said. "His office Christmas party was last week. You just met *last week*?"

Megan Wheeler laughed as if Molly had just told the funniest joke in history.

"No, no! *Last* year's Christmas party," she said.

"But we didn't start seeing each other until this fall," Alex's dad said—too quickly, Alex thought.

Alex wanted to be fair. He'd just met the woman. But already he didn't like her. And it wasn't just because she was marrying his dad.

"So what do you study in college to become a party planner?" he asked, realizing too late the question was rude. Megan Wheeler realized it too.

"I majored in art history," she said coolly. "I worked in New York at MOMA until I moved to Boston and my partner and I started our company."

"MOMA?" Alex said. "What's that?"

"The Museum of Modern Art," she answered.

The waiter came back with her drink.

"Davey, you never told me you had such inquisitive children," she said.

"*Davey?*" Alex and Molly said together.

The waiter asked if they were ready to order. "I need a minute to look at the menu," Megan Wheeler said.

"Why don't you bring me a scotch and soda," Davey said. "And then we'll order."

Alex had never even thought about ordering a drink before. But for one split second he was tempted to say "Make it two."

■ ■ ■

Alex's dad had tried to make conversation through the rest of lunch—telling Megan Wheeler all about the accomplishments of his two children. Alex supposed she could have looked more bored, but he wasn't sure how. The plan had apparently been for Megan to come to the train station and see them off, but as they were leaving, she said, "Davey, I have one of my headaches. I'll just go home from here." She turned to Alex and Molly and said, "I'll see you both again soon, I'm sure," and Alex wondered if that was a promise or a threat. At least she made no attempt at a phony kiss goodbye for either one of them. He was pretty sure that Molly would have screamed at the top of her lungs if she had.

Once they were all back in the car, heading for the train, Molly lost it.

"Dad, how could you?" she yelled, and then burst into tears. She was crying so hard she was shaking.

"Moll, I'm sorry," their dad said. "But I did tell you both I was seeing someone. And Alex tells me your mom is seeing someone too."

"*One date!*" Alex yelled, surprised at how loud his voice was inside the car. "She's not *engaged!*"

"It just happened," Dave Myers said. "I never planned it that way."

"But, Dad, she's *horrible*," Molly wailed.

His dad looked at Alex in the rearview mirror for support. "She's right, Dad," Alex said. "I mean, what a snob."

"You don't know her yet," their dad said.

"We know enough," Molly answered.

■ ■ ■

The hugs at the train station were quick and awkward. Alex's dad pulled over to the curb and jumped out of the car just long enough to help Molly get her bag and to wish them a

Merry Christmas and tell them he would see them in Philadelphia soon.

"You okay, Moll?" Alex asked as they walked inside to get out of the frigid wind.

She was rolling her bag behind her and wiping the tears away with her free hand.

"No, I'm *not* okay," she said. "How can I possibly be okay?"

"He has the right to move on with his life, just like Mom does," Alex said. "I know this is kind of quick—"

"Quick?" she scoffed. "Quick? He had her picked out before we even left town. But that's not the worst part. That woman is *awful*! What is he thinking?"

Molly had always been a precocious little kid. She was right too—what was their dad thinking? He was still young, he was a good-looking guy, and he was a very successful lawyer. Why would he get engaged so fast? And to a woman who might be attractive but was clearly an absolute snob. It was baffling—and upsetting.

They both slept for most of the train ride, totally wiped out. Alex was actually happy to see the skyline of Philadelphia come into view.

He had never thought anyplace but Boston would be home. Philadelphia might not be home either, but after the last twelve hours, he felt a lot more comfortable being here than there.

■ ■ ■

Christmas was a long day for Alex.

Opening presents in the morning with Molly and his mom was nice. But then they went to his aunt and uncle's house. His cousins were six and four, and Alex had no desire to sit on the floor and play games with them. But that might have been better than the adult conversation about who the likely presidential nominees were going to be.

He finally escaped to the den, where he was able to turn on an NBA game. Unfortunately, the one he cared about wouldn't be on until late that night: the Celtics and his new best friend, Brad Stevens, were playing the Lakers in Los Angeles.

He tried not to think about his father and Megan Wheeler. His mom, who had clearly been briefed by his dad while they were on the train, brought it up on the car ride home from the station, causing Molly to burst into tears yet again.

"I'm sure she isn't as bad as you think," Linda Myers said. "She was probably just as nervous as you were."

"We weren't nervous, Mom," Alex said. "We were mad—at *Dad*."

His mom tapped the rearview mirror for no reason—a nervous habit. "Well, I told him his timing wasn't great. He should have just introduced you and then told you about the engagement later—without her there. But he said she wanted it that way."

"Yeah," Molly said, sniffling. "Whatever Megan wants, Megan gets."

Alex hadn't disagreed.

Now he took comfort in calmly watching a basketball game by himself—no one crying, no one arguing, no one demanding he play with trains or listen to talk about presidential politics.

"Thank God for basketball," he murmured.

■ ■ ■

On Sunday afternoon, Alex went to watch his teammates practice. Coach Archer had asked them all to be back on Sunday unless they were on extended family vacations. They were cramming in three more nonconference games—two before school even started again. There were games on Tuesday and then Friday (the day after New Year's) and then the next Tuesday. Then on Friday the ninth, they'd start their conference schedule. Alex was hoping to play in the last nonconference game as a warm-up. He *would* be playing in the conference opener.

Everyone had made it back, including, sadly, Zane Wakefield. He and Alex exchanged nods, nothing more, when he walked on court before practice began. Everyone else came over for left-handed shakes or hugs, including Jonas, who he knew had been in New York for Christmas. They had texted regularly, so Jonas knew about his dad's engagement.

"You doing okay?" Jonas asked.

"Been better," Alex said, before they were interrupted by Steve Holder coming over to say hello.

Both coaches came over too.

"It's really nice of you to show support for the team by coming," Coach Archer said. "You didn't have to do that."

"I know; you told me," Alex said. "But I thought I should see what you're working on, since I'll be playing in a week."

"When do you go back to the doctor?" Coach Archer asked.

"Tomorrow morning. I'm hoping the cast will come off then."

Coach Archer nodded. "Good. Call me or text when you have news."

"I will. Thanks."

Coach Archer turned to whistle everyone to the circle to start practice. He hadn't asked about Alex's mom. Maybe, Alex thought, he didn't need to ask.

■ ■ ■

Dr. Taylor was waiting in the outer office the next day when Alex and his mom walked in.

"Technically, we're closed until next week, except for emergencies," he said, answering their question before they could ask. "But I knew you'd really want to try to get that cast off today, Alex." He smiled. "Plus, Pete keeps telling me how much the team needs you back as soon as possible."

"That's really nice of you, Dr. Taylor," Alex's mom said.

"Anything for the cause," he said. "Come on back and let's take a look."

He took the cast off, then carefully began poking his fingers around various places on Alex's hand, wrist, and arm. When he got to what he called the "hot spot," he pressed down lightly. Alex felt nothing. He pressed a little harder, and Alex felt a little pain. He tried to mask it, but the doctor saw the look on his face.

"It's okay, Alex. It should still hurt a little bit when I do that. But it's nothing like it was two weeks ago. I want to do a quick X-ray just to make sure nothing shows up."

"You don't need an MRI?" Alex's mom asked.

Dr. Taylor shook his head. "No, we'd only need an MRI if there might be something hiding we can't see on the X-ray. But I think he's pretty close to healed. I'm only really doing the X-ray as a precaution."

It didn't take Dr. Taylor long to come back with the films. He put them up on the light box on the wall, then smiled and pointed at a tiny spot on one of the pictures.

"That's where you felt the pain," he said to Alex. "You're just about there. No need to put the cast back on. You can start rehab today."

"Rehab?" Alex said.

"Hold your wrists up next to each other," Dr. Taylor said.

Alex did as he was told. Both he and his mom gasped. His left wrist—normally the weaker wrist—looked to be twice the size of the right one.

"Your wrist atrophied after being in the cast for two weeks," Dr. Taylor said. "That's totally normal. But it will take some rehab to build it back up. Start slow—just get some five-pound weights and increase your reps slowly. Maybe three sets of ten today; then add one set per day."

"But when can I play? We have games on Tuesday and Friday. . . ."

"No basketball until the weekend. Then you can start doing drills—dribbling, passing. If that goes well, if you're feeling no pain, then you can try to practice Sunday. But come back next Monday and I'll check it one more time."

"There's another game next Tuesday. . . ."

Dr. Taylor held up a hand. "I'm well aware," he said. "That'll be up to Coach Archer. My guess is you won't be really game ready until next Friday, but that's the one that matters, right—conference opener?"

"Right," Alex said. "I'd just like to play a game before—"

"See if you're ready for practice Sunday afternoon. See how quickly your strength comes back. If your coach thinks it's a good idea and you're able to practice, then you can play Tuesday. But don't rush it, Alex. You don't want to reinjure yourself by coming back one game or even one day too soon."

Alex knew the doctor was right. He also knew that watching two—and maybe three—more games would be torture.

■ ■ ■

The game Tuesday night was against Bishop O'Connell, a team that played in Washington, DC's, high-powered Catholic league. Coach Archer had worked for Joe Wootten, O'Connell's coach, and they had agreed to a home-and-home series—the first game taking place at Chester Heights since O'Connell was en route to a post-Christmas tournament in New York.

From his seat on the end of the bench, Alex could tell in less than a minute that O'Connell was a much better team than Mercer—which was bad news for the Lions. The only thing that kept the game from becoming completely humiliating was that Coach Wootten, probably out of respect for his friendship with Coach Archer, didn't press the entire game. That allowed Wakefield to get the ball upcourt and start the offense, but it didn't matter much.

Even when the Lions ran a play perfectly, they had trouble getting a shot off because O'Connell was so much quicker than they were at every position. On several occasions, the Lions made perfect passes to set up wide-open layups—until an O'Connell defender recovered quickly and blocked the shot.

The only Lion who looked remotely like he belonged on the court was Steve Holder. He had ten points at halftime—

six of them on offensive putbacks. The problem was the rest of his teammates also had ten points—combined. Even Jonas looked helpless, trying to go head to head with a shooting guard who was about six four, a senior, and even quicker than he was. O'Connell led 54–20 at the break.

"I scheduled this game so you guys could see up close the kind of team that we want to be someday," Coach Archer said at halftime. Alex stood in a corner of the locker room and listened. "This is one of the best teams in the country. Joe told me he's got six guys on the team he expects to be Division I scholarship players when they go to college. LeGares is being recruited by every big-time school in the country, and he's only a junior."

Alex wasn't surprised that Juan LeGares was coveted by colleges. He looked to be about six eight. Alex figured the Chester Heights starters might be able to take him in a game of five on one. If the Lions played really well.

The second half was like a slow-motion scrimmage. LeGares, who'd had twenty-two points at halftime, never saw the court. Because they were on a two-city holiday trip, Coach Wootten had brought fourteen players—several of them JV players, no doubt. He didn't play any of his starters in the second half. Even so, the final score was 84–48, meaning O'Connell had only outscored the Lions by two points in the second half. Alex guessed that if Coach Wootten had played his starters and pressed the whole game, O'Connell would have won by eighty.

Coach Archer didn't say that after the game; he emphasized the positive—the more competitive nature of the second half. He told the players they would practice at one o'clock the next day, since it was New Year's Eve.

As everyone headed for the showers, Coach Archer beckoned Alex. "Come into my office for a second, Myers," he said.

Alex followed him to the tiny office.

"You want a soda or something?" Coach Archer asked.

"I'm fine," Alex said. "Thanks."

Coach Archer grabbed a Coke and pointed Alex to the chair across from his desk.

"What did you think tonight?" he asked.

"Honestly?" Alex asked.

Coach Archer sipped his Coke. "Yes, honestly. You saw that Joe didn't play his starters in the second half. How much do you think they would have won by if he'd left his starters in?"

Alex shrugged. "If he left his starters in and didn't press like in the first half, probably about sixty or so," he said. "If he'd wanted to press, it might have been eighty."

Coach Archer smiled. "Alex, if he'd pressed, with Wakefield playing point, we might never have crossed midcourt," he said. "You're being kind. If we'd had you, *then* we might have lost by sixty or so if they'd pressed."

"Are we that bad, or are they that good?"

"Both," Coach Archer said. "They're ranked fifth in the country in the *USA Today* poll right now, and it isn't an accident. Without you, we're pretty bad. With you, we're better. When you get healthy, and Jonas gets more comfortable, and Steve Holder is hot, we can be competitive. But"—he leaned forward in his seat—"we're going to get a transfer in here next week who I'm told is as good or better than any of the three of you."

"A transfer, in midseason?"

Coach Archer nodded. "He's like you. Parents are divorcing. He and his mom and sister are moving here from Detroit. His mom and dad are both lawyers, and apparently they worked together. That isn't going to work anymore, and she got offered a job with a firm here."

"How do you know all this?"

"The kid's coach was a college teammate of mine, so he called me."

It occurred to Alex that Coach Archer might not have been a stand-out player in college but he certainly knew a lot of people.

"I probably shouldn't be telling you, but his situation sounded so much like yours—I thought you might reach out to him."

"What's his name?"

"Max Bellotti. He's about six four, which means he can play small forward. So by the time we get into conference play, assuming your wrist keeps getting better, we should have four solid players in the starting lineup. And some of the guys who are playing too many minutes now can come off the bench instead and do okay in more limited roles."

"We won't be good enough to beat O'Connell," Alex said, smiling.

"No." Coach Archer returned the smile. "But we might only lose to them by about twenty-five."

■ ■ ■

Jonas's mom had volunteered to drive Alex home since his mom was at a concert with Molly, so Alex filled Jonas in on Max Bellotti during the ride.

"We could use another player," Jonas said. "I'll tell you what, though—some of those guys who'll be sitting down won't be happy."

"They'd rather lose by eighty?" Alex said.

"And play? You bet. You think Wakefield is going to be happy going to the bench when you're back just because it makes us better? Dream on."

Alex thought about what Jonas had said when he got home and heated up the dinner his mom had left for him. The guys who had been on the team last year were *used* to losing. When he had walked back into the locker room to find Jonas after his talk with Coach Archer, most of the older guys had been joking and laughing and talking about their plans for New Year's Eve.

Alex knew Jonas was right—Zane Wakefield and Tony Early and Cory McAndrews, who was currently playing small forward, would not be happy to lose their starting spots. Coach Archer had started Early that night, but it was clearly a token gesture: Jonas was going to be the star shooting guard and play the most minutes, and everyone, including Early, knew it. If Max Bellotti was as good as Coach Archer said he was, McAndrews would be on the bench too. What's more, the three seniors who had been the team's main backups a year ago—Pete Taylor, Larry Ceplair, and Arnold Bogus—would hardly play at all. They wouldn't be happy either.

That would mean, no doubt, a divided team. Though really, the team was already divided. Wakefield, Early, and McAndrews couldn't stand the fact that he and Jonas were better than they were. Holder, as the captain, was trying to get along with everyone and to get everyone to get along— but it wasn't working.

Alex thought about Matt Gordon and the fact that he had recognized right away that Alex was a threat to him at the quarterback position. But Matt had never been anything but supportive, and in the end, he had only hurt himself— not the team—when he started taking steroids. There was another difference: Matt Gordon was an excellent player on one of the best football teams in Pennsylvania. Wakefield, Early, and McAndrews were lousy players on a lousy team. Actually, McAndrews and Jameer Wilson, who was currently the team's sixth man, weren't awful. But Wakefield and Early were pretty bad.

Alex looked down at his wrist. He couldn't wait to get back on the court and have the chance to humiliate Wakefield in practice. But the arrival of Max Bellotti gave him something more positive to look forward to. He might help the Lions be really competitive once conference play began. Or he might be the final wedge that would divide the team for good.

Alex put his dishes in the dishwasher and headed up to bed. It wasn't up to him to figure out how to get the newer, more talented players to mesh with the older, less talented ones. That was Coach Archer's job.

Alex didn't envy him.

■ ■ ■

Christine called early the next morning. She had gotten back from a visit to her family in Chicago the night before—but too late to get to the game.

"How bad was it?" she asked.

"Could have been much worse," Alex said. "If they had pressed the entire game, we might have lost by a hundred."

She laughed as if he were joking—which he wasn't. "Well, if it makes you feel any better, the team you're playing on Friday night is probably almost as good."

Alex had heard that. He knew that West Philadelphia was also ranked in the USA Today top twenty-five.

"So we'll get killed," Alex said.

"I would think so," she said. "How's your wrist? Jonas texted me to say you were out of the cast."

He had? Alex hadn't texted Christine except to say Merry Christmas. He'd kind of thought she would check in with him, since she knew he was seeing Dr. Taylor on Monday. Now he felt bad somehow.

"Yeah. I'm rehabbing it slowly. The doctor says I can start to play by Saturday, so I should be able to practice Sunday."

"And play in the game on Tuesday?"

"That'll be up to Coach Archer."

"Do you wish you were playing Friday, or are you glad you don't have to deal with it?" she asked.

He thought that was an odd question. "Of course I want to play," he said. "Why wouldn't I?"

"Because this way you don't get embarrassed."

"Yes I do," Alex said. "That's still *my* team out there, my teammates."

"Even Wakefield?"

He sighed. "Yes," he said finally. "Even Wakefield. I will happily kick his butt in practice, but when he's wearing *Lions* on his uniform we're on the same side."

"You really feel that way?"

"Yes, I do."

At least, he thought, I *hope* I do.

■ ■ ■

West Philadelphia wasn't as good as Bishop O'Connell, but they were plenty good enough to humiliate Chester Heights. They lived up to their nickname—Speedboys—from the start, darting around the court and making both Zane Wakefield and Tony Early look helpless trying to bring the ball upcourt. Coach Archer finally brought Steve Holder back to help handle the ball, and at least some of the time, he was able to get the ball into the frontcourt.

The final score was almost as embarrassing as the O'Connell score had been: 77–51. Their coach had left his starters in for a little while in the second half but backed off the press and played his second team the entire fourth quarter. Just as well that the gym was practically empty. Lots of people were still probably away for their holiday breaks. But they'd all be back next week. The Lions were now 2–3, with one nonconference game left to play.

There were a number of reporters waiting outside the locker room when Alex came out, some of them familiar faces from football season. He noticed Dick Jerardi, who worked for the *Philadelphia Daily News* and appeared regularly on Comcast SportsNet–Philadelphia, standing off to the side. Jerardi waved at him.

"Why would you be at *this* game," Alex said, using his left hand to shake hands with Jerardi, since he still wasn't taking any chances with his right.

"Doing a profile on Tim O'Donnell, West Philly's point guard. He committed to Saint Joseph's in November. A lot of people think he could be the best guard they've recruited since Jameer Nelson."

Alex certainly knew who Jameer Nelson was. He was a graduate of Chester, the Lions' crosstown archrivals. He had gone on to be the national player of the year at Saint Joseph's and was still playing in the NBA. O'Donnell had dominated the game, but Alex hadn't really thought that much about it since the guards he was playing against—Wakefield and Early—were so bad.

"Tough to tell much from this game," he said to Jerardi.

"True," Jerardi said. "But the kid came ready to play against a team he knew wasn't any good." He paused. "No offense."

"None taken," Alex said. "We're terrible."

"I'm sure the team is better with you out there. Freak accident in practice, right?"

That was the way the story had been told. The local media had all done short stories on Alex's injury, in large part because of the notoriety he had gained during football season.

"Yeah, I just fell funny on a fast break," he said. "I might be back for Tuesday, but definitely for the conference opener next Friday."

Christine walked up. Like Jerardi, she was waiting for those who had played in the game to shower, dress, and come out of the locker room. The two knew each other, in part because Jerardi had covered the football team during the state playoffs and also because her dad was an editor at the *Philadelphia Inquirer*—which was in the same building as the *Daily News*.

"You want a quote from Coach Archer on O'Donnell, right?" she said to Jerardi. "Should I try to talk to the two guards too?"

"They may be shell-shocked, but sure," Jerardi said.

"Stark's tomorrow?" she asked Alex. "Usual time?"

"Okay," Alex said, feeling like he should have thought to ask her first. Why was he always a step behind with her?

"Best reporter in the building," Jerardi said, causing Christine to blush. "I'm sure you'll get better quotes from your guys than I would."

"I'm not sure Wakefield or Early are that quotable," Alex said. "Jonas and Holder might be better."

Christine nodded in agreement.

"Well, that'll be enough for me," Jerardi said. He spotted West Philly's coach coming out of the visitors' locker room. "Gotta go. Hope you're better soon, Alex. I'll tell Stevie you said hello, Christine. I'll see him tomorrow at the Palestra."

"Stevie?" Alex asked.

"You remember," Christine said. "He helped me out on your case last month."

Alex remembered. "Oh yeah, the famous teenage reporter with the really hot girlfriend."

Alex mentioned the girlfriend, whose name he couldn't remember, to see how Christine reacted.

"Susan Carol Anderson," she said, without batting an eye. "You're right; she is hot. Also an Olympic swimmer and a *great* reporter. Stevie said he'd try to introduce us the next time she comes to Philadelphia."

That was fine with Alex. He changed the subject.

"Did you hear we've got a transfer coming soon who Coach Archer thinks can help us a lot?"

"Max Bellotti," she said. "Actually, I'm a little bit mad at Coach Archer because he wouldn't give me his phone number. He said I can talk to him after practice on Sunday. I guess that'll work for the Wednesday *Roar*."

That tidbit made Alex smile, if only for a moment. "Well, we can't get much worse," he said. "Even if the guy is just okay, he'll help. That was embarrassing tonight."

"Yeah," she said. "Dick told me during the game that West Philly is probably only the fourth or fifth best team in the Public League this season. They beat you by twenty-six, with the starters playing zero minutes in the fourth quarter. Unless Max Bellotti can play like LeBron James or Kevin Durant, it's going to be a long season."

They spotted Coach Archer coming out of the locker room.

"Gotta go," she said. "Don't invite Jonas tomorrow. I was thinking we'd bike to the mall after lunch."

He was trying to think of a clever answer—maybe, *Wow, that sounds great*—but she was gone, heading over to where Coach Archer was standing.

He wondered if anyone noticed he was standing there with a stupid grin on his face. He might be a step behind, but he still had a date on Saturday.

15

Alex and Christine had wandered the mall, drifting in and out of different places, catching each other up on their holidays. They hung out in a bookstore for a while, talking their way through the books on the sports shelves. Alex and his dad had done that often, and they always came home with something they both wanted to read. But every time Alex pointed out a book now, Christine's response was, "Yeah, that was good."

Finally he made her pick a favorite for him and something she hadn't already read for her.

They took their books upstairs to the food court. They had time for an ice cream before his mom was due to pick them up. Watching Christine eat her ice cream, Alex made an important decision: he was going to kiss her. The question was where and when and—perhaps most important—how to do it.

"You think you'll be able to practice tomorrow? Are you worried about your wrist?" she asked, bringing him back from his strategizing.

"Maybe a little," he said. "Jonas and I are going to get to practice early, so I'll have a chance to see how it feels. And Coach Archer wants to watch me before he decides whether to let me scrimmage or not."

"I wonder how good the new kid will be," she said.

Alex shrugged. "Coach doesn't compliment players too often, and he seems pretty excited. He has to be better than what we've got, right?"

Christine pointed her cone at Alex for a second. "Dick Jerardi says he's never met a coach who didn't like the guys *not* playing for him better than the ones who are."

Alex actually remembered reading something like that in a book about the infamously angry former coach Bob Knight. His best players always seemed to be those who had already left the Indiana program or hadn't yet arrived.

"Well, we'll find out soon enough," Alex said.

They got up and started walking in the direction of the escalators that would take them to the lower parking deck, where they'd locked their bikes and where they were supposed to meet his mom. Down they went, heading for the doors. Alex's heart was pounding, and he found himself walking slower and slower. The doors loomed. His mom could already be waiting, or she could pull up at the worst possible time. It was now or never.

He stopped and reached out for her arm. "Hey, hold on a minute, Christine."

She turned and looked up at him.

Then, almost before he knew what was happening, she stood on her tiptoes, pulled his head down, and kissed him—quickly, but firmly, on the lips.

"Thank you for the book, and the ice cream, and the great day."

She stepped back, smiling her dazzling smile.

"Thank *you*," he whispered.

He couldn't think of anything else to say. But judging by her smile, that seemed to be okay.

■ ■ ■

It turned out Alex wasn't the only Myers to have a date on Saturday. After they had dropped Christine off, his mom told him she was going out to dinner with Coach Archer.

"He called after you left to meet Christine," she said. "I wasn't holding out on you."

Alex laughed. "You aren't going to get engaged or anything, are you?" he said. "As long as you don't do that, it's all good."

She laughed, then said, "Still mad at your dad?"

Alex shrugged. "I don't know how to feel. He's texted a couple times this last week to check on my wrist, but that's it. I think he's afraid to talk to me. Or Molly."

She stopped at a red light and looked right at him.

"You're probably right," she said. "I think he wants to talk to the two of you in person the next time he's down here."

"Which will be when?" Alex asked.

"Good question," his mom answered, and the light turned green.

■ ■ ■

The weather was frigid on Sunday morning, with snow expected later in the day. Alex's mom picked up Jonas and dropped the two boys off at the gym. She had gotten home after Alex had gone to bed on Saturday, and they only talked briefly about her date at breakfast.

"It was fun," she had said. "He's definitely a jock at heart, like you and . . ."—she paused—"like your dad."

Alex didn't know what to think about that. . . .

■ ■ ■

Alex and Jonas walked into the gym to find Coach Archer shooting jump shots by himself. He looked at his watch and said, "It's 11:01—you're late. I should make you go outside and run."

If he hadn't been smiling, Alex would have been worried.

As Alex and Jonas began peeling off their jackets and sweats, Coach Archer flipped them the ball he'd been practicing with. "Remember, Alex, nothing too physical at first. Go slow. Just do some shooting drills and *maybe*, if you feel okay, some noncontact one on one. You understand what noncontact means, Jonas?"

"I should knock him on his butt before he makes contact with me?" Jonas asked.

"Exactly," Coach Archer laughed.

Alex felt no pain when he shot the ball, but he was completely rusty. And despite all the reps he'd put in with free weights, his wrist still wasn't built back up to full strength, so he found himself pushing his shot to get it to the basket.

Coach Archer noticed. "That's not your shooting motion," he said. "You're trying too hard."

"I know," Alex said. "My wrist is still a little bit weak."

"Right," Coach Archer said. "Not surprising. Let's just work on dribbling and passing and do some fast-break stuff. That way you won't get into any bad habits with your shot. When practice starts, we'll get you in some drills, but I think we'll wait until after Tuesday's game to let you scrimmage."

"So, you're saying I'm not going to play Tuesday?"

"Do you think you're ready to play?"

Alex glanced at Jonas. He wanted to say yes, but he knew the answer was no. He finally shook his head. Coach Archer walked over and put an arm around him.

"Smart call, Alex. Take it slow. Passing and dribbling . . ."

Alex and Jonas did that, running up and down the court throwing passes to one another and doing ball-handling drills—mostly with Alex on offense, because he needed the work—and then forming their own two-man layup line, so Alex could ease his way back into shooting the ball. His wrist felt fine attempting simple layups.

At noon, Coach Archer looked at his watch.

"Okay, fellas, we should stop. You've got to be back here at three o'clock for practice. I don't want to wear either one of you out. Jonas, you need a ride?" Alex's mom and Molly were ice-skating, so Coach Archer was giving Alex a ride home.

"My mom's picking me up in fifteen minutes," Jonas said. "We've got a big family lunch. We've got relatives who are still in town."

Coach Archer nodded. "Sounds good. I'll see you back here at three for practice."

Jonas gave Alex a gentle high five and headed to the locker room for a quick shower.

"You hungry?" Coach Archer asked Alex.

Alex was always hungry. "Sure," he said, thinking maybe Coach Archer was going to offer a McDonald's stop on the way back to the house.

"Good," Coach Archer said. "Let's go get some pizza. We should talk."

Alex sighed. The pizza sounded good. The talk he wasn't so sure about.

They went to a place called Tony's that Alex had never been to before, but it certainly smelled good when they walked in.

"One of the teachers told me the pizza here is good," Coach Archer said as they sat down at a table in the corner. "I figure a place called Tony's has to have good pizza."

They ordered a large with sausage. Alex asked for ice tea. Coach Archer decided on coffee.

"So, I just thought before school and practice and games start again that you and I should talk about your mom," Coach Archer said once they had ordered.

He waited to see if Alex had anything to say and then plowed on. "How do you feel about your basketball coach going out with your mother?"

Alex grimaced. But the guy seemed nervous, so he decided to cut him some slack. "Well, I'm not sure how I feel about *anyone* going out with my mom," he said. "But that's a different question. As for you going out with her . . ." He paused. "Honestly? I don't know. It's kind of a jumble right now."

"That's honest," Coach Archer said. "If it makes you feel better, I'm not sure how she feels about it either."

"She likes you," Alex said. "At least, I think she does."

That seemed to make Coach Archer happy. "Well, I like her too," he said. "She's smart and funny and . . ."

"Pretty," Alex said.

"That too," Coach Archer said.

Alex sighed. "She's probably told you about what's going on with my dad. He's moved on with his life—for better or worse—so I guess my mom is entitled to do the same thing."

"But it would probably be easier for you if your basketball coach and your mother's boyfriend weren't the same person."

Alex winced at the word *boyfriend*.

Coach Archer noticed. "Sorry, that's probably premature. We've only been out twice."

"But you want to go out with her again."

He nodded. "I do. But I'm not joking about this even a little: your mom and I both agree if it's at all uncomfortable for you, we won't go out anymore."

Alex thought about that for a minute, then took a deep breath.

"Look, Coach, let's be real. It *is* weird for me. But it would be way worse if she started going out with some jerk—like my dad is doing."

"Or got engaged to one," he put in.

"Yeah, that too."

Their pizza arrived. It looked very good.

"Of course, a month ago, you thought *I* was a jerk," Coach Archer said, taking a slice.

"Much worse than that," Alex said, causing his coach to laugh.

Alex took his own slice of pizza. "Coach, if you like my mom and she likes you, then you should keep seeing her. I just want her to be happy."

"You sure you're fourteen?" Coach Archer said. "You sound more like forty."

Alex thought about that for a second. "Well, there has to be one man in my family who acts like an adult," he said. "I guess, for now, it's me."

He took a bite of the pizza. It was excellent. He held the slice up: "Besides, you discovered a really good pizza place. That gets you big points with me."

They ate and talked about the game coming up and whether the Celtics or the Sixers might have a chance this year. When they were down to the last slices, Coach Archer looked at his watch.

"Gotta get you home," he said. "I'm supposed to meet your new teammate and his mom back at school. Give them the lay of the land a little bit. I hope you guys will help him out tomorrow. Dropping into a new school in the middle of the year isn't easy."

"Dropping into a new school at the *start* of school isn't that easy either," Alex said. "We'll look out for him. I promise."

■ ■ ■

Alex didn't have much time at home after Coach Archer dropped him off. He watched some football until his mom and Molly came home. Then they picked up Jonas for a second time and got back to school at a few minutes before three.

As Alex and Jonas walked in the direction of the locker room, Coach Archer came out of his office trailed by a tall, wiry kid with almost shoulder-length blond hair who could only be Max Bellotti. He looked to be about six four and moved easily like a natural athlete. What that meant was hard to describe. The walk was fluid, almost a strut, filled with the confidence of someone who knew people were looking at him and he was completely comfortable with that.

"Perfect timing," Coach Archer said, waving Alex and Jonas over. "Guys, this is your new teammate. Max Bellotti, meet Alex Myers and Jonas Ellington." He paused a moment and then added, "They're going to be your guards when the game's on the line."

That made Alex feel good.

"When did you get to town?" Alex asked.

"We started from Detroit on Tuesday and got here late Wednesday. My mom really wanted to start the new year in our new place."

He had an easy smile and a friendly manner. Alex, who had a tendency to make snap judgments, decided he liked him.

"Since they're both juniors, I'm asking Steve Holder to try to guide Max through his first few days," Coach Archer said. "But I'd appreciate it if you guys could make him feel welcome too."

"Sure," Jonas said with a smile. "Long as he can play."

"I can play," Bellotti said, smiling too. "At least, I think I can."

Coach Archer said, "Well, your last coach is definitely a fan."

"That might be because we won twenty-five games last season," Bellotti said. "Coach was a fan of all of us for that."

"Did you make the state playoffs?" Alex asked.

Bellotti nodded. "Lost by six points in the sectional final to the team that won it all. They had two starters who are at Michigan State this year and one who's at Florida State. Of course, we had two guys who got D1 scholarships too."

He had just the right mix of cockiness and modesty, Alex thought. Clearly, he was a good player and knew it—but he didn't feel the need to get in your face about it.

"Can you guys take Max to the locker room?" Coach Archer said. "I set up a locker for him. We need to hustle."

The rest of the players were already changing. Steve Holder spotted them, and said, "Hey, Max, come on over here. I want to introduce you to everybody."

"It's a new year," Holder said when he had rattled off all their names. "Let's get going in the right direction. Max was averaging twenty-one points a game for his team in Detroit."

Alex saw some wide eyes when Holder said that.

"There's only one ball," Tony Early murmured in a stage whisper everyone could hear.

"So that ball better get to Max a lot," Holder said.

Happy New Year, Alex thought as they headed in the direction of the court.

17

It was apparent very quickly that Max Bellotti was the real deal.

Alex noticed it in the shooting drills Coach Archer ran them through before they started to scrimmage. The ball came off Max's hands softly as it arced toward the basket. He stepped into three-point shots with the confidence most players showed when going in for an open layup. Even when he missed, the ball seemed to go around the rim several times before dropping off.

Coach Archer put both Max and Alex with the white team when they started to scrimmage. Max was still feeling his way, learning the offense, and Alex was pretty tentative on his first day back at practice. Even so, when they were both in, the whites held their own against the reds.

Coach Archer pulled Alex to rest him on several occasions

so that he didn't try to do too much too soon. And even with Early at point, Max managed to score.

As they walked off the court at the end of practice, Holder caught up to Alex and Jonas.

"Fellas," he said, "I think we might just have ourselves a basketball team."

Zane Wakefield, a couple of steps in front of them, turned when he heard that. He started to say something but apparently thought better of it, then kept walking.

■ ■ ■

The first sign of trouble came Monday morning, when Alex walked out of his third-period math class and was almost thrown against the wall by Hope Alexander.

He had actually been enjoying the morning—thinking about how nice it was to start a new semester at a school where he now had friends, knew his way around. Plus, he couldn't wait to get to basketball practice.

And then Hope literally put her hand on his chest and pushed him up against the lockers.

"Okay, who is he?" she asked. "And don't give me any runaround."

Alex thought that Christine Whitford was the prettiest girl in the school. But Hope Alexander was tops on a lot of other guys' lists. She was tall (at least five ten) and impossible to miss as she sashayed down a hallway with her long blond hair appearing to blow in the wind—even indoors.

Now she was looking him right in the eye—which was a little unnerving—and saying, "Did you hear me, Alex? I want details."

Alex was genuinely confused. "Who are you talking about?" he asked.

"The Greek god walking around with Steve Holder," Hope said in a tone that implied Alex was perhaps the densest person she had ever met.

Ah. Alex probably should have predicted this. "You mean Max?" he said casually, as if he were talking about his cat. "He's the new kid from Detroit. Transfer. Plays basketball. He's a good shooter; I think he's going to help us—"

"Who *cares* if he's any good," said Kelly Clark, a very pretty redhead, who was standing just off Hope's shoulder. "Do you know if he's dating anyone?"

"Since he just moved here, I doubt it," Alex said. "But I really don't know. I only met him for a few minutes yesterday before practice. Seems like a good guy—"

"Introduce me," Hope said instantly.

Alex looked at her for a second and smiled. "You're not shy, Hope. Introduce yourself," he said. "And while you're at it, introduce him to Matt too."

Hope and Matt Gordon had been dating since the middle of football season. Alex had actually been impressed that even after Matt's fall from grace, Hope had stuck with him.

Her face clouded for a second; then she brightened. "Maybe he's got a sister for Matt," she said.

"Maybe he's got a twin brother," Kelly said.

Alex had heard enough—more than enough. "I gotta go," he said. He squirmed free from Hope's grip and fled down the hall.

■ ■ ■

It got worse at lunch.

Alex was sitting at his usual table with Jonas, Matt, and Christine when he saw Steve Holder and Max approaching. Maybe it was his imagination, but he swore he could hear sighing as Max and Steve carried their trays through the cafeteria.

"Wow," Christine murmured. "Kelly wasn't kidding. . . ."

"Max, I know you've met Alex and Jonas," Steve said. "This is Matt Gordon and Christine Whitford."

Max said hello, and Alex was convinced his smile had widened when he saw Christine. Which was understandable.

"So, word is you're going to turn our basketball team around," Matt said as Steve and Max sat down.

Max laughed. "Well, I hope I can help," he said. "From what Coach Archer has told me, getting Alex back will be key too."

"Very modest of you," Christine said. "But you were averaging twenty-one points a game before you transferred—"

"How did you know that?" Alex said, breaking in.

She shrugged. "It doesn't take a genius to go on the Internet and check out the stats for Wildwood High School in Detroit," she said, giving Alex her *you're too stupid to live* look. She looked directly at Max and gave him her megawatt smile. "I work for the student newspaper, the *Weekly Roar.* Would you be up for an interview?"

"For you?" Max said, returning the smile. "Of course."

Alex was feeling a little bit sick.

"Great," Christine said. "Give me your number and I'll call to set up a time."

Alex was staring at his green beans as if they held the

secret of life. Inside his head, Alex heard the words of an old Grateful Dead song his parents both loved: "Trouble ahead, trouble behind. . . ."

He kept staring at the green beans. It felt like the right thing to do.

■ ■ ■

The good news was that Alex felt great at practice that afternoon. He still wasn't one hundred percent, but he felt more confident handling the ball and shooting than he had on Sunday. He had no trouble dealing with Zane Wakefield when the second team was on offense. Coach Archer started the day with Alex and Max still in white but then began giving each one time with the red team.

Max seemed to be feeling more comfortable too. There was no doubt about it—Max was the best player on the court. Even Holder, easily the team's best defensive player, couldn't guard him. Max was giving away a couple of inches to Holder, but he was a lot quicker.

Alex's mind was racing: with Max, they could be a good team—compete, he thought, with just about anyone in the conference. At the same time, he envisioned Max making game-winning plays while the entire female population of Chester Heights—including Christine Whitford—swooned.

Before practice was over he had gone through the five stages of *about to lose a girlfriend* grief. For a while he was in denial: Christine liked him; she wouldn't fall for another guy just because of his looks. Then came anger: she better *not* fall for him because of his looks. He bargained: maybe he could convince Max that he was better off with Hope Alexander;

maybe the tall girl would appeal to him more than the petite one. Depression set in while the team was shooting free throws: *why* did this have to happen? He was just starting to feel confident with Christine and then *this* guy shows up. And finally, acceptance: if she wanted to dump him for Max, there was nothing he could do.

He'd just focus on basketball and move on.

Or at least try to.

■ ■ ■

Coach Archer called them all to the center jump circle at exactly 5:29—meaning he had one minute before the girls' team would take over the court.

"Good practice today, guys," he said. "I think we all agree we're a better team with Alex healthy and Max wearing red or white. I don't want some of you guys on the second team to get discouraged because you think you're going to lose playing time. We're going to need everybody if we want to have a chance to win the conference.

"But we *can* win the conference with the thirteen of you standing here right now. . . ."

He paused for a moment.

"Be here at five o'clock tomorrow," Coach Archer continued. "Starters will be Holder, Gormley, Ellington, Bellotti, and . . ." He waited a beat before saying, "Wakefield."

Alex could see Wakefield smirking. Apparently he thought he was starting because Coach Archer thought he should, not because Alex wasn't quite ready to play.

Holder walked to the middle of the circle and put his hand in the air. "New year, new start. Let's go one and oh," he said. They all put their hands in with Holder and said, "One and oh," then started in the direction of the locker room. Alex paused to pull his socks up—and so he could linger long enough to talk to Coach Archer.

"You need something, Alex?" he asked.

"Coach, I know we agreed I wouldn't play tomorrow, but I felt pretty good today. . . ."

Coach Archer smiled. "Be patient, Alex," he said. "You dress for the game and we'll see how it goes, but I'd like to give you the extra time."

Alex understood. He just hated the idea that Wakefield thought he was still the starter.

"Did you ask him?" said Jonas, who had waited by the steps and, as usual, could read Alex's mind.

"Yeah," Alex said. "He said I can dress tomorrow, and we'll see as the game goes on."

Jonas smiled. "So that's good, then."

"Yeah, but Wakefield still starts—"

Jonas waved him off. "You know that doesn't matter. Coach knows who his point guard is. We all know who the point guard is."

He smiled and then added, "We've got a real team now. Our boy Bellotti can *play*."

Alex nodded. He was looking forward to being on the same team as Bellotti. Whatever else Max's presence was going to mean, he'd worry about later.

■ ■ ■

In his pregame speech on Tuesday, Coach Archer made a point to remind his team that Main Line had made the state playoffs a year earlier and was off to a 5–2 start. What he didn't mention—as Steve Holder pointed out later—was that they'd graduated four seniors and played in a much weaker conference than the Lions did.

It wasn't as if the Bears were awful. They just weren't good enough to compete with the revamped lineup of the Chester Heights Lions. There were some rough spots—especially on offense, with Bellotti still learning the plays and Wakefield running the offense.

The score was tied in the second quarter when Coach Archer waved at Alex to sit next to him on the bench.

"Tell me the absolute truth," he said. "Are you ready? Because Friday's a lot more important. . . ."

"I'm ready, Coach," Alex said. He wasn't lying. He *knew* he was ready to play.

"Okay," Coach Archer said, pointing to the scorer's table. "Go for Wakefield."

Alex was on his way before the word *go* was out of his coach's mouth.

He put up his hand to give Wakefield a high five as he entered the game, but Wakefield put his head down as if he didn't see him.

Alex felt strong even though his shot, at least when guarded, was a little rusty. He settled for getting the ball to Max, Jonas, and Steve—which proved to be the right thing to do.

The game was close for three quarters, Chester Heights leading by just 49–45. But the fourth quarter began with Bellotti and Jonas making back-to-back three-pointers to stretch the lead to 55–45. The Bears didn't give up, but they never got the margin back within single digits, and the Lions won 67–55.

Coach Archer didn't come close to living up to his promise to make sure that the two former starters—Tony Early and Cory McAndrews—would see plenty of playing time. McAndrews got into the game on a number of occasions, and so did Jameer Wilson, who had been the sixth man before the arrival of Alex, Jonas, and Max. Early got in midway through the second quarter, missed a three-point shot, and was back on the bench at the next dead ball. Jonas played thirty of a possible thirty-two minutes. Holder and Bellotti played twenty-eight minutes apiece. Among the starters, only Patton Gormley and Wakefield sat for any extended period of time. And Wakefield played more than he probably would in the future, because the coach was going easy on Alex.

Which might have explained the strange dynamic in the locker room after the game. Coach Archer told them he was proud of the way they had all approached the game and that they had a lot of work to do before the conference opener at Bryn Mawr Tech on Friday night. As soon as he walked out of the locker room, the seven players who had gotten serious minutes high-fived one another, then backslapped Bellotti—who had scored nineteen points—and welcomed him to the team. The other five players—all seniors—went to the showers without a word.

Alex and Jonas looked at one another—both thinking the same thing.

"Never a dull moment around here," Jonas said.

"Yup," Alex said. "Winning isn't going to keep those five guys happy."

Which, he had to admit, didn't make him terribly *un*happy.

There was a small cluster of reporters waiting outside the locker room when Alex and Jonas climbed the steps back up to the gym floor. They had apparently already talked to Coach Archer, who was now talking to Alex's mom, Jonas's mom, and a woman Alex didn't recognize.

This was one situation where Alex didn't mind talking to reporters. He had played well. According to the stat sheet he'd had thirteen points and seven assists with just one turnover. He'd only been one of five shooting threes but had made all six of his free throws. Jonas's numbers were almost identical: thirteen points, four assists, and four rebounds. Alex had only had one rebound—something he knew he'd hear about in practice the next day. His shooting could easily be attributed to rustiness. Rebounding was another story.

But no one in the cluster of reporters moved toward Alex or Jonas. Then the door opened behind them and Max Bellotti came through it. The cluster, TV cameras included, made a beeline for him.

"Looks like the new guy is the new star," Jonas said, smiling.

Alex didn't really mind that *too* much. What he did mind was seeing Christine standing at Bellotti's shoulder, scribbling notes as he talked and smiled and talked and smiled.

"Well, he was the leading scorer," Alex said.

"And he looks like a young Brad Pitt," Steve Holder said, coming up behind them. Holder had been the best player on the court, with sixteen points, fourteen rebounds, four blocks, and an excellent defensive job on Main Line's center and best player.

Holder was grinning when he said it.

"It doesn't bother you that Max is getting all the attention after the way you played tonight?" Alex said.

"Not even a little," Holder said. "You weren't here the last two seasons, Myers. We won a total of twelve games. I don't care if they write that Max won the game playing one on five as long as we won."

"Easy for you to say," Jonas put in with a wide grin on his face. "That's not *your* girlfriend standing at his elbow."

Holder glanced at Alex. "True. But even if it was my girlfriend, I'd still be happy to have him on the team."

"I *am* happy to have him on the team," Alex said, louder than he meant to, since a few people glanced in his direction. He lowered his voice and said, "But I do wish it was your girlfriend standing over there, Steve."

He looked at Jonas. "Come on, let's go talk to our moms."

Holder went off to find his family too.

"What's worse," Jonas whispered, "Christine checking out Max or your mom dating your coach?"

Alex had told Jonas and Christine about his mom and Coach Archer, but no one else. Christine, not surprisingly, had taken the rational approach: your parents are divorcing *and* your dad's acting like a jerk—you should be happy for your mom. Jonas's reaction was closer to Alex's: there's like a million guys your mom could date—she has to pick *him*?

Alex was still pondering Jonas's question when they arrived to a round of applause.

"Coach was just saying he's never seen two freshmen work together so well," Jonas's mom said as she gave her son a quick hug and a peck on the cheek.

"Alex, Jonas, this is Andrea Bellotti—Max's mom."

Alex saw the resemblance instantly. Mrs. Bellotti was tall—Alex guessed close to six feet—and had Max's blond good looks. Or, more accurately, Max had her good looks.

"Nice to meet you both," she said, shaking hands. "You were both terrific tonight."

"They were *all* terrific," Jonas's mom said. She was about the same age as Alex's mom, trim and tall—much like her son. Alex wished Coach Archer could be dating her. The problem being that she was happily married to Jonas's dad. Mrs. Bellotti, on the other hand, was getting divorced. Maybe Coach Archer might want to date her?

"Looks like we have a new star," Alex said, forcing a smile and nodding in the direction of Max Bellotti and the gaggle of reporters still surrounding him.

"He's managed to fit in incredibly quickly," Coach Archer said. "He played an outstanding game."

"So did Steve Holder, and no one's talking to him," Alex said—then wished he'd kept his mouth shut.

He saw his mother open her mouth, but Coach Archer beat her to it. "If we're going to be good, all of you have to work *together*. I'm betting Steve's not really upset."

"You're right, Coach," Jonas said. "He was psyched we won."

"So am I," Alex said, looking at Mrs. Bellotti. "I'm sorry, I didn't meant anything—"

"I know you didn't, Alex," she said. "Max doesn't actually like the spotlight. I'm sure people are just interested now because he's new."

"Time for you guys to get home," Coach Archer put in. "It's a school night."

There were handshakes all around. Alex was relieved when Coach Archer didn't give his mom any sort of kiss good night. Though he guessed his coach wouldn't do that with people standing all around them.

When they got in the car, Alex's mom asked, "Are you jealous of the new boy?"

"No. Well. I don't know," Alex hedged. "Ask me next week."

By then he would have a chance to see what happened with Christine.

■ ■ ■

Steve Holder and Max sat with them at lunch again, so the talk was about the game and about the conference opener at Bryn Mawr on Friday.

"Stevie Thomas told me they're the only team in the

conference with a chance to beat Chester," Christine said. "They've got two senior guards who are both being recruited by D1 schools."

"Who's Stevie Thomas?" Max asked.

"He's a reporter for the *Daily News*," Christine answered. "He's only fifteen, but he's done some really huge stories."

"And he's got a hot girlfriend," Jonas said.

"I can't believe she's better-looking than Christine," Max said, causing Christine to turn about fifty-eight shades of red.

Alex's heart sank.

"How about we get back to the game?" Alex said, afraid that Max and Christine might dive across the table at one another if the conversation continued in this vein.

"Christine's right about Bryn Mawr's guards," Holder said. "Posnock and Morgan. They killed us last year."

Thank God, Alex thought, for Steve Holder. Max asked about Bryn Mawr's frontcourt players, and the rest of lunch was bearable.

Later, walking out of French class, Alex caught up with Christine.

"Look, can I ask you a favor?" he said.

"Sure," she said. "What is it?"

"If you're going to go out with Max, I understand. I know he's like the best-looking guy this school has ever seen. But just tell me now straight up so I can deal with it."

She stopped and looked at him with a very serious expression. It took her a moment to respond.

"First of all, Alex Myers, I'm a little bit hurt that you think I'm going to throw myself at whatever good-looking guy shows up. Max seems perfectly nice, but I'm going out with you and I *like* you. Or I do when you're not being a doofus. And besides that, even if I *was* interested in him, which I'm not, he has no interest in me. So stop asking for stupid favors and stop worrying."

Alex actually felt a little dizzy. "Hang on, what do you mean he has no interest in you? You heard what he said at lunch."

She laughed. "He was just being nice—that's all."

"Then why'd you turn so red?"

"Because it was flattering and sweet. And you're right, he's gorgeous. But I like you." She paused. "You're smart and you're funny and, whether you know it or not, you aren't bad-looking yourself."

Now *he* was turning red.

"Well, that's really . . . cool," he said, stumbling a bit. "*Amazing,* actually. But there's no way he's not interested. I mean—look at you—who wouldn't be?"

Christine shook her head. "Trust me, I know when a guy's interested. It's the way they look at you, talk to you, even the way they walk up to you." She smiled. "I knew you liked me the very first time you tried to talk to me after French class. There wasn't any doubt about it at all.

"There's none of that with Max," she added. "I guess I'm not his type."

Thank God, Alex thought, although he was stunned and thrilled about what she had said about him.

"I've got one last question," he asked, deciding to push his luck.

"Shoot."

"That first day . . . did you like me?"

"Absolutely," she said with that great smile. "I have to get to the newspaper office. And you have to get to practice."

She turned and walked down the hall. It might have been the happiest moment of Alex's life.

■ ■ ■

Practice that afternoon was rough.

The seniors could clearly see the handwriting—or the future lineup—on the wall, and they weren't happy about it. That included Wakefield, who was technically still a starter but spent most of the practice in white along with Early and the other seniors. Even when Coach Birdy was having the second-team walk through Bryn Mawr's offense, there was pushing and shoving during what were usually half-speed drills. When they started scrimmaging, things began to get out of hand.

After a few red possessions with Wakefield playing the point, Coach Archer had him switch with Alex. On the very first play after the switch, Wakefield bumped Alex from behind and Alex lost control of the ball. Coach Archer and Coach Birdy were, as usual, refereeing. Alex heard the whistle and Wakefield was called for the foul.

It was that way for about ten minutes. Every time one of the backups couldn't stay with one of the starters, they fouled. It was as if they had gotten together before practice and said, *If we can't guard 'em, we'll foul 'em.*

It didn't take long for Coach Archer to figure out what was going on. After Early practically mauled Jonas as he was releasing a three-point shot, Coach Archer blew his whistle and didn't even bother calling the foul.

"Everyone to the jump circle," he ordered.

Coach Archer walked into the middle of the circle and looked at all his players.

"We've got a problem here, and we might as well address it right now," he said. "There are three guys on this team today who were not on it when we started practice in November. As it happens, they've all earned the right to play a lot of minutes.

"Wakefield, my plan right now is to keep starting you, because I want a senior out there to start the game and because Alex gives us a burst of energy coming in off the bench.

"But I am *not* going to tolerate this constant chippiness." His voice was low, but intense, and he was looking at Wakefield and Early and the other three seniors. "We already lost Myers for a handful of games because you"—he pointed at Wakefield—"resorted to dirty play. And that will not happen again."

He stopped and looked around the circle of players. "Try to remember we're all on the same team. I know everyone wants to play—I respect that; I like that. And, as I said to you before, we need everyone in this gym to contribute if we're going to be a good team. But the next time *anyone* commits a cheap foul or pushes or shoves for any reason other than to try to get to a loose ball or a rebound, you aren't playing the next game. Maybe two. If you think I'm bluffing, try me."

He looked at each of them again, pausing to look Wakefield, Early, McAndrews, and Wilson right in the eye. Only Wakefield, Alex noticed, held his gaze. None of the four said anything.

"Okay," Coach Archer continued. "I'm going to take your silence to mean you understand. I know I'm new to you older guys and you are still learning about me just as I'm learning about you. But I seriously doubt any of you think that I'm going to do anything but play the guys I believe give us the best chance to win.

"I know the presence of Myers, Ellington, and now Bellotti means that some of you are going to play less. I know firsthand that doesn't feel good. Check my playing time in college. It was, to put it mildly, limited. But I contributed to my team. I came to practice and played hard—and clean—every day. I pulled for my teammates. I learned the opponent's plays so I could run them as effectively as possible during practice. I'll say this one last time: every one of you standing here right now can make us a better team—a pretty good team from what I saw last night.

"But it's up to you. It all depends on your attitude. You want to come in here and be disruptive by fouling on every play or by not paying attention when we walk through things—that's fine. I'll bring some kids up from the JVs who will do what we ask, even if they can't do it as well as you guys can.

"It's your call. All I ask is that you be fair with me and with your teammates, and I promise I'll be fair with you."

He looked at all of them again.

"Anyone want to say anything?" Coach Archer asked. "If you do, say it right now. I don't want this to linger." It was the proverbial *you could hear a pin drop* moment.

Nothing. He clapped and put his whistle to his lips to

send everyone back to their positions. But just before he could blow his whistle, Alex heard Zane Wakefield's voice.

"Coach, I do have one question," he said.

"Fire away, Wakefield."

"Do you think you can be fair to everybody on the team if you're dating the mother of one of your players?"

For a moment, the gym was completely silent, everyone seemingly frozen on the spot where they were standing. Coach Archer let the whistle drop and stared at Wakefield for a few seconds—which felt to Alex like several minutes.

Then Coach Archer smiled and folded his arms. If the thought crossed his mind to deny what Wakefield had just said or to express shock or outrage, it didn't show. Alex felt himself shaking. How in the world had Wakefield found out? He wanted to deck him, but there was no time because Coach Archer had quickly found his voice.

"Tell you what, Wakefield, let's do this," he said. "Let's take a vote on who your teammates think should be getting the most minutes at point guard. In fact, I'll take it a step further. I'll leave the gym while you guys vote. So will Coach Birdy, so no one feels like they're going to be in trouble for disagreeing with the lineup Coach Birdy and I believe gives us our best chance to win."

He nodded at Steve Holder. "Steve, you're in charge of the vote. Come and get us in my office when you're finished."

He turned and started walking away.

"Coach, you don't have to . . . ," Wakefield said, but the two coaches were already leaving.

Holder waited until the door was closed, then turned to his teammates. "I'm not going to say a word until we vote," he said. "Then, as captain, I'd like to say a few things before we ask the coaches to come back. So, let's get this over with.

"Everyone who thinks Myers should play the majority of minutes at the point, raise your hand."

The hands of four starters went up instantly—Holder included. Alex also put his hand up. After a brief pause, McAndrews and Wilson put their hands up too. That gave Alex seven of twelve votes.

"Just for the record, those who think Wakefield should be playing more, raise your hands."

Wakefield and Tony Early both put their hands up. Holder looked at the other three seniors—Pete Taylor, Larry Ceplair, and Arnold Bogus. "You guys haven't voted."

"I abstain," Bogus said. "I understand how Zane and Tony feel. I also understand what Coach is trying to do."

Taylor and Ceplair both nodded.

Holder shrugged. "Fine. The official vote is seven for Myers, two for Wakefield, three abstentions." He looked at Wakefield. "Want a recount, Zane?"

Wakefield said nothing, and Holder shook his head in disgust.

"Wakefield, Early, if you don't like the way this team's being coached, you should quit. We can take a vote on that too, if you want."

"I never asked for a damn vote," Wakefield snapped.

"No—you just brought up an issue that has nothing to do with basketball just to embarrass your coach or to try to make one of your teammates feel bad, or both. If you don't want to be *part* of this team, get the hell out of here. If anyone disagrees with me on that, say so."

He looked around. No one said a word.

Holder turned to Todd May, the team manager, who had been standing off to the side.

"Go tell the coaches we're ready to play basketball," he said. "Reds, it's our ball. Alex, stay in red. Whites, you better be ready to play some defense."

■ ■ ■

There was little life to the rest of practice. Told not to play dirty, or semi-dirty, the whites responded by not trying very hard. Alex could tell by the look on his face that Coach Archer was seething, but apparently one confrontation per day was about all he could handle. With little competition from the whites, the reds got sloppy and lost focus. The last hour of the practice was pretty much a waste of time.

Clearly, Coach Archer could see that. At 5:10—twenty minutes before they had to give up the court to the girls' team—he called a halt.

The team gathered around him at midcourt. He had little

to say. "If we practice like this tomorrow, I can promise you we won't win on Friday," he said. "Which will be too bad, because even though Bryn Mawr's good, it's an eminently winnable game, and that would be a big deal for all of us.

"You all have to decide what kind of team you want to be." He looked directly at Wakefield and Early. "And if you don't want to be part of this team, and I mean *part* of it, you need to come see me. Like I said before, we've got guys on the JV who would love to have your uniforms.

"Steve."

He turned and walked away as Holder stepped into the middle of the circle, his right arm in the air. "Let's hear it on three," he said. "Team!"

They put their arms up and said, "One, two, three, team!"

Alex noticed that Wakefield and Early had simply walked away without taking part in the end-of-practice cheer. He was neither surprised nor disappointed. Maybe, he thought, they were going to talk to Coach Archer.

■ ■ ■

No such luck.

Wakefield and Early were at practice the next day, and little changed. A couple of times Coach Archer stopped practice and had everyone run suicides. All that did was sap their energy—already lagging—a little bit more. The team was now clearly divided into four different cliques: the four starters and Alex, the sixth man, who were all in agreement with their coach and wanted things to go better; McAndrews and Wilson, who didn't like losing minutes but weren't bailing completely because they still wanted to get playing time;

the three seniors at the end of the bench, whose roles hadn't really changed in the new order but who felt obligated to somehow stand up for Wakefield and Early; and of course, Wakefield and Early, who were mad at the world.

It made for a very unpleasant—to say the least—feeling in the gym, and Coach Archer seemed to have no answer for it. Alex sensed that if the coach kicked Wakefield and Early off the team for bad attitudes, the other three seniors would walk with them. Sure, they could bring up JVs to fill the uniforms, but as a coach with a grand total of three career wins, Archer didn't really want the dissension inside his team to become a public spectacle. Alex also suspected that he was hoping as long as Wakefield and Early were still on the team, they wouldn't go public with the gossip that the coach was dating the mother of a player.

Alex hadn't told his mom what had happened at practice on Wednesday because he figured she would stop going out with Coach Archer if he did. He didn't want to be responsible for that, even if it might make his life easier.

With all that on his mind, he didn't practice especially well on Thursday. He was almost afraid that Wakefield might ask for a recount. But when Alex said so to Jonas after practice, his friend laughed and said, "On your worst day, with one hand tied behind your back, you're still better than Wakefield."

■ ■ ■

The bus ride over to Bryn Mawr was pretty quiet. What's more, the Lions struggled to get it together when the game began. Unfortunately, the same could not be said for Bryn

Mawr's guards—Posnock and Morgan, both seniors, were every bit as good as Steve Holder had said they were. And the rest of their team was solid. They came out in a zone defense, which forced the Lions to shoot from outside, and their shots just weren't dropping.

By halftime they trailed 31–21, and Alex honestly wouldn't have blamed Coach Archer if he had decided to play Wakefield and Early for most of the second half. Alex had been dominated by Posnock and had four turnovers and zero assists. Part of the reason he didn't have any assists was because on the occasions when he had been able to get the ball to either Jonas or Max Bellotti for an open shot, they had missed: Jonas was zero of five and Bellotti one of six—the one on a breakaway layup when Steve Holder had managed to poke the ball free from the Chargers center and Bellotti had scooped it up on the run for an easy basket.

Much to Alex's surprise, Coach Archer didn't read them the riot act at halftime.

"I don't want to say this was totally predictable," he said, "but this was totally predictable. You can't succeed at any sport if you feel like your teammates are your opponents. Let's face it, that's what we've got here, right? We're a team divided, and some of that's my fault. I'm willing to own it.

"But all of you," he added, moving his finger in a circle so he could point at all twelve of them, "have to own it too."

He paused. "Look, they're good. No one really expected us to come out here and win, so if we lose it'll be a blip on the radar at school and in the league. Heck, we haven't come close to beating anybody good yet, have we?

"But I *know*, and I think you all know, we're plenty good

enough to beat this team. Just calm down. Alex, you don't have to beat Posnock off the dribble on every possession—especially when they're in zone. Recognize what you've got out there. Jonas, Max, you're both rushing your shots. This is a good high school team we're playing, not the Spurs. Take your time when you catch the ball and you're open. If you get a shot blocked, it's on me—okay?

"Steve, keep doing what you're doing. You other guys, what's he doing? Just playing—that's all. That's why we're in the game. Patton, Cory, Jameer, just do what you need to: play defense, rebound, and keep the ball moving on offense. If you've got a shot, take it; don't be scared to do that."

He looked at them all again. "Answer me honestly, guys—is there anyone in here who doesn't think we're good enough to win this game?"

Alex almost expected Wakefield and Early to say something, but the locker room was completely silent.

"Good," Coach Archer said. "Then let's go out and do it."

■ ■ ■

Bryn Mawr's gym was tiny even by high school standards, maybe half the size of Chester Heights' gym, which seated about thirty-five hundred. Because of that, it had been packed to the rafters even with a lightly regarded opponent. It was a Friday night in January, and there was no snow to keep people home, so anyone who cared at all about the Chargers had packed the place.

The crowd had been loud in the first half with their team in control of the game. But they clearly weren't prepared for what took place in the third quarter. It began when Alex, helped by a solid Patton Gormley screen near the top of the key, got a step on Posnock and then, spotting Bellotti in the corner, got the ball to him for an open three. The shot was off Max's fingertips almost as soon as he caught the pass, and it hit nothing but the bottom of the net.

Coach Archer had told them in the huddle that Alex would start the second half. "No screwing around now," he said—to everyone but also, it seemed, as a reminder to himself that he simply couldn't chance letting the deficit grow by starting Wakefield. "Let's go out and set a tone—our tone."

Max's basket did exactly that. It wasn't so much that Bryn Mawr came out playing worse but that Chester Heights came out playing better. Bellotti's opening shot seemed to loosen everybody up. Jonas hit a three from the corner a moment later, and then Alex went all the way to the rim, made the layup, and got fouled by a late-arriving Charger defender.

Meanwhile, Morgan missed a contested jumper and Posnock threw a pass too hard to center Jason Adams and it went off his fingertips. In under two minutes the Lions had put together a 9–0 run and a one-sided game went to 31–30. Bryn Mawr's Coach Splaver called time to settle his team down. Posnock and Adams worked a perfect pick-and-roll off the time-out, and the Chargers rediscovered their rhythm. But the Lions were locked in now, understanding that their coach was right—this was a winnable game.

The game rocked back and forth, both teams making plays. Alex remembered football season when he had entered games with his team trailing and the game seeming to hang in the balance on every play. This wasn't all that different. As the point guard, he was still the quarterback, but the decisions he had to make were more split second: Dribble and penetrate, or pull up for a shot? Find Max or Jonas on the perimeter, or push the ball inside to Holder? McAndrews and Wilson came in to relieve Gormley and, for short spells, Jonas and Max. Neither Holder nor Alex came out at all. Alex didn't think about his wrist once—which he guessed meant it was fully healed.

Wakefield and Early might as well have been nailed to the bench. Alex didn't think it was because Coach Archer was making any sort of point. The coach just didn't believe they could compete in this game.

Holder picked up his fourth foul with 4:53 to go and the score tied at 56–56. Coach Archer decided to take him out in the hope that the team could hang in without him for a couple of minutes. He put Gormley on Adams. Coach Splaver knew what he was doing. Twice Posnock found Adams in the low post. Twice Gormley—giving away four inches—had no chance to stop him, fouling him as he scored the second time. When Adams made the ensuing free throw to make it 61–56, Coach Archer called time to get Holder back into the game and to calm his team down.

By now the gym was so loud he had to pull his players close to him in the huddle and shout to be heard.

"Those last two baskets are on *me*—not you, Patton—understand?" he said. "Steve, you gotta play with four fouls. I shouldn't have taken you out." He looked at Alex. "They've killed us with pick-and-roll all night. You ready to give 'em some of their own medicine? We haven't run one the whole game. You do it right and Steve will get a basket *and* get fouled—I promise."

He looked at all of them. Alex noticed that all eyes were locked on him. None of the players who had been in the game were thinking about cliques or playing time or who they liked or disliked. The others were leaning into the huddle, listening intently.

As the horn sounded to send the players back on court, Alex felt someone pat him on the back. To his surprise, he turned and saw Tony Early.

"Come on, Myers, we need this basket right now," he said. "Go do it."

Alex almost did a double take. But there was no time to wonder what was going on. They had a game to win.

The pick-and-roll had become the offense du jour of the NBA. It wasn't as easy for younger players to run because the timing and the execution had to be perfect or it would lead to a certain turnover. The play itself was basic: big guy comes up to screen—or set a pick—and little guy uses the screen to create space, while the big guy rolls in the direction of the basket and waits for a pass. If the man guarding him tries to stop the little guy, the big guy should be open.

When Holder came up to screen, Posnock tried to get over the screen, thinking Alex was going to shoot a three. He had hit two already in the second half. But as soon as Posnock came up, Alex took one hard dribble to his right and away from him, then saw Adams take a step to help guard him as he turned in the direction of the lane. Holder was already rolling to the basket. Alex put the ball in the air toward the rim, and Holder grabbed it and laid it in, getting fouled by one of the Bryn Mawr forwards just as he released the ball. Suddenly the margin was 61–59, and Alex felt a surge of adrenaline and confidence.

The problem was that with Holder playing with four fouls, he was just as vulnerable to Adams inside as Gormley had been. Twice Adams scored, and twice the Lions answered. Then, when Gormley tried to drop down and help Holder, Adams found Morgan wide open. Fortunately for the Lions, Morgan was just inside the three-point line when he released the shot. Even so, the eighteen-footer made it 67–63 with forty-one seconds to play.

Alex looked over to Coach Archer as he brought the ball upcourt to see if he wanted a time-out. All Alex saw was three fingers pointing downward, which meant Coach wanted the three man—Max, playing small forward and thus the designated three man—to curl behind a high screen, which Gormley would set, and shoot a three. Gormley would set the screen so Holder would have a chance to rebound in case of a miss. It would be up to Alex to get enough penetration to allow Max to get around the screen without a Bryn Mawr defender switching to guard him.

Alex pulled up long enough to signal the play, then charged at Posnock as if he were going to try to beat him into the lane. Posnock stayed in front of him, and Alex penetrated to the foul line. He saw Max's man crash into Gormley's screen and instantly released the ball to Max. Max had already made three shots from beyond the arc in the second half. He made a fourth one, cutting the margin to 67–66.

Now, before Bryn Mawr could inbound, Coach Archer called time-out with twenty-six seconds left.

"That was my last time-out," he shouted above the din. "We'll look to steal on the inbounds, but if we don't get it, try to foul number twenty—he's their worst foul shooter. They'll just run down the clock, so let's try to get the ball in his hands and foul. If the clock gets under ten seconds, foul whoever has the ball.

"When we get the ball back, remember, *no* time-outs. If they've made two, Alex, Jonas, Max—one of you needs to find space for a three. If we're down one or two, just get to the basket for a shot as quickly as you can."

He looked around. "Everyone understand?"

Alex was pretty certain that neither Posnock nor Morgan was going to give up the ball, since both were excellent foul shooters. Number twenty was Tab Winters, the power forward who was Bryn Mawr's Patton Gormley. Alex couldn't remember him taking a shot since the first quarter—and that had been an open layup.

Sure enough, Winters screened Alex on the inbounds so Morgan could inbound to Posnock. As soon as Alex and Jonas tried to double-team, Posnock coolly found Morgan, who raced into the frontcourt and threw the ball crosscourt to Adams. Before anyone could get close to Adams, he flipped the ball back to Posnock. Alex charged at him, glancing at the clock. Posnock dribbled to the middle of the court to avoid a double-team. Alex had no choice. He reached in and fouled with eight seconds left.

"Hey!" Posnock screamed as Alex wrapped his arm around him. "How about intentional, ref?"

The referee ignored the plea for an intentional foul.

"You're kidding, right?" Alex said. "Afraid you can't make one and one?"

"Just watch me, football boy," Posnock said.

He'd been trash-talking on and off throughout the game—more so in the first half, when he had constantly reminded Alex that "We aren't playing football here, no linemen to protect you." He'd quieted down when the game became close and tense.

Now the two of them exchanged glares as Posnock walked to the foul line.

Alex stood directly behind him as close as he was allowed to—just outside the top of the key—and yelled, "Be ready to rebound after he misses!"

They lined up. Posnock took the ball from the official, dribbled it twice, and calmly swished the first shot to make it 68–66.

He turned to Alex and pointed. "Be ready to *in*bound."

Alex didn't flinch. "Rebound coming!" he yelled.

The gym grew quiet as Posnock dribbled twice again and flicked the ball at the basket. It did a 360 around the rim and rolled . . . off! Holder—always ready—grabbed it, and Alex took a step in his direction to get the ball. There was no time to do anything but turn and fly upcourt as quickly as possible. He could see Max and Jonas racing up the wings and Posnock scrambling to get back and block his path to the goal. Adams was behind him, meaning even if Alex got by Posnock he would have to shoot over a six seven center with long arms.

Alex could see the clock over the basket as he crossed

midcourt. It was at four seconds. He drove directly toward the lane, knowing that Posnock would stop at the three-point line to deny him a shot from there. The clock in his head told him that there were two seconds—or a tad less—left as he reached the three-point line. Posnock was waiting, hands up. He took one more dribble to go past him and saw what looked like the entire Bryn Mawr team collapsing into the lane to stop him.

Without even looking at the basket, he flicked a pass to Max, who was somehow completely unguarded on the right wing. Max caught it and was in the air in a split second. Alex saw the ball come off his hands and then saw the red light go off behind the basket. He was sure Max had released the shot in time.

Max was holding his pose the way shooters do when they know they've made one. The ball splashed through the net with the buzzer still sounding and the red light on. Alex's arms went into the air. Posnock and the other Chargers were all waving their arms in the baseball "safe" sign, which in basketball meant "no good."

Alex saw the referee on the perimeter with his arms up in the touchdown signal, indicating the shot was good for three points. Alex and his teammates engulfed Max. As they were celebrating, Alex saw Coach Splaver racing at the two officials. One of them was waving for Coach Archer.

Alex knew that all the gyms in the conference had equipment for video replay. Unlike in college or pro games, it was only used to determine questions involving the clock or to decide who had started a fight. Now Alex heard the public address announcer say, "The final play of the game is under video review."

The gym, which had gone quiet except for the screams of the Chester Heights players, erupted in cheers.

Alex and his teammates headed for Coach Archer, who was waving them over.

"Stay calm, everyone," he said. "They have to review it by rule. You got it off, Max; don't worry."

They stood and waited, as did everyone else in the building. One of the officials had put on a headset to talk to the video coordinator, no doubt asking for as many angles on the clock and the shot as possible. Alex's heart was pounding. He rarely felt nerves when playing. It was only when things were out of his control that he felt nervous.

The wait dragged on. And on. The crowd began to buzz and then to boo. Finally, the official wearing the headset took it off and waved the two coaches over. Alex sneaked up behind Coach Archer so he could hear. He noticed several security guards lurking not far away.

"Gentlemen," the official said. "The shot was good. Beat the buzzer clearly." He turned to Coach Splaver. "I'm going to ask you, if your crowd gets angry when I give the signal, to take the PA and ask everyone to stay calm."

Alex saw Coach Splaver nod. "Great game, Coach," he said, shaking Coach Archer's hand. As he did, the referee put his arms up to indicate the shot was good.

The gym erupted in boos. Four security guards quickly surrounded the officials, who began running off the court. Alex saw a couple of fans on the far side of the court moving as if to block their exit. True to his word, Coach Splaver had grabbed the PA. "Folks, this is a tough loss, but please listen to me: the officials got it *right*. So let's not do anything silly."

If there was going to be trouble, it stopped right there. The fans who had moved in the direction of the officials stopped. The coaches shook hands again and then the players did too. When Alex got to Posnock, he stiffened for a second, but Posnock had his hand out.

"You're really good—especially for a freshman," Posnock said. "Can't wait to play you again."

"Same here," Alex said, and they mini-hugged one another.

They raced to the locker room, filled with the kind of joy that comes from an improbable—and draining—win. Coach Archer went straight to the grease board in the locker room, where he had written the lineups during pregame. He wiped it off and wrote in large red numbers, 1–0. He pointed at it for a second and said, "Fellas, that's what we are in conference, and that's all that matters. You just showed everyone—most important, yourselves—what kind of team you can be. Every one of you contributed to this win. We'll take the weekend off. You've earned it."

They all cheered at that, happy there would be no practice on Sunday.

Coach Archer turned to Alex for a moment. "You did a great job understanding the clock on the last possession, Alex," he said. "I just wish you hadn't cut it *that* close. You aged me about ten years right there."

Everyone laughed.

"And, Max," Coach Archer continued. "You're not a cool customer; you are an *ice-cold* customer."

"He's ICE!" Patton Gormley yelled, and they all began chanting, "ICE, ICE, ICE!"

It was a great night.

■ ■ ■

It was a little after ten o'clock when the bus arrived back at school. Alex was exhausted and ready to go home. But as the bus pulled into the back parking lot, Jonas showed Alex a text he had gotten from Hope Alexander: *Party's at my house. Heard you guys won! Bring Max!*

Jonas translated. "I think what she meant to say was, 'Couldn't care less about you two guys, but will put up with you if you bring Max.'"

Alex laughed.

"Is Christine going?" Jonas asked

"Don't know—let me call her."

When Christine answered, he could tell she was at a party because he could hear loud music in the background.

"Where are you?" he yelled.

"Hope's," she said. "Are you coming?"

"Maybe," he said. "I'll text you."

They got off the bus, and Alex and Jonas corralled Max and told him about the party.

"I'm not sure," Max said. "I really don't know that many people."

"*That* will not be a problem," Jonas said. "Everyone's dying to meet you."

"Well, if you guys will come with me in my car so I can find the place, I'll take you home after."

Alex had forgotten that Max had a car and a driver's license. He knew he had to call his mom, and he also knew what her first question would be if he was going to drive with Max.

"So, mom question. Do you drink?" Alex asked.

"Soda," Max answered with a smile. "I have a mom too."

Jonas snorted. "Same here." And all three of them called home to let their mothers know where they'd be.

Much to Alex's surprise, he, Max, and Jonas were greeted by cheers when they walked into the packed living room at Hope Alexander's house. Hope didn't throw a party every Friday night, but she threw them often enough that Alex was familiar with her house—which was massive. Her parents were two floors up most of the time—far enough away, Alex guessed, to not be driven crazy by the music but close enough that everyone knew not to do anything crazy.

Alex had learned early that if you were a football star at Chester Heights, you were always on the invitation list for parties. Basketball wasn't even close—largely because the team had been lousy for so long. The win that night had clearly raised their cred a bit. Alex was happy to see that Steve Holder and Patton Gormley had just walked in. He was less happy to see that Zane Wakefield and Tony Early were also there.

As always, Hope was the official greeter.

"Alex, Jonas, MAX!" she screamed. "Hey, people, let's hear it for our basketball heroes!"

Everyone cheered. Hope, who was wearing impossibly high heels that made her look about eleven feet tall, came over and hugged Alex and Jonas. Then she turned to Max, hugged him, and kissed him on the lips. Max looked stunned. Alex almost laughed out loud. Hope was accustomed to getting what she wanted, and it was pretty clear what she wanted at that moment.

He wondered if Matt Gordon, who had ostensibly been Hope's boyfriend before the Christmas break, was around anywhere. He was about to go look for Matt and for Christine when he heard Jonas hissing in his ear.

"Hey, you think we need to rescue Max?" he asked.

Hope was pulling Max by the arm in the direction of the dance floor—a large open area in the next room where all the furniture had been pushed aside. Alex noticed several other girls following them, clearly ready to make Max feel welcome if Hope moved from his side.

"Well, he wanted to meet people," Alex yelled back in Jonas's ear. "I think he can probably take care of himself."

"I'd be happy to take any of them he doesn't want," Jonas said, laughing.

"Don't think that option is available," Alex said.

"Yeah. Let's get something to drink."

"And find Christine."

"Good by me."

Finding Christine turned out to be fairly easy. She was

standing not far from the drinks table, talking to Matt Gordon.

"Hey, Goldie, what were you thinking bringing the golden boy with you?" Matt said. "The rest of us have no shot as long as he's in the room."

Alex felt guilty, especially looking across the room, where Hope now had her arms locked around Max's neck, since a slow dance was playing.

"Matt, I'm sorry. I didn't know. . . ."

Matt broke into a grin. "Alex, I'm kidding. Hope and I were done about fifteen minutes after our first date. We just went out for a while because, well, look at her."

"Yeah, but that passes as a serious relationship for her," Christine said.

"Me-ow, Christine," Jonas teased, but Christine just laughed.

Alex was relieved that Matt didn't appear to be upset that Hope had turned her gaze to someone new.

"Christine says he hit a big-time shot tonight to win the game," Matt said.

"After Alex set him up with an amazing pass," Christine added quickly.

"He still had to make the shot," Alex said.

"Guy can *play*," Jonas said.

Matt grinned and nodded back at the dance floor. Max was in the middle, like the sun, with no fewer than four girls orbiting around him.

"Apparently so," Matt said. "Apparently so."

■ ■ ■

They all ended up on the dance floor by the end of the night, and Alex actually got to dance with Christine this time. Neither Matt nor Jonas had any trouble finding partners either. Matt danced with Kelly Clark. Good for him, Alex thought.

Jonas had been seeing someone, but as of Christmas he was "single" again.

"Chelsea wanted to get, you know, serious," he had said, laughing. "I said, 'I'm fourteen! Check back with me in ten years!'"

"That's what you get for dating a sophomore," Alex had said.

Max had finally escaped the dance floor and was sitting on a couch while wave after wave of girls came to sit with him, talk to him, offer to get him a drink. Hope was practically glued to him, but that didn't seem to deter the others.

"Never seen anything quite like it," said Matt, who'd had his share of female admirers as the captain of the football team. "Guy's like a magnet. You guys better let me take you home, or you could be here all night."

Alex fought through the gaggle of girls around the couch and got Max's attention.

"Hey, Max," he said, grateful that the music had stopped for a moment. "We're going to catch a ride home with Matt, okay?" he said.

Max extracted himself from the couch with difficulty.

"I can take you guys," he said. "I'm ready to go now. I'm really tired."

"No! You should stay, Max," Hope said.

He leaned down and gave her a kiss on the cheek. "Thanks

for inviting me, Hope. But I promised my mom I'd be home by midnight."

"I'll walk you to the door," she said, standing up.

Max started to protest, but she had already linked her arm in his.

They walked to the front hallway, where Matt, Jonas, and Christine were waiting. Hope again made a production of kissing Max good night, while they all pretended to look the other way.

"I'll call you," she said to Max, and walked away, remarkably graceful given the high heels.

Matt was clearly thinking the same thing. "You gotta give it to her," he said. "Girl looks good coming and going."

"A-men to that," Jonas said, causing Christine to elbow him—hard—in the ribs.

"Can you guys stop objectifying her for *one* minute," she said.

"Oh come on, Christine," Matt said. "That girl lives to be objectified."

He had a point.

They decided that Jonas would ride home with Max, since they lived near one another, and Matt would take Christine and Alex.

They dropped Christine off first, and Alex and Matt rode in silence for a couple of minutes until Matt said, "Hey, Goldie, can I ask you a question?"

"Sure," Alex said, figuring the question would be about which girl Matt might want to date next, since he was now clearly single.

"You ever think about what it would be like to *not* play a sport?"

"I thought about it when I was suspended for that week because of the false-positive on my test," Alex said.

"Yeah, that sucked," Matt said. "I still feel guilty about that—"

"Why?" Alex broke in. "*You* had nothing to do with it. . . ."

"Yeah, but my dad had everything to do with it."

"Doesn't matter. You were innocent. . . ."

"Of framing you. Not of taking steroids . . ."

"And you're paying the price for it right now."

"That's what I'm saying," he said. "I'm a jock. I need to play. I know I wouldn't be playing basketball right now, but I'd be working out, getting ready for baseball, keeping in shape. I can't even go in the weight room at school. It's killing me."

"Can you go to the Y? Is there a town baseball team you could play for? I know it sucks, but it's just until next fall, right?" Alex said.

"That's what I thought," Matt said. "Then I got a letter today from the school board informing me that, after further review of my case, they decided my suspension would extend through next football season."

"What!?"

"Yeah. They said I had only missed one football game— the championship game—and since I admitted I'd been using most of the season, they believed I should be suspended for next season."

They were pulling into Alex's driveway.

"Thing is, if I don't play as a senior, no college is going to recruit me."

"Matt, I don't know what to say," Alex finally said.

"I'm going to fight it," Matt said. "I said I'd accept whatever penalty I received, but this isn't fair. I *have* to play football next fall."

"Is there some way you *can* fight it?"

"My mom knows a lawyer who will help," he said. "We're going to see him on Monday after school."

"What's your dad think?" Alex was almost afraid to ask the question.

"I don't know," Matt said. "He and I really don't speak anymore."

"I'm sorry," Alex said.

"I'm not," Matt said. "Listen, Goldie, do me a favor and don't tell anyone—not even Jonas or Christine—okay?"

"Sure," Alex said. "But you'll let me know how it goes, right?"

Matt nodded.

Alex got out of the car and walked into the house. His life wasn't exactly smooth sailing right now, but he was suddenly grateful to have *his* problems and no one else's.

■ ■ ■

Alex's phone buzzed at 7:50 the next morning. He couldn't believe that *anyone* would call him so early on a Saturday. He reached to turn it off and saw it was Christine.

"*Why* would you call me at this hour on a Saturday?"

"I'm fine, thanks for asking," she responded.

He sighed. "What's up?" he asked. "Besides me, now."

"I forgot to ask you last night about Stark's."

"You mean lunch?" He was still a little groggy.

"Yes," she said. "Mr. Hillier wants me to do a big story about Max for Wednesday's paper, and I want to talk to you about him."

"So you woke me up to make a date to talk about Max?" he said.

"Well," she said. "I'd also like to see you."

Alex sighed again. She always found a way to turn things around. . . .

"I'll be there at eleven-thirty," he said.

"Don't sound so enthused," she said, and was gone.

Alex looked out his window. The sun hadn't been up for very long, and everything was sparkling with frost.

He thought about going back to sleep. Then it occurred to him that if he got up, he could read the newspaper accounts of last night's game. He groaned loudly and stumbled in the direction of the shower.

When Alex came downstairs, his mom asked him what in the world he was doing up and showered so early.

"Christine," he answered. "She woke me to say she needs to talk with me for a story she's doing on Max."

His mom laughed. "He did make the winning shot last night, right?"

"I passed him the ball," Alex answered.

She walked over and kissed him on the top of his head. "And she asked *you* to lunch, not him."

"Yeah," Alex said, actually feeling better.

"By the way, I taped Comcast's late-night news just in case they mentioned the game," she said. "Turns out they somehow got tape of the last shot. It's cued up on the TV if you want to look at it."

"You're the best, Mom," he said, heading for the family room.

"That's right," she said. "And if you have any doubts, I'll make you some eggs."

Dei Lynam had anchored the show the night before.

"Everyone knows Chester Heights has always been more of a football school than a basketball school," she said. "In fact, that's freshman quarterback Alex Myers with the ball as the last seconds are ticking away with the Lions down 68–66 to Bryn Mawr." The tape ran as Alex dribbled to the frontcourt. "Then Myers finds transfer Max Bellotti on the wing, and just before the buzzer"—she paused as Max released the shot and the red light behind the basket came on with the ball in the air—"and SWISH!" Lynam said. "Chester Heights' biggest win since Ben Franklin invented basketball."

It was a running joke on Comcast that Ben Franklin had invented everything—including basketball. Poor James Naismith, Alex thought, but he was smiling as he turned off the TV and returned to the kitchen, where his eggs awaited.

■ ■ ■

Jonas and Christine were both waiting in their usual booth in the back when Alex got to Stark's.

"Awake yet?" Christine asked as Alex slid in next to her.

"Thanks to you," he answered.

She smiled, which always left Alex a little weak-kneed, even when sitting down. "Max is coming too," she said. "I've done the background stuff on him, so I thought I could talk to all three of you about last night and about the team at once."

It figures, thought Alex. "Are we waiting to order?" he asked. "I'm hungry."

"Nope," Christine said, waving. "He's here right now."

"I didn't think anyplace could be colder than Detroit," Max said, taking his coat off and putting it on the hook next to the booth. "But I might have been wrong." He sat down next to Jonas. The waitress came over, and Alex, Jonas, and Christine told Max he'd be crazy to order anything but a hamburger—Stark's was famous for them.

"Thanks for inviting me," Max said once the waitress was gone. "It's nice to have friends in a new place."

Jonas laughed. "There were a lot of girls last night who seemed like they wanted to be your *best* friend."

Max grimaced. "Yeah, but that's different. It's flattering—I mean, very flattering, but also really uncomfortable. I'm more interested in making real friends."

"You better get used to it," Jonas said. "I don't see it stopping anytime soon."

"Hope can be pretty relentless," Alex agreed.

Max laughed uncomfortably. "She's not really my type."

"She *is* a bit over the top," Christine said.

Max smiled. "She's, um . . . direct. And she's got a certain style. But like I said, not my type."

Alex cringed inwardly. That probably meant Christine *was* his type. Alex was convinced that Christine was everyone's type.

"Well, you've only got about half the girls in school to choose from," Jonas said. "I'm sure you'll find someone."

Max was shaking his head. "You guys don't understand," he said finally. It seemed like he wanted to say more, but then the waitress delivered their lunches and everyone dug in. Except Max.

"See, the thing is . . ."—Max took a deep breath—
"I'm gay."

Alex choked a little on his milk shake and started coughing.

Jonas stared at Max for a second and then said, "Come again?"

"I'm gay," Max repeated.

They were all quiet for a moment. Alex knew plenty of people who *were* gay, but this was the first time someone had actually come out to him. He had no idea what to say.

"Are you upset, Alex?" Max said. Alex realized his only response had been to choke on his milk shake.

"No!" Alex said. "Not at all. Surprised? Yes. It just never occurred to me—"

"Why would it occur to you?" Christine asked, which was a good question, but one that seemed to come out a bit hostile.

"I just meant I never thought—"

"Because Max is good-looking and girls like him, right?" Christine said.

Alex was baffled. Why was Christine attacking him for being surprised by surprising news?

Jonas clearly felt the same way. "Christine, what is Alex doing wrong here? Why are you on his case?"

"I . . . ," Christine faltered. "I don't know, really."

"It's okay," Max said. "It's okay if you're surprised. I've never really told anybody. . . . Well—a few people knew at my old school.

"But moving here . . . starting somewhere new . . . Chester Heights seems like a pretty liberal school. I know there's a GLAAD chapter in the school with about a hundred members."

"Remind me what GLAAD stands for," Alex said.

"Gay and Lesbian Alliance Against Defamation," Christine answered quickly.

"I was . . . thinking of joining," Max said.

Alex thought about that for a second, then understood the implication.

"You mean you're thinking of coming out publicly," he said.

Max nodded. "Jason Collins did it in the NBA, Michael Sam in the NFL, and Derrick Gordon did it in college basketball up at Massachusetts," he said. "More and more athletes are coming forward. Things have changed a lot."

"Have you talked to your parents about it?" Alex asked.

"About being gay or joining the GLAAD group?"

"Both," Alex answered.

"Yes to being gay, no to GLAAD."

"How did they react?" Jonas asked.

"I think my mom kind of knew," he said. "My dad's trying very hard to not be upset, but I know it bothers him. I think at first he thought I was somehow trying to get back at him because of the divorce. But I just didn't want to leave Detroit without him knowing."

"So how's he going to react if you come out?" Alex asked.

"It's not *if*; it's *when*," Max said. "I'm going to come out at some point. And I just thought, new city, new school, new friends. Why not just be honest from the start? It's really hard to lie all the time. The party last night kind of reinforced it for me."

"That makes a lot of sense," Christine said.

"Yeah, but my question is, how do you think the other guys on the team will react?"

Alex looked at Jonas.

"You can probably guess," Jonas said. "The smart ones won't care. The dumb ones probably will."

"You mean Wakefield and Early?" Max asked.

"I wouldn't count on those other three seniors either," Alex said.

"Bogus will be fine," Christine said. "He's quiet, but a good guy. I don't know the other two that well."

"And you guys?" Max asked, looking at them all. "Are we okay?"

"Of course," Christine said.

"It's fine by me," Alex agreed.

"Fine?" Jonas scoffed. "Alex is *psyched* you won't be hitting on Christine."

Alex practically choked on his milk shake again, but then laughed. "Fair point," he admitted, while Christine rolled her eyes (and blushed just a little).

"I tell you what, though," Jonas continued, shaking his head. "Hope Alexander is going to be seriously put out."

With that they all laughed and went back to their burgers.

■ ■ ■

They talked through the possible ramifications of Max's joining GLAAD and whether he should come out in the *Weekly Roar*. They all figured it would be a big story locally and nationally.

Max had mentioned that he had started to receive recruiting letters from colleges in the fall. Derrick Gordon, the University of Massachusetts guard, had come out in 2014, but Max might end up being the first highly recruited high school athlete to be openly gay.

They talked about timing. Max was just one week into a new school. And this story might blow up in ways none of them could predict. Did he want to take that on right now?

Max listened and nodded and groaned. "Look, I'd rather not be in the center of some media frenzy. The more you talk about it, the worse it sounds. But I can't go through another night like last night," he said. "I was embarrassed, and to be honest, I felt sorry for Hope."

Max continued: "Maybe it won't be that big of a deal. I mean, it shouldn't be, right?"

They all nodded. It shouldn't be a big deal. But they all knew that it would be.

■ ■ ■

Alex got home to find his mom getting ready to go out again with Coach Archer. It still made Alex a little queasy, but he wasn't going to ask her to stop. She seemed so happy. Throw in the whole dad–and–Megan Wheeler debacle, and there was no way he was going to criticize any relationship his mom was in.

Still. He wanted to talk to his mom about Max, but he felt compelled to make her promise not to say anything to Coach Archer, which was weird.

She looked at him very seriously. "Alex, there's *nothing* you can't tell me in confidence—whether with Evan or anyone else. You can always trust me on that."

He nodded and told her what had happened at Stark's.

"Christine's right—Max should take his time and think it through," his mom said. "It's good that he feels confident enough to want to come out, but there *is* going to be a lot of publicity. Maybe it shouldn't be that way, but it is—even now."

Alex nodded.

"He'll need friends to help him through," she added, and came over to put an arm around him. "He's lucky to have you guys."

He noticed she was more dressed up than she had been for her other dates with Coach Archer.

"What are you doing tonight?" he asked.

"We're going to see *A Chorus Line*," she said. "There's a new revival of it in Philadelphia."

"I thought you hated musicals," Alex said.

"I do," his mom said. "Going to see *Cats* eleven times as a kid turned me off them forever. I'll never forgive my mother for that. But Evan loves *A Chorus Line*."

"Really?"

"Yup. Says he cries every time he hears 'What I Did for Love.'"

Alex had a hard time picturing Coach Archer getting weepy about anything, much less a song from a musical.

Then, without really thinking it through, he said, "You must really like him."

She smiled. "Yes, I do," she said. "Evan's a very nice guy, and he's fun to go out with. But I don't want you to worry. I'm nowhere close to getting serious with anyone."

"So, you aren't going to do anything like Dad. . . ."

She laughed. "Absolutely not," she said.

"But you do think he's good-looking."

"Oh, he's *very* good-looking. But there's a lot more to life than that."

"So I don't need to worry about being coached by my stepfather?" he asked.

"Only if Chester Heights hires George Clooney to coach baseball," she said. "Then all bets are off."

Alex laughed. He could live with that.

23

The crowd for Tuesday's game against Lincoln was easily the biggest of the season.

"Is it us beating Bryn Mawr, or is it the Max Factor?" Jonas asked as they went through their pregame layup drills.

Alex answered by nodding in the direction of the student section. About ten rows up, twenty girls were wearing red-and-white T-shirts that said THE MAX PACK on them.

"Nice," Jonas said.

Max jogged by—clearly not happy. "The longer I wait, the worse this is going to get," he said.

"Let's talk about it later," Alex said. "We *do* have a game to play."

Fortunately, the game wasn't all that difficult. If Max was distracted, it didn't show. He scored twenty-two points and had twelve rebounds. Holder had identical numbers: twenty-two and twelve, but there was less shrieking when he scored.

Alex came in three minutes into the game and didn't come out until the game was in hand. He scored fourteen points and had eleven assists. Jonas had eighteen points. Zane Wakefield had two. The Lions eased to an 81–62 win.

The win made the Lions an unimpressive 5–3 on the season but 2–0 in the conference, which, in a very real sense, was all that mattered.

"Back on the road for the next two," Coach Archer said. "We're looking good, but let's not rest on our laurels. We aren't going to sneak up on people anymore."

Alex wasn't worried about that. He *was* worried that if Max decided now was the time to come out, all the commotion around the announcement might slow down—or completely stop—the momentum they had built since he had joined the team.

"Maybe we should ask Max to keep quiet for a while longer," Alex said to Jonas as they climbed the stairs from the locker room back to the gym floor.

"How long?" Jonas said. "I kind of understand where he's coming from. How would you feel if guys were throwing themselves at your feet?"

"What?"

"Think about it. For Max, all those girls shrieking and throwing themselves at him is about the same as it would be if you or I had fifty guys doing that."

"Come on, it's different."

"Is it?"

Alex thought a moment, then decided Jonas was right.

"Okay, I see your point. But I still wish we could get a few more games behind us before we get hit with a media frenzy."

Jonas shook his head. "Not really up to us."

Alex knew he was right.

■ ■ ■

Christine had done a short feature on Max for the *Weekly Roar* on Wednesday about how his presence gave the team a whole new dynamic on offense and made them a team to watch in the league. And as if to prove her right, the Lions won again easily at Thomas Jefferson on Friday.

Max begged off the Friday-night party, telling Alex, Jonas, and Christine to let everyone know he had a bad sore throat. Alex knew that excuse would work—*once*.

The four of them met for lunch again on Saturday. They talked about the game and the week; and it was Jonas who finally asked Max if he had made any decisions about coming out.

"I don't know. I talked to both my parents—separately—about it this week. My mom says I should do whatever feels right. Which is nice, but not much help. My dad was cooler about it than I expected, but he seems to think as long as everything is going well here, why rock the boat? He's got a point, I guess."

Alex actually felt a pang of jealousy that Max could have a conversation like that with his father. He and his dad hadn't spoken—unless brief texts counted—since the Christmas disaster. His dad *had* left a voice mail after the Bryn Mawr win, and Molly had told Alex he'd tried to call her on several occasions.

"I just can't talk to him about it yet," she'd said, sounding very grown-up and very sad. Alex felt pretty much the same way.

"Okay," Christine said, bringing Alex back to the here

and now. "But how do you feel about it, Max? What is your gut telling you?"

Max laughed. "Nothing," he said. "Everything. Part of me wants to do it and move on. Another part of me says my dad is right. Things *are* going well. Maybe I should keep quiet and just play."

He looked at the three of them, clearly seeking their thoughts.

Alex looked at Jonas, who just shrugged as if to say, *You take this one.*

"Look, Max, I'm not in your shoes," Alex said. "So if you think I'm out of line in any way, just tell me."

"No," Max said. "I'd really like to know what you think."

"I *think* we're playing really well right now. With you here, we're a real team. We're three and oh in the conference, and we beat Bryn Mawr, who was picked to finish second. I'd hate to mess up that momentum. . . ."

"So you think I should wait," Max said.

Alex nodded, then shook his head. "No. I'm being selfish. I want you to do whatever you think is best for you," he said. "This is your life, and you're the one who's going to have to deal with it—whatever 'it' happens to be."

Max thought a moment. "Actually, you're wrong," he said. "This is part of your life too. And Jonas's. It will affect everyone on the team. Because it is going to be a big story—I know that. And there are going to be some guys on the team who will be upset—I know that too."

"You shouldn't worry about those guys—" Jonas began.

"Yeah, but I do," Max said. "I don't want this to divide the team. . . ."

"The team's already divided," said Christine, who had been surprisingly quiet. "This will just give them something else to focus on. Some people won't care at all. Some will have mixed emotions but will stay quiet. And some will say stupid things like, 'I don't want him in the shower room.'"

Max smiled. "I've heard that one before about other guys," he said. "And they were even talking about it on the news after Jason Collins and Michael Sam came out. Why do people assume that gay people can't control themselves and straight people can?

"But that's the least of it, really," he added. "I've been reading a lot of the coverage from when other athletes came out. . . . Some of it is inspiring, and some of it is pretty ugly.

"The point is, you're right, Alex; this is bound to affect the team. And I like winning too. I can wait."

"Are you sure?" Christine asked. "If you keep playing well and the team keeps winning, the Max mania is only going to grow."

"Let's see how it goes," Max said. "For now, let's just play basketball."

■ ■ ■

The next couple weeks were the most enjoyable Alex could remember since the midseason stretch during football, when Matt Gordon had been hurt and Alex had been the starting quarterback and the team was winning easily.

They stretched their record in the conference to 7–0, with three easy wins and one narrow escape. The escape came at King of Prussia on the last Friday in January. The Lions trailed

57–52 after three quarters, largely because Steve Holder had gotten into foul trouble and because Max had lost his temper.

Max had gone to the party the previous Friday night, with Christine acting as his bodyguard. They figured if Christine hung out with Max a lot that people might get the wrong idea and give Max some space. They figured wrong.

"Hope Alexander did everything but head butt me to get to him," Christine reported later. "You'd think by now she'd get the hint he's not interested."

"I don't think Hope takes hints," Alex said.

"Or no for an answer," Jonas added.

Max survived the night, but he didn't come to lunch the next day at Stark's. And it was pretty clear that he was up-tight at practice on Sunday. He didn't hang out at all when practice was over, dressing fast and leaving the locker room with a quick "See you guys tomorrow." The same had happened on Monday.

They got through an easy win on Tuesday, and Max seemed more himself. But Wednesday and Thursday he seemed stressed, and then came the game at King of Prussia. KOP was 5–1 in the league, having lost on the road to Chester, who, like Chester Heights, was undefeated. That the game was close surprised no one. KOP had lost 55–51 to Chester, which meant they could play.

Early in the third quarter, with Chester Heights leading 41–38, Max caught a pass on the wing, made a pretty shot fake to get around his defender, and drove to the basket. Seeing Max with a lane, Pete Sessa, the Cougars center, scrambled to cut him off. He was too late, slamming into Max as he laid the ball in. The whistle blew, and Alex pumped his fist because Max would be going to the line to try to give the Lions a six-point lead.

Except he wasn't. The official came out from under the basket with his hand behind his head, signaling a charging foul on Max. It was a brutal call. Sessa hadn't even been close to being in position to take the charge. Alex had a perfect view from across the key of him arriving a full step late and initiating the contact with Max.

"NO WAY!" Alex screamed, causing the official to give him a look. Alex turned away so he wouldn't get into trouble.

But Max was having none of it. Alex heard him screaming, "Are you kidding me? You have to be kidding!"

Now Alex turned and saw Max in the official's face.

"Back off, son. He established position on you."

"WHAT?!" Max screamed. "There's no way!"

Steve Holder, always the cool head, got between Max and the official. "Come on, Max, we'll get it right back," he said, trying to move Max away.

"He was at least a step late!" Max yelled. "What were you looking at?!"

The official, who had started to walk away, turned back to Max, pointed his finger, and said, "That's enough."

Then he walked to the baseline with the ball, blew his whistle, and said, "Let's play."

Max was still seething. On the inbounds pass, he reached his hand in and knocked the ball loose. The whistle blew again—another foul, Max's third. Alex had dropped back on defense, so he couldn't see whether the call was correct or not. It didn't matter to Max. He jumped up and went right at the official.

"Have you ever seen a basketball game before?" he demanded. "EVER?!"

That was it. The official made the *T* sign for a technical foul, and Holder and Jonas and Alex all rushed in to pull Max away.

Alex saw Jameer Wilson sprinting to the table to report in for Max. Coach Archer had to get him out of the game—in part to calm him down but also because the technical counted as his fourth foul, meaning he was one away from fouling out. Alex, Jonas, and Steve escorted Max to the bench to make sure he didn't try to get in one more shot at the official.

"I'm fine," he kept saying. "I'm fine."

"*No*, you're not," Holder said. "You gotta calm down, man, or you're going to get tossed, and we *need* you."

That seemed to bring Max back to earth. He walked to the bench, where Coach Archer put an arm around him and began talking quietly to him as Ernie Gulbis, KOP's point guard, went to the line to shoot the technical free throws.

The rest of the quarter went badly, the Lions' three-point lead turning into a five-point deficit. Max came back at the start of the fourth quarter, and Coach Archer switched to a zone defense, in part to force the Cougars to shoot more from outside but also to try to protect Max from picking up his fifth foul.

Both strategies worked. Max's expression never changed throughout the last eight minutes. When he went up for a jumper in the lane and clearly got hacked across the wrist but didn't get the call, he said nothing, sprinted back on defense, and made a clean steal at the other end. He hit two key threes in the last four minutes and had five rebounds.

With the defense keying on Max, Jonas found some open space and scored eight points in the quarter. A Holder layup with 3:12 to play put the Lions ahead for good, and they ended up with a 77–72 win.

As soon as the buzzer sounded, Coach Archer sprinted after the official Max had tangled with.

"I just want to say one thing," Alex heard him say. "My kid was right. You let people foul him all night. You shouldn't be officiating."

He didn't wait for an answer, instead heading for the handshake line with his players.

"That was a bad move," said Steve Holder, who was standing behind Alex in the line and had also heard the comment.

"Why?" Alex said. "Game's over. He's standing up for his player."

"*This* game's over," Holder said. "Chances are, we'll see that dude again."

He had a point.

Alex was worried. The ref had clearly missed the call, but Max didn't usually lose his temper. Besides Holder, Max was usually the calmest guy on the court. He never showed any emotion when he made a shot and had never argued a bad call beyond a quick look at an official before.

Alex suspected Max mania was part of the problem. At home games, the "Max Pack" was now close to a hundred girls, and they all made a point of shrieking rock-concert-style when he was introduced with the other starters. Max was trapped: the team was playing well, and he wanted to keep riding that wave. But clearly another part of him was drowning.

Max went straight home after the King of Prussia game, leaving Alex and Jonas to fend off Hope Alexander at the afterparty.

"Where's Max?" Hope asked, without so much as a "hello" or "nice win."

"He was tired," Alex said.

"And he got teed up and nearly thrown out of the game," Matt added.

Alex and Jonas had filled him in on the game after arriving.

"What's teed up?" Hope said, looking exasperated.

"It means he got into an argument with one of the refs," Jonas said. "Cut the guy some slack."

Alex looked at Jonas. It wasn't like him to snap at people.

"Cut him some slack?" Hope said. "What's that mean? I'd just like to see him come out and get to know more people."

"He was beat," Alex said, deciding he'd better cut off the argument before it got out of hand. "He just wanted to go home. No big deal."

Hope raised an eyebrow but then turned and walked away, her entourage following.

Matt was shaking his head as she walked away. "You have to admire her spirit," he said, smiling.

He turned to Alex. "For the record, though—if I were Max, I'd be here, not hiding out. I mean, look at those girls. He can have his pick of any one of them."

"I'm pretty sure he knows," Alex said. And left it at that.

■ ■ ■

On Saturday morning, Alex woke up early and decided it was time for him to play the role of Christine Whitford. He called her and said he thought they all needed a lunch at Stark's.

"Did something happen last night?" she said.

"At the party?" he said. "Nothing important. But you saw what happened in the game. Max isn't Max right now, and he's not talking about it. I don't think that's good."

"Okay, I'll be there," she said.

Jonas was in too.

Max hedged. "I'm okay, Alex. I'm sorry I blew up last night—"

Alex cut him off. "You don't need to apologize, Max. Just come to lunch."

When they were all assembled, before Alex could say anything, Max said, "I know why you wanted to talk, Alex, and you're right. It's time."

It was Christine who spoke first. "Max, are you sure? Just because you lost your temper for a moment over a bad call—"

Max waved his hand. "It wasn't just a moment," he said. "I've been uptight for a while now. It's harder than I thought to hide. I thought keeping quiet would be better for the team. But I could have cost us the game last night. . . ."

Jonas tried to jump in. "You were right about the bad call, though. Any of us could have lost it."

"But it was me who did. No, I think it's time.

"Christine, are you still willing to let me write something for the *Weekly Roar?*" Max added. "If it's in next week's paper, the news won't break until after we play Chester on Tuesday, so it won't affect that game. Except that I'll feel better, so I'll probably play better."

Their hamburgers arrived. Max picked his up and grinned. "You know how I know this is the right thing to do?" he said. "Because I feel better already."

■ ■ ■

Max was nowhere in sight at lunchtime on Monday when Christine sat down at their table. She handed printouts of something to Alex, Jonas, and Matt.

"You might as well read this too," she said to Matt.

The headline at the top of the printout was self-explanatory: MAX BELLOTTI: I'M GAY.

The byline said, BY MAX BELLOTTI, AS TOLD TO CHRISTINE WHITFORD. It was written in the first person and got right to the point.

I'm gay. I've known for a while, and I've been out with my family and a few friends, and now it feels like time to be out more publicly.

Coming out is, for me, a great relief. It means I can be who I truly am every day at school and out of school. I'm planning to join the GLAAD group here at Chester Heights, and I hope that my coming out will encourage other gay high school athletes to do the same.

I don't think it takes any great courage to do what I'm doing. Athletes like Jason Collins, Michael Sam, and Derrick Gordon have already blazed this path for me and for others who will follow.

The story went on to talk about his friendships with other gay athletes who were still closeted and that he hoped they would feel comfortable coming out too at some point in the near future. He offered special thanks to Alex and Jonas.

They have known for weeks and haven't pressured me one way or the other about when or even if I should come out. If my being gay has affected the way they feel about me, I certainly haven't seen evidence of it. They're great teammates and wonderful friends. And they've given me hope that my other teammates and schoolmates will see this as no big deal too. Time will tell.

All three boys finished reading at about the same time. Alex had heard Matt say "Whoa" when he saw the headline, but beyond that, he didn't seem fazed.

"When did he tell you guys?" he asked.

"The day after the Bryn Mawr game," Alex said. "You remember how Hope and the girls were all over him at the party that night? He told us the next morning. He was thinking about coming out right then but decided to let it ride awhile. I guess awhile is up."

"It'll cause a stir around here, that's for sure," Matt said.

"Maybe in all of Philadelphia," Christine said. "He's the leading scorer in the conference right now. I think it'll get picked up on TV, radio, the Internet, newspapers. . . ."

Matt looked at Alex. "What is it with you, Goldie? Trouble follow you everywhere?"

"You call this trouble?" Alex said with a grin. "And Jonas has been here all school year too, you know."

"Jonas didn't have the false-positive on his drug test," Matt said.

"True," Alex said. "But seriously, do you really think this is trouble? I mean, what's the big deal? There are probably gay players on the football team too."

"Not *openly* gay," Matt said. "Look, I couldn't care less, but Max is a star player and he's movie-star handsome. This is going to go viral in about two minutes."

■ ■ ■

The win over King of Prussia meant that Tuesday's game against Chester would be a showdown between the two unbeaten teams in the conference. The game would also mark the halfway point of the conference season. Each school played home and away against the other eight conference schools.

Chester had been everyone's preseason pick to win the conference title. Chester Heights had been picked eighth.

But here they were at midseason—neck and neck.

Chester's gym was packed. It looked to Alex like people were practically hanging from the rafters and sitting in the aisles during warm-ups.

"Guess they don't have any fire marshals around here," Jonas said.

Alex and Jonas had talked to Max at lunch about when and how he was going to tell the team about the story they'd see in the *Weekly Roar*.

"I told Coach Archer this morning," he said. "I thought he should know, and he was great about it. He suggested I tell the guys after the game. No need to distract them before."

As it turned out, it probably wouldn't have mattered. For the first time since December, the Lions were completely outplayed.

Zane Wakefield couldn't even last his usual three to four minutes. He turned it over twice and forced a terrible shot, and Coach Archer had to call time-out to get Alex into the game. By then, Chester was already up 9–0. Alex was better than Wakefield—someone playing with a hockey stick would have been better than Wakefield—but not good enough. He had serious trouble dealing with the Clippers' senior point guard, Avery Jackson, at both ends of the court. This was hardly surprising given that Jackson had already committed to Villanova and was clearly a D1-caliber player.

He wasn't that much taller than Alex but probably outweighed him by at least twenty pounds. Alex simply couldn't keep him out of the lane, and that meant his teammates had to cover for him or let Jackson go to the basket for an easy layup. At the other end, Jackson was quick enough to stay in front of Alex, which meant Alex could force shots from deep or move the ball on the perimeter. Neither of which did much good.

The only Lion having any success was Max. Even though he couldn't get inside any more than Alex could, he kept stepping back farther and farther and making threes. The closest Chester Heights came was at the end of the third quarter, when Max made an NBA-distance three just before the buzzer to close the gap to 58–48.

Chester promptly started the fourth quarter with a 9–0 run, and that was the ball game. Coach Archer let the subs play out the last few minutes, and Chester coach Robert Sprau did the same. The final was 81–66. But it hadn't really been that close.

"So now we know how much we have to improve," Coach Archer said in the quiet locker room. "We've got seven games to go before we get to play them at our place to finish the season. We have to keep winning against the other teams *and* keep getting better. We can do that. I know we can do that. I put you in a hole tonight, and we never dug out of it. Next time we'll be ready."

Alex knew he was referring to the 9–0 start that had happened largely because Wakefield simply couldn't handle the Clippers' pressure. Alex glanced at Wakefield, who had his head down and was staring at the floor as if he wasn't listening.

"Okay, fellas, listen up for one more minute." Coach Archer paused and then said simply, "Max?"

Max stood up in front of his teammates. The locker room

was tiny, so they were packed in tight. Alex could tell by the look on everyone's faces that they were baffled.

"I just wanted to let you guys know . . ." Max hesitated. He looked at Jonas and then at Alex. Both nodded at him.

Max took a deep breath. "I wanted to let you know there's a story in the *Weekly Roar* tomorrow about me. Actually, it's by me—sort of."

"Bellotti, what makes you think we care?" Wakefield said. "Can we just get out of here? We've all got school tomorrow, in case you forgot."

"Shut up, Wakefield," Alex said. "Let him talk."

"No, he's right, Alex," Max said quickly. "Zane, you're right. I'll spit it out. The headline on the story is, 'I'm Gay.' You can read it, and if you have any questions, feel free to ask. I just wanted to give you a heads-up. Thanks."

For a split second no one moved, except for Max, who walked over to his locker and opened it. Everyone looked at Coach Archer.

"Usual practice time tomorrow," he said. "We won't go very long."

He turned and walked out.

Alex stood up to shuck his uniform and head for the shower. Max patted him on the shoulder.

"Thanks for that," he said quietly. "Tough night."

"I have a feeling tomorrow's going to be tougher," Alex said.

"It'll be okay," Max said. "I promise."

Alex trusted Max. It was the rest of the world he wasn't so sure about.

Alex was up before the sun after sleeping restlessly most of the night. It was pretty warm for the fourth day of February, so he decided he would bike to school. That way he wouldn't have to wait for his mom.

He pulled up to the bicycle rack at school at the stroke of seven o'clock and was surprised—though he shouldn't have been—to hear a familiar voice call his name.

"Can't wait to see the paper?" Alex asked.

"Can you blame me?" Christine answered.

They walked into the empty front lobby together and found the papers stacked up and waiting. Not surprisingly, Max's story was on the front page. Alex read through it quickly—it wasn't different from what Christine had shown them on Monday. But reading the final line of the story again gave Alex a little chill.

I am so happy to begin again. Keeping this secret locked
up inside me for the last couple of years has been difficult.
Right now, I feel as free as I've ever felt in my entire life.

Alex read the last line aloud as he and Christine walked
in the direction of the freshman lockers. "I just hope he feels
that way tonight," Alex said.

"It was going to come out sooner or later," Christine said.
"At least this way—"

She was interrupted by the sound of an angry voice calling her name: "Christine Whitford!"

They looked up and saw Mr. White, the school principal. Mr. White was generally regarded as a buffoon by most
of the students—especially by Alex, who had watched him
disappear under his desk during his drug-testing crisis in the
fall—and as someone content to cite rules rather than try to
help a student in trouble.

Now Mr. White was striding down the hall, pointing a
finger at Christine. The ever-present phony smile on his face
was nowhere to be found.

"Good morning, Mr. White," Christine said, cool as ever.

Mr. White ignored her greeting and Alex. He was holding
a copy of the *Weekly Roar*. Clutching it, really.

"Did Mr. Hillier approve this story?" he asked.

"Of course he did," Christine said. "He reads everything
that goes into the newspaper. He—"

Mr. White cut her off again. "He had no right to do that
without consulting with me. This is a school-wide issue, not
just some silly story about a ball game."

Alex thought that was pretty funny coming from Mr.

White, who loved to play the role of head cheerleader at pep rallies. He didn't seem to think ball games were silly then.

Christine put her hands on her hips, which Alex knew meant one of two things: she wanted something or she was angry. In this case, Alex figured it was the latter.

"Mr. White, Max isn't the first gay student at Chester Heights or even the first gay student to come out."

Mr. White's face twisted into a sneer. "Then why," he said, waving the paper, "is it front-page news?"

Whoops. He had her there.

Christine hesitated—and was lost.

"I'm going to see Mr. Hillier right now. I want to see him *and* you in my office during lunch hour."

He stalked away.

"And good morning to you too, Mr. White," Alex said to the principal's back—though not loud enough for him to hear.

Christine looked like she might cry. That was 180 degrees from her normal demeanor, even under pressure.

"Hey, take it easy; he's being a jerk," Alex said, putting his arm around her.

She shook her head. "I don't care about him. What's he going to do—yell at me some more? But if that's the reaction of the principal, how is the rest of the school going to react?"

■ ■ ■

It didn't take long to find out.

Everywhere Alex went, kids kept coming up to him asking how he felt about Max being gay. Alex had rehearsed his answer lying in bed the night before, because he knew the question was going to come.

He'd finally settled on, "I don't care what he is; I care who he is. He's a great kid and a terrific teammate."

Naturally, Hope Alexander was the one person who made his life difficult. He was on his way to lunch when she cut him off in the hallway. Surprisingly, she was alone.

"You knew and you didn't tell me?" she said.

"Wasn't my story to tell, Hope. It was Max's."

"But you let me throw myself at him at the parties; you knew I was texting him all the time. . . ."

"Actually, I had no idea you were texting him all the time," Alex said. "Max never told me that. And I'll bet he didn't tell anyone else either."

For the first time since he had met her in the fall, Alex saw Hope Alexander blush. It made him wonder what had been in her texts. She recovered quickly.

"I should have known," she said. "I've never had a guy be so completely uninterested in me. Now I know why."

Much to Alex's relief, she stalked away.

The cafeteria was abuzz, and Alex knew it wasn't about last night's game. Max was at their usual table, with Matt hovering protectively, so Alex rushed over to join them. He hadn't seen Max all day.

"How are you doing?" he asked.

"Okay, I guess," Max answered. "It's kind of surreal, actually. Where's Christine?"

"She's meeting with Coach Hillier and Mr. White."

"Ah."

On a couple of occasions, Alex saw kids start over to the table only to turn away when they saw Matt glaring at them.

Only Zane Wakefield and Tony Early made it past Matt's force field. Both were holding their trays.

"You owe us all an explanation," Wakefield said.

"You going to quit?" Early added.

Before Max could respond, the others did.

"Why should he quit?" Jonas said.

"What is there to explain?" said Matt. "Even you two guys can read."

"He's gay," Wakefield said. "You think we're going to have any chance playing against teams who know we've got a fag on our team?"

Alex jumped up, right in Wakefield's face.

"Shut up, Wakefield," he said. "The only reason we're seven and one in the conference is because he's on our team. It sure as hell isn't because of you."

Wakefield was still holding his tray, and for a second Alex thought he was going to dump it on him. He didn't get the chance because Matt jumped in between them.

"Wakefield, do us all a favor and go crawl back under your rock," Matt said.

"Figures a cheat would stand up for him," Wakefield said. "My dad's on the school board. We'll see what happens next."

He and Early walked away. Matt, a little red-faced, sat down.

Max hadn't said a word.

Now he did. "Listen, you guys. I appreciate you wanting to stand up for me. But I'm fine. I know I'm going to hear stuff like that."

"You shouldn't have to hear it from players on your own team," Alex said.

Max shrugged. "Do I really care what Zane Wakefield thinks? If I let guys like that get to me, teammate or not, that's on me."

"If it were me, I'd have decked him," Jonas said. "Alex and Matt were right—"

Max put a hand up. "So, Jonas, no one has ever thrown a racial slur at you?"

"Of course they have," Jonas said. "But it's different."

"How's it different?" Max asked. "Because you can't hide the fact that you're black, and I *can* hide the fact that I'm gay? Do you lay out everyone who says something idiotic to you?"

Jonas shook his head. "No, I wouldn't give them the pleasure of knowing they got to me. . . ."

He stopped, understanding.

Max smiled. And the rest of them did too.

■ ■ ■

Coach Archer walked into the locker room with Max just as everyone was getting into their practice gear. Max was already dressed for practice.

"Okay, fellas, listen up," he said. "Grab a chair as if we were having a game-day talk."

They all pulled their chairs forward. Only Max didn't sit, standing off to the side.

"We didn't talk last night about what Max told you because it was late and he and I agreed you should all read the story first.

"Before I tell you what I think about it, I'd like to ask if anyone in this room has an issue with it. Raise your hand if you do."

For a moment, no one moved. Then Zane Wakefield put

his hand up. So did Tony Early and, to Alex's surprise, Larry Ceplair. Coach Archer waited to see if anyone else wanted to join in. He was about to begin speaking again when Ceplair spoke up.

"Coach, I don't have a problem with Max or anyone being gay," he said. "But the shower—"

Max started to say something, but Coach Archer put up his hand. "Larry, I hear you. We'll get to that."

He turned in the direction of Wakefield and Early. "Zane, Tony, I'm not here to tell you how to feel on any issue other than basketball. You have two choices right now: you can leave the team or you can stay. I hope you will stay. But if you do, I want you to understand: Max is a member of this team and he will be treated with respect.

"If he was our twelfth man, I would deal with this exactly the same way I'm dealing with it now. The fact is, he's the leading scorer in our conference, which means we're going to have to deal with a lot of outside factors going forward. So it's important that we're together on this."

He pointed at Wakefield and Early. "You guys don't have to give me a decision now, but I need one before the game on Friday."

"Coach, my father's going to want to talk to you about this," Wakefield said. "He's on the school board, and—"

"I don't care if your father is on the school board," Coach Archer said. "Of course I will talk to him, like I'd talk to any parent. Have him call me anytime. But I'll say the same thing to him that I'm saying to you. Max is a member of this team."

He looked Wakefield square in the eye. Wakefield didn't hold the gaze.

Coach Archer waited a couple of beats, then moved on.

"Okay, the shower question." He shook his head for a moment. "Max actually brought this up to me, because he doesn't want anyone to be uncomfortable, but I think it's a nonissue. For the record, you've all been taking showers in the same room as Max for a month now, and nothing's happened, right? For all any of you know, the guy sitting next to you might be gay too. Right?"

He looked around the room. "Okay," he said. "One other thing—dealing with the media. I am never going to tell anyone what to say, but I would *recommend* you tell the truth: Max is part of our team. He's a terrific player and a good guy. His social life is his own business just like my social life is my own business."

He looked around again. "Any questions?"

He looked at Max. "Anything you'd like to add?"

"I want to thank you, Coach, for supporting me," he said. "You guys who might feel a little uncomfortable at first, I understand. I'll give you some space." He nodded at Ceplair, who nodded back. "Zane, Tony, let me put your minds at ease. Neither one of you is my type."

It took a split second for the comment to register. Then everyone broke up laughing. Even Wakefield and Early. It was the perfect tension breaker.

Max sat down, and Coach Archer said, "Okay, guys, let's take a look at some of the tape from last night's game. There's a lot we can learn from it."

It was time to get ready for the next game.

Of course it wasn't nearly that simple.

By that evening, the word was all over the local media about the fact that the leading scorer in the South Philadelphia Athletic Conference had announced in the school newspaper that he was gay. Fortunately, the word hadn't gotten out before the end of practice, so they didn't have to deal with any media on the way out.

"It'll happen tomorrow," Christine told Alex on the phone that night. "My dad said it didn't hit the Internet or Twitter until about six o'clock, because no one checks high school student newspapers looking for news. How did it go at practice today?"

"Practice was okay," he said. "Coach Archer made it pretty clear that anyone who has a problem with Max is free to quit."

He asked her about the meeting with Mr. White and Coach Hillier. She started to laugh.

"White was beside himself," she said. "He kept saying, 'Haven't we had enough trouble around here after the Myers-Gordon PED debacle?' Mr. Hillier reminded him that *you* had nothing to do with the 'debacle,' that you were the victim. Mr. White said, 'You're missing the point!' And Mr. Hillier said, 'No, Mr. White, *you're* missing the point.'"

"Sounds like fun," Alex said. "What did Coach Hillier say the point was?"

"He said it was a legitimate story because Max is a star basketball player, and athletes coming out has gotten a lot of press lately. He said that Max was going to make an announcement somehow. And that by having an article in the *Roar*, he got to tell the story in a way that he found comfortable.

"The best part, though, was when he said, 'Mr. White, is this about what's best for the student or what's easiest for you?' That pretty much ended the conversation."

"Good," Alex said. "White's a clown."

"I'd go for buffoon."

"That's because you're a writer," Alex said.

She laughed again. "You know what I've been thinking?" she said. "Coach Archer has turned out to be a pretty good guy."

Alex knew she was right. If his mom had to date someone, she could do a lot worse. His father certainly had.

■ ■ ■

At lunch the next day, Max told everyone that he and Coach Archer were working on a plan for dealing with the media. "He figures it'll be a mob scene this afternoon. I said I wanted to talk to anyone who shows up, so he's trying to find a way to do it so it won't affect practice."

"Is Coach going to let them talk to the rest of us?" Jonas asked.

"What difference does that make?" Christine asked.

"What if they talk to Wakefield and Early?"

Max shook his head. "Who cares? Let them say what they want."

"*That's* why Coach may not want us to talk," Jonas said. "Because they will."

■ ■ ■

They practiced that afternoon with the gym doors locked and a couple of security guards keeping an eye on the entrances. Even so, everyone was a little on edge. Alex hoped that dealing with the media today would allow them to be mentally ready to play at Haverford Station the next night. Coach Archer was apparently thinking the same thing.

"Okay, this is how it's going to work," he said when practice was over. "There are a bunch of reporters outside, and Max and I are going to talk to them now. But I want the rest of you to keep your minds on tomorrow's game. So go home, get your homework done, and get some rest. If you're approached by a reporter, just say, 'Coach doesn't want us to talk until after tomorrow's game.' You're free to say anything you like tomorrow, but until then, I want you focused on Haverford Station. We beat them pretty easily the first time around, but they've improved, and playing at their place will be different. Remember, we need to be ready to go by four-thirty tomorrow."

Alex and Jonas did as they were told, bolting through the lobby and out a side door before anyone could stop them. Even as they breezed in the direction of the exit, Alex could see that the lobby was packed with cameras and media.

"That looks worse than the press conference when Matt confessed to the steroids," Jonas said as the cold evening wind hit them in the face.

"Yeah, but this isn't the end of the story; it's just the beginning."

He was grateful to see his mother waiting for him in her usual spot in the parking lot. This was one night when he was glad to not be riding his bike.

"I'm guessing all those TV trucks are about Max," she said as he climbed into the car. Alex saw one that said Comcast–Philadelphia. That was no surprise. The one next to it brought him up a little short.

"CNN is here?" he said.

"I know," his mother said as she put the car into gear. "I also saw trucks from MSNBC and Fox News."

"Oh boy," Alex said.

He tried to think of something to add to that comment. Nothing came to mind.

■ ■ ■

While his mom was making dinner, Alex turned on Comcast–Philadelphia to watch their six o'clock sports update show. The lead was Max Bellotti. Michael Barkann, normally the host of *Daily News Live*, was the reporter on scene at the school.

"Max Bellotti, the leading scorer in the South Philadelphia Athletic Conference, met with the media after his Chester Heights team practiced this afternoon to discuss the story he cowrote in Wednesday's student newspaper. The first two words of the story—'I'm Gay'—explain why Chester Heights was overrun this evening with local *and* national media."

While Barkann was talking, the on-camera shot went from him to the TV trucks to the packed lobby. Then, almost abruptly, Max was standing at a podium, talking.

"This is something I've thought about doing for a while, even when I was still living and playing in Detroit," he was saying. "I'm grateful to live in a time when gay athletes can be honest about who they are and not be made into an outcast for it."

Alex heard a reporter ask, "How did your teammates react to the news?"

Max smiled. "The ones I've talked to are absolutely fine with it," he said—an honest answer, since Alex was certain Max hadn't talked to Wakefield or Early after practice. "But there hasn't been much talk, really. We're pretty focused on basketball."

Someone else asked if he was worried about hearing taunts when the team played on the road.

"We got taunted pretty good Tuesday night at Chester because we played lousy," he said, shaking his head. "I feel worse about that than anything anyone might say about me personally. I don't think it will be a big deal."

Max faded from view, and Barkann was back on camera. "None of Bellotti's teammates were available to talk this evening, but I did get a chance to speak with Coach Evan Archer."

Just like that, Coach Archer was on camera with a Comcast microphone in front of him.

"I'm really proud of Max," Coach Archer said. "He knew there was going to be a lot of attention focused on him when he decided to do this, and he's prepared to deal with it. I know that someday soon this sort of thing won't be newsworthy anymore. But for now, we'll take it as it comes."

Alex heard Barkann's voice off camera: "How concerned are you about how this will affect your team? You were seven and oh in conference play before you lost at Chester Tuesday. Do you think your guys were affected because they knew this was coming?"

Coach Archer smiled. "No—most of the team *didn't* know. Max told me Tuesday morning, and he and I decided to wait until after the game for him to tell his teammates. Max wanted to be sure the news *wouldn't* affect Tuesday's game. What affected us was Chester—they're a strong team, and they beat us fair and square. Going forward, we'll win or lose based on our ability to improve—nothing more, nothing less. Our last two practices have been very good."

Alex wasn't sure about that last line. The rest made sense.

Barkann was back on camera again wrapping up. "Time will tell how the rest of this season will play out for Chester Heights, which has been one of the surprise teams in the Philadelphia area ever since Bellotti transferred here. The Lions play tomorrow night at Haverford Station."

He threw it back to the anchors from there. Alex turned and saw his mom standing in the doorway.

"What did you think?" he asked.

"I think Evan looks great on camera," she said. "Especially when he smiles."

She turned and walked back into the kitchen.

Very helpful, Alex thought.

He clicked off the TV set.

■ ■ ■

Haverford Station was probably the perfect place for Chester Heights to go on the road after Max's press conference. The Red Wave was 1–7 in conference play, and it looked like there were more media members than fans in the gym. Apparently the media wanted to see how Max and his teammates would play with the spotlight on them.

The answer was just fine. Haverford Station started the game in a zone. On the game's first possession, Zane Wakefield—who had not quit the team to protest the presence of a gay teammate—found himself wide open for a three-point shot in the corner. Without hesitating, he took the shot and, much to everyone's surprise, made it. Sitting on the bench, Alex caught himself grinning. He leaned over to Pete Taylor and said, "Maybe Zane is inspired by Max's courage in coming out."

He thought it was funny. Taylor did not. "Shut up, Myers," he said. "Lay off Zane."

Alex was tempted to say that Zane should lay off everyone else, but he resisted. At least now he knew where Taylor stood.

Despite Coach Archer's warnings about Haverford Station having improved since they last played them, the Red Wave looked pretty helpless from the start. Coach Archer let

Wakefield play the entire first quarter—which didn't thrill Alex. He understood, though: with the Lions leading 18–9, he could quiet some of the carping from the bench players by giving Wakefield and Tony Early more minutes than normal.

Max had missed his first two shots of the game, and Alex had heard a couple of predictable taunts from the crowd. But when he came off a Steve Holder screen and drilled a three late in the quarter, Alex heard a huge cheer go up from a contingent in the far corner of the gym. One person held up a sign that said, WE'RE GLAD THAT MAX IS PART OF GLAAD.

Interesting. Max clearly had a new group of fans.

Alex played the second quarter and was content to set up Holder, Jonas, and Max most of the time, building to a 41–22 halftime lead. Coach Archer started both Wakefield and Early in the second half, and they played the entire third quarter.

"What do you think he's doing?" Jonas asked Alex as they watched from the bench.

"Trying to make them happy," Alex said quietly.

"Why?"

"So they won't rip Max when they talk to the media after the game."

That was Alex's theory, anyway. Jonas nodded.

The final was 76–54, with Coach Archer finishing the game with Wakefield, Early, Taylor, Larry Ceplair, and Arnold Bogus on the floor. Wakefield finished with sixteen points, which had to be a career high for him. Max ended up with ten points, by far his lowest output since arriving. Some people would make a big deal of that, but he simply didn't *need* to score more. Alex, who only played twelve minutes all night, had just four points—but eleven assists. Steve Holder had been unstoppable, scoring twenty-nine.

"Okay, fellas, good job," Coach Archer said afterward. "You made it clear right away who the better team was, and that helped us a lot. That's what you need to do on the road." He paused. "Especially tonight."

Another pause.

"Now, you all know that was the easy part of the night. The place is swarming with media, and they've been told that all of you are available to answer questions about Max tonight. After this, it will be basketball only."

He paused, and Alex saw his eyes wander in the direction of Wakefield and Early, who had been celebrating as if the team had just won the state championship.

"I'm not going to tell any of you what to say. And you don't have to talk to the media at all if you don't want to. But if you do, please remember that we're a team. A good team. A team that has a great chance to stun everyone by winning the conference championship. Think about that before you speak."

He nodded at Holder, who came to the middle of the room. "Bryn Mawr next Tuesday," Holder said. "We know how good they are." He held his arm up in the air, and they all moved in to surround him, arms up. "On three," Holder said. "Beat the Techies!"

They repeated after him and turned back to their lockers. But they couldn't focus on the next game just yet. . . .

27

The TV lights were almost blinding when Alex and Jonas walked back onto the gym floor. There were reporters and cameras everywhere. There was a riser set up, Alex assumed for Max and Coach Archer.

Alex heard several people calling his name and turned in the direction of a squadron of reporters and cameras. The questions came quickly.

"Alex, tonight was easy, but how do you think the team will do going forward now that one of your teammates has come out and admitted to being gay?"

He looked at the questioner, who was holding a microphone that said FOX NEWS on it.

Alex took a deep breath. "First of all, I don't think of being gay as something you 'admit to,'" he said. "It's just something that you are. As for the team, I think we're playing well, and we're all looking forward to the rest of the season. To us, Max is no different now than he was before the story came out on Wednesday."

"Then how do you explain his performance tonight?" another microphone-wielding person asked.

"What was the final score?" Alex said, then tried to soften that with a smile. "He didn't need to do any more than he did. Steve Holder was unstoppable inside tonight, so we all got him the ball."

In his peripheral vision, Alex saw a tall blond woman coming at him. She hadn't been there for the first couple of questions. Now, before anyone else could ask a follow-up, she stuck her microphone, which said ESPN, in his face and said, "Alex, one of your teammates just told us that you and Jonas Ellington both knew about Bellotti's sexuality long before Wednesday. That true?"

Alex glanced to his left to see where the woman had come from. Not surprisingly, Wakefield was standing there talking.

He shrugged. "If you read Max's story in the paper, you'd know that. Max has only been here about a month, so I don't know that I'd say we knew 'long before' Wednesday. But yes, Jonas and I knew."

"Why did you stay quiet?" It was the guy from Fox News again.

That question made Alex angry. "Because it was Max's story to tell whenever he chose to tell it."

"Why did he tell you and Ellington?" It was the ESPN blonde again.

"You'd have to ask him that. I guess because he trusted us."

"Do you wish he had waited until the end of the season to make this announcement?"

The question came from someone in the back who didn't have a microphone. Alex peered through the lights to see the face. He recognized who it was: Stevie Thomas, the kid reporter who worked for the *Philadelphia Daily News*. It was the one question he honestly didn't know the answer to.

"It's easy to say yes," he said, "because if Max had waited, I wouldn't be talking to any of you right now." That drew a laugh. "But I'm not Max. It had to be his decision, and I understand why he made it."

"Why *did* he make it?" someone else he couldn't see asked.

"You should really ask him," Alex said. "But my sense from talking to him is he felt he'd be happier after he came out."

Alex heard a commotion behind him and saw Coach Archer and Max walking toward the podium. The lights in front of him went out and the microphones disappeared. Other players were just as quickly abandoned, leaving them scattered alone across the court.

One reporter stayed and came up to say hello.

"I don't know if you remember me," he said, putting out his hand.

"Stevie Thomas," Alex said. "You helped Christine out in November when I was being framed. *Thank you.*"

Thomas nodded. "You handled yourself great just now."

"Thank you, again."

"I do have one more question, if that's okay."

"Sure."

"Do you think you'll ever get through a season here without a media circus?"

"There's still baseball," Alex said.

They both laughed—which, after the last few days, felt awfully good.

■ ■ ■

Alex watched the various TV reports on Friday night and into Saturday. They were all pretty much the same—predictable questions and predictable answers. Max was cool and smart and so was Coach Archer.

"Anyone who sees an issue here has a problem," Coach Archer said. "We don't have a problem. Max is comfortable with who he is, and so are his teammates."

Alex's only uncomfortable moment came when the Fox News report—which his mom had advised him not to watch because it was bound to upset him—ended with Alex saying on camera that he thought the reason Max had chosen to come out was because he would be happier being out.

Transitioning from that quote, the Fox reporter came on camera and said, "Mr. Myers's naïveté is understandable— he's only a freshman. But if he and his Chester Heights teammates think that sharing a locker room with a gay teammate isn't going to be an issue, then Mr. Myers is in for quite a shock these next few weeks."

"EVERY TEAM ON EARTH SHARES A LOCKER ROOM WITH GAY TEAMMATES, YOU MORON!" Alex shouted at the TV.

His mom had been right—he never should have turned on Fox.

In spite of that, and the stupid online headlines, and some of the ludicrous comments and tweets Alex read, things did calm down the following week. The only comments he heard in the hallways on Monday were from kids saying they had seen him on TV. The only bad moment came when he turned a corner and bumped smack into Zane Wakefield and Tony Early—never a pleasant experience under the best of circumstances.

"Hey, Myers," Wakefield said. "Saw you on Fox the other night. Boy, did they nail you!"

"Actually, I think they got it wrong," Early said. "You aren't naïve—you're flat-out stupid!"

Alex just looked at them and shook his head. "*I'm* stupid? You guys own a mirror?"

He kept walking without waiting for a response. He really wanted to punch Wakefield, but he knew it was a bad idea—especially in a crowded hallway.

Things were almost back to normal by lunch, where the only comments anyone made walking by the table were things like, "Nice win Friday."

"I think the worst might be over," Christine said hopefully as they were getting ready to leave.

"Have you been reading the Internet?" asked Max, who had been cheerful but quiet through most of lunch. "Things may be okay here—which helps—but there are some truly vicious, bigoted people out there."

"Cowards," Matt said. "They'll spew that stuff online, where they're anonymous, but they won't dare say anything like that to your face."

"Your lips," Max said, "to God's ears."

■ ■ ■

God must have been listening, because there were very few issues over the next couple weeks.

When the Lions came onto the court prior to the Bryn Mawr game, Alex was pleasantly surprised to see that the Max Pack was still out in force. Except now it also contained some boys. There were now two BELLOTTI IS A HOTTIE signs—one being waved by a guy and the other being waved by none other than Hope Alexander.

Wow, Alex thought, maybe there's more to Hope than I thought.

Alex's other surprise came when Mark Posnock, the Bryn Mawr point guard who had given him so much trouble a few weeks earlier, hobbled up to him on crutches.

"What happened to you?" Alex said. He knew Posnock had played in the previous Friday's game, because he'd watched the game tape.

"Fluke," Posnock said. "Someone came down right on my ankle going for a rebound. Tore a tendon. I'm done for the year."

"That sucks" was all Alex could think to say.

Posnock nodded. "So how you guys dealing with all this Bellotti stuff?"

"I think we're okay," Alex said. "Worst is probably over. Least we hope so."

Posnock raised an eyebrow, indicating surprise. "Look, you didn't hear this from me, but my dad knows your boy Wakefield's dad," he said. "He says this is *not* over."

Alex had heard Wakefield's "my dad is on the school board" threat in the locker room but hadn't thought much about it. "What can he do?" he asked Posnock.

"Don't know, but I'd be on the alert. My dad says Wakefield's old man is . . . well, not the nicest guy ever."

That might explain a lot about Wakefield, Alex thought. He and Posnock shook hands. "You know where you're going to school next year?" Alex asked.

Posnock smiled. "I got offered by a bunch of schools, you know, midlevel D1s like Lafayette, Holy Cross, William and Mary, and some others. My grades are pretty good. Now, I guess, we'll have to see. Good luck tonight."

As it turned out, Alex and the Lions didn't need that much luck. Bryn Mawr wasn't the same team without its point guard. Plus, Chester Heights was a better team than it had been a month ago. The most-improved player was Jonas: he'd learned to take advantage of the openings created for him by the defense's need to key on Max. Jonas was a good open shooter, but that wasn't his best skill. He had a great first step to the basket, much the same way he had a great first step as a receiver. If you gave him even the smallest of openings, he was by you in a heartbeat. He scored twenty-four against Bryn Mawr, most on drives to the basket.

Alex was comfortable now with his role as a feeder. He didn't need to shoot that much with three strong scorers in the lineup. Max was deadly from outside, Jonas could shoot from beyond the three-point arc but could also get to the goal, and Holder was very tough to guard when he got the ball in the low post. Patton Gormley and even the guys off the bench were all more effective because they were often left open by double-teams.

The final was 71–59, and it never felt that close. Alex finished with eight points and fourteen assists.

Any concern that Max's decision to come out might hurt the team was now behind them. It wasn't as if the issue completely disappeared; it just became more of a scattered annoyance than anything else.

There were a couple obnoxious signs in the stands at Thomas Jefferson that Friday. One said, WHEN YOU MEET GOD HE WILL TELL YOU WHY YOU HAVE SINNED, MAX BELLOTTI. Another said, STRAIGHT IS THE ONLY DIRECT ROUTE TO HEAVEN. But they were quickly taken away by security people.

If anything, those signs seemed to galvanize Max, who had his best shooting night of the season and finished with thirty-one points in a 79–60 win. The margin was nice and so was the fact that Coach Archer didn't put Wakefield back into the game.

"You may set a record for minutes played by a sixth man," Jonas said on the way home.

"Yeah," Alex said, smiling. "And Wakefield may set a record for fewest minutes ever played by a starter."

The funny thing was that Wakefield didn't seem bothered by his lack of minutes. Holder had told Alex that he'd been at a few parties with kids from other schools, and Wakefield always introduced himself to girls as "the starting point guard for Chester Heights."

"How's that work out for him?" Jonas had asked.

Holder laughed. "Mostly they ask, 'Do you play with Max Bellotti?'"

"Even now?" Alex asked.

"Yup," Holder said. "More now than ever."

■ ■ ■

After the Lions had beaten Lincoln to raise their conference record to 12–1 and their AMCO ("After Max Came Out") record to 5–0, the usual group agreed to meet at Stark's on Saturday to celebrate. Max's dad had come to town both weekends since the story had broken, so Max hadn't been around to join them.

Alex was actually jealous of the fact that Max's dad cared enough to fly in and spend time with him. He had finally spoken to his own dad, who had made more of the same empty promises to come to Philadelphia and had insisted that once Alex and Molly got to know Megan better, they would like her.

Alex's answer had been blunt: "What makes you think she wants to get to know *us* better, Dad?" he said. "And when might that happen even if she did?" Alex's dad stumbled through an answer, until Alex finally cut him off and said he had to go.

Alex was the first one to show up at Stark's. It was still cold, but it was a sunny day, and compared to late December and the early days of January, it almost felt balmy on the ride over. Philly was definitely warmer than Boston, which he knew was being pummeled by snow almost every day.

"So," Jonas said to Max when they were all together, "how's life in the superstar business?" Jonas always got right to the point.

Max, who had been the subject of a story in *Sports Illustrated* the previous week, laughed. "Some good, some bad," he said. "Some funny."

"What's funny?" Christine asked.

"I'm still getting texts and notes from girls," he said.

"What do they say?" Christine asked.

"Stuff like, if you ever change your mind . . ."

"Well," Jonas said. "It's good to know you've got options in life, right?"

"Some options are more appealing than others," Max said, laughing.

"Are people still tweeting stuff at you?" Alex said.

Max shrugged. "Oh yeah. And I see stuff on the Internet about these groups who want to stage protests to 'balance' the GLAAD supporters. But nothing serious.

"You know what got to me, though?" he added. "There have been a couple stories on sports websites that said I came out to call attention to myself. They weren't written by crazies; they were written by legitimate guys. That hurts a little."

"Did they call you to talk to you about it?" Christine asked.

"One did, one didn't," Max said. "The guy who did kept asking me why I couldn't wait until the end of the season, that it seemed to him it was a 'me, me, me' move. I tried to explain that wasn't what it was about, but he didn't buy it."

He shrugged, clearly trying to shake it off. "There have been some nice surprises too."

"Like what?" Jonas asked.

Max smiled. "Early came up to me last night as he was leaving and said, 'Nice game.'"

"Wow," Jonas said. "That's bigger news than us being twelve and one."

"You get Wakefield to say it too and we'll put out a special edition of the *Roar*," Christine added.

They laughed their way through lunch. It was all good.

The last week in February would decide the season. Chester Heights, Chester, and King of Prussia all had conference records of 13–1 with two games left. KOP had beaten Chester in their second meeting in double overtime. The game had been extremely controversial because three Chester players had fouled out during the first overtime on what were described in the *Philadelphia Inquirer* as "ticky-tack calls."

King of Prussia had outscored Chester 13–4 in the second overtime in large part because the Clippers were out of players.

On Monday, before practice, Coach Archer explained where the team stood.

"We're basically in postseason right now," he said. "One and done. If we beat King of Prussia tomorrow, then it will be us against Chester for the conference title on Friday night.

"Chester plays Lincoln tomorrow, and we all know they aren't going to lose that game. So, they'll come in here fourteen and one, and we need to be fourteen and one too.

"If we lose tomorrow, Myers can start getting his pitching arm loose."

He looked at Alex. "You ready to start baseball next week, Myers?"

"No, Coach, I'm not," Alex said. "I'm not big on baseball when there's still snow on the ground."

That got a snort and a smile from Coach Archer.

"Okay, so, in the spirit of keeping Myers from freezing to death, we need to be completely focused on King of Prussia. You know how good they are. And you know if we don't beat them, the Chester game is for nothing but pride."

"Gay pride?" Wakefield blurted, causing everyone to stare at him.

"Good one, Wakefield," Max said, and the tension broke. Everyone laughed.

Coach Archer sent them out to warm up. As Alex walked to the ball rack, he turned to Jonas. "Why do I have a bad feeling about this week?"

Jonas shrugged. "They're both tough games. We barely beat KOP at home; going on the road won't be easy."

"I'm not talking about the games," Alex said.

"Then what are you talking about?" Jonas asked.

"I'm not sure," Alex said. "I really don't know."

He picked up a ball, glanced at Wakefield, and felt something turn in his stomach. His gut—literally—told him there was trouble ahead.

As the teams warmed up Tuesday evening, King of Prussia's gym was almost full—a solid twenty minutes before tip-off. That was to be expected. What bothered Alex was what he saw in the stands.

In one corner, near the Chester Heights bench, was the group now dubbed "Max's Army of GLAAD." Alex had first noticed them several games ago. There'd be anywhere from fifty to a hundred people, usually dressed in pink, showing their support for Max. Some were students, some not. They were completely different from the Max Pack. That group had swollen to about two hundred students, and they were in the stands too, already starting their various pro-Max chants.

But there was a new group on the other side of the gym that worried Alex. They were *not* dressed in pink—in fact, many of them were dressed in black.

When Alex heard *their* first chant, he knew it was going to be a long night.

"Max, Max, he's our man—NOT!"

There were signs informing Max that he was a sinner. And there was a group of shirtless guys in the front row, each with a letter on his chest spelling out, GO HOME F——.

This was the worst thing they'd seen so far. And it didn't seem like the King of Prussia security people were going to do anything about it.

Alex looked at Max. If he was concerned about what they were seeing and hearing from that corner, he wasn't showing it. The dueling chants went back and forth while the teams continued to warm up. The atmosphere in the gym seemed to grow more hostile as the clock ticked down toward tip-off.

As always, the Lions left the court when the clock went under fifteen minutes to return to the locker room for a final pregame talk.

"Okay, fellas, you let me worry about what's coming out of that far corner, okay?" Coach Archer said. "I'll take care of it."

"Coach, don't worry—" Max started to say.

Coach Archer put a hand up. "Max, with all due respect, this isn't just about you. It's about everyone in this gym. I know how passionate your army is—and that's fine. But there's some real ugliness coming from the other side of the gym, and the people here need to get it under control. Coach Birdy is talking to their coaches right now."

He then moved on to game strategy, but Alex was pretty certain no one was listening. He wouldn't say he felt scared, exactly—but like everyone in the room, he was nervous.

When they went back on the court, roundly booed by everyone except those in Max's Army and family and friends sitting behind the bench, Alex saw Coach Archer walk to the scorer's table, where Coach Anderson from King of Prussia and several men in suits were waiting for him. He also noticed that the pregame clock had been stopped at four minutes.

One of the men in suits was Mr. White, the Chester Heights principal. Alex couldn't ever remember seeing him at a game before.

The KOP players were half warming up, half watching what was going on at the scorer's table. Alex heard Steve Holder's voice: "Come on, guys, let's get ready to play. Let Coach deal with this."

They went through their layup line. As Alex circled back near the scorer's table, he caught a snippet of what Coach Archer was saying: "At the very least, you have to get extra security over there. My kids need to be protected."

"What about extra security to protect our kids from the gay group?" Alex heard one of the suits say.

Alex paused before he started back in the direction of the basket, so he could hear Coach Archer's answer. "They've been to a half dozen of our games and never caused any trouble. . . ."

Alex took a pass and drove in for a layup. As he jogged back to midcourt, he heard another chant coming from the far corner: "Gays, gays, go away—do NOT come again some other day."

Three-year-old stuff, Alex thought. But in this context, really creepy.

He jogged past the scorer's table again. One of the suits—he assumed it was King of Prussia's principal—was saying, "They're not our students. They bought tickets. Unless they interfere with the game, there's nothing I can do."

Great, Alex thought. If they come on court and attack us, *then* someone will do something.

■ ■ ■

When Alex watched the tape of the game the following day, he was amazed by how poorly both teams played in the first half. No one, it seemed, could make a shot outside five feet. The energy level, especially for such a critical game in front of a packed house, was surprisingly low. It was almost as if both teams had one eye on the court and the other eye on the bleachers.

It was tough to focus during time-outs because the chants being exchanged were ringing in their ears. On a couple occasions, Coach Archer snapped at his players to get their attention. "I need your eyes, ears, and minds right here!" he said.

The score was tied 29–29 at the half. As they left the court surrounded by more security than Alex had ever seen, it occurred to him that the Lions would be shooting directly in front of the antigay group in the second half.

Coach Archer wasn't focused on any of that during the break.

"We're lucky," he said. "We're lucky because they're letting what's going on off the court bother them as much as we are. Fellas—STOP! Forget the politics and forget the idiots in the stands!"

He talked for the next few minutes about the need to get Steve Holder involved in the offense—which was true. Holder had only taken two shots in the half, largely because Alex, Jonas, and Max had been guilty of settling for outside shots without even looking inside.

Both teams came out more focused. Apparently Coach Anderson had said much the same thing to his team as Coach Archer had. On the Lions' first two possessions, Alex and Holder ran perfect pick-and-rolls, resulting in layups for Holder. The game swayed back and forth, still tied—at forty-nine apiece—after three quarters. Alex was dimly aware that the chanting and yelling was still going on, but he was caught up in the adrenaline of the game now.

Max made a three-pointer from the corner to start the fourth quarter—his third of the second half—bringing wild cheers from his army. Then, Alex made a steal and fed Max for a layup and a five-point lead—the biggest margin either team had been able to build all night.

Coach Anderson called time. As the teams headed for their benches, Alex heard Mike Lesco, KOP's center, yelling angrily at his teammates, "Hey, we're not letting this fairy beat us!"

Alex started to say something to Lesco, but Max, who had also heard the comment, grabbed him.

"No, Alex," he said. "Let's keep our cool and win the game. That's the best way to shut them up."

Alex knew he was right. But hearing it from another player and not just the idiots in the stands made him very angry.

Coach Archer clearly hadn't heard what was said, because he was all business in the huddle. "We've got them on their heels right now," he said. "Keep attacking. Myers, great play on defense, but don't get steal-happy. Let's make sure we aren't giving them anything easy."

King of Prussia was too good a team to just go away—especially playing at home with the season on the line. Lesco might have been a bigoted dope, but he could play. He scored from the low post and drew Steve Holder's fourth foul with 4:07 to play. His free throw tied the game at sixty all. Alex looked to the bench to see if Coach Archer might sub for Holder for a minute or two.

No way. He couldn't risk playing anyone but the five "starters"—Alex hadn't come out since replacing Wakefield three minutes into the game—at this stage. The final minutes were as intense as anything Alex had ever experienced, including the state championship football game.

Every possession was played as if *it* would decide the game. If anyone was tired, it didn't show. When Chester Heights scored, the building was loud, but when KOP scored, the place exploded. Alex couldn't hear himself think. Coach Archer reminded them during a time-out that they had to be ready to communicate with hand signals alone because there was no way to hear one another.

With just under a minute to go, Roy Appleman, who had been a tough matchup at point guard for Alex all night, tripped over Alex's foot as he tried to start a drive to the basket. Alex waited to hear the whistle—whether he had intended to trip Appleman didn't matter; it was still a foul—and heard none. Almost everyone had stopped playing, expecting the call.

Everyone except Jonas. He scooped up the loose ball

at the top of the key and went the length of the court untouched for a layup that put the Lions up 67–66 with fifty-three seconds left. Coach Anderson called time-out for the express purpose of screaming at the officials. Alex knew he was right but didn't really care. He'd been hammered a few times during the game and hadn't gotten the call, so he really didn't mind if the officials missed one that favored his team.

The officials let Coach Anderson rant for a solid thirty seconds—leading Alex to believe they knew they'd blown the call. When Coach Anderson finally calmed down, the time-out was over. The gym was starting to feel like a powder keg. It wasn't just the home crowd booing; it was the angry shouts—some directed at the officials, some (still) at Max, and others at all the Lions. If Alex had a dollar for every person who had yelled "How can you guys live with yourselves?" he could have retired at the age of fourteen to a life of leisure.

None of that mattered now. The game—and the season—was on the line in the last fifty-three seconds.

King of Prussia took its time setting up on offense. For a split second, Alex wondered if the Cougars were going to play for one shot. That didn't make sense when you were losing. Better to lengthen the game than to shorten it when you were behind—even by one.

Finally, with the clock under twenty seconds, Alex saw Lesco curl around a baseline screen and get position in the post on Holder. As soon as Appleman dropped the ball into him, Alex left Appleman to double Lesco and try to steal the ball from him rather than let him attack Holder—and his four fouls.

Lesco saw Alex coming and quickly picked his dribble up

and flipped the ball right back to Appleman on the perimeter. Because Alex had left him, the point guard was wide open. He caught the pass just outside the three-point line, took one quick dribble to square himself, and fired. Alex's heart sank as he saw him release the ball. He knew it was going in by the way Appleman was posing on his follow-through.

Sure enough, it swished with twelve seconds to play. KOP led 69–67. Jonas grabbed the ball as it came through the basket and quickly inbounded to Alex. The Cougars had dropped their defense back as soon as Appleman made his shot, so Alex was able to quickly get the ball to the front-court, where Coach Archer called time with eight seconds left.

It was now so loud that Coach Archer told everyone to get as close to him as they possibly could while he talked.

"We're going to run option-down," he said, shouting to be heard even though he was no more than a foot from any of his players. "Got it?"

They all nodded. He grabbed his grease board and drew up the play even though they all knew it. Max would inbound to Alex and run to the left wing as a decoy. Alex would look at Max and then throw the ball to Holder in the low post. Steve's job was to get a shot up as soon as possible so the Lions would have a chance to follow his shot if he missed. When they ran the play in practice, Holder regularly got a shot up in three to four seconds after the play began. They had eight seconds left.

Plenty of time.

"Steve, you even have time for a shot fake if you need it," Coach Archer said. "No need to rush. Make the shot, get fouled, we'll get out of here. If not, make it and we'll win this thing in overtime."

He was shouting to be heard, but the look on his face was one of complete calm, which helped settle Alex down. Coach Archer looked around at all of them as the horn sounded, meaning the time-out was over.

"We've done this in practice a thousand times," he said. "Close your eyes for a second and see an empty gym. Just us." They all did as they were told. Alex actually *did* see an empty gym for a split second.

Then he heard the referee's voice just outside the huddle. "Come on, guys, let's play," he said.

Alex opened his eyes and looked around. The gym was anything but empty.

They had to inbound from the far side of the court, which meant that Max had to stand within a few feet of the homophobe section. Never once during the game had he so much as flinched at the barbs being hurled at him. Now he looked to Alex as if he were still seeing an empty gym. Alex couldn't imagine what must be going through his head.

The official handed Max the ball, and Alex took a jab step in the direction of the basket, then stepped outside to catch the inbounds. As instructed, Max ran to the wing, hand up in order to look like he wanted a quick pass back. Alex looked at him as if he intended to pass him the ball, took one quick dribble to force Appleman backward, then picked the ball up and tossed it to Holder, who had quickly established position to the left side of the basket.

Holder grabbed it, turned to his right, and had space to

shoot. He was up in the air, open because Lesco wouldn't dare go near him and risk a foul. Alex saw the clock above the backboard slide down to four seconds as Holder released the shot. Instinctively, he ran in the direction of the basket, right into a mosh pit of bodies trying to get position.

Holder's shot was too strong. It hit the back rim and bounced in the air, everyone scrambling for it. Someone got a hand on it, and Alex saw it, still well above everyone's heads, spinning almost right at him. Without even thinking, he jumped as high as he could and tried to tip the ball to his left—to the wing, where he could see Max waiting.

Max was always the designated "tip-back" guy. Coach Archer often repeated a quote he had read from Duke coach Mike Krzyzewski years earlier: "In a close game, if you can get three tip-back threes, you'll almost always win the game."

Alex wasn't thinking about that line or anything else as he tried to direct the ball to Max. All he knew was there was no way for him to get two hands on the ball and this felt like their only chance.

Max took a step to his left to grab the spinning ball. Alex almost couldn't look—or listen. He was turned away from the basket, so he couldn't see the clock, and he was afraid he was going to hear the buzzer before Max could shoot.

In one lightning-fast motion, Max got the ball into his hands and was in the air, and the shot was off his fingertips. At that instant, Alex *did* hear the buzzer, but the ball was already in the air. The ball seemed to float toward the basket in slow motion, and the air seemed to be sucked out of the gym while everyone held their breath.

Finally, the ball hit the rim, sat there for a split second, and then crawled over the orange paint and into the basket. Alex heard screams coming from every direction. His arms were in the air and he started toward Max.

But Max had turned his back on the basket and his on-rushing teammates. He was facing the homophobe section, pointing and screaming. Then he threw his arms into the air and shouted above the din: "Hate loses!" It was an awesome line, but completely out of character for Max. But then, this game hadn't been like any other they'd played.

Jonas and the rest of the team were converging on Max, but before they could get to him, Alex saw something come hurtling out of the stands. It caught Max square in the head, and Max went down as if he'd been shot.

Out of the corner of his eye, Alex saw something bouncing on the floor and realized it was a baseball. Someone in the stands had thrown a baseball at Max. A baseball? There was no time to think about that. Jonas and Alex were the first ones to get to Max, and Alex could see that he was out cold with blood trickling from his temple. He could hear screaming all around and heard someone—he didn't know who—yell, "Get the EMTs out here!"

Kneeling by Max's head, Alex was suddenly aware of the stands emptying on both sides of the gym.

"Oh my God!" he heard himself say. He and Jonas both turned their bodies to shield Max, and hoped they wouldn't be trampled.

Alex had never prayed much. Now he made an exception. "Please," he said urgently in a voice he knew no one else could hear. "Please get us out of here alive."

The shouts grew louder. He felt Jonas put an arm around

him and pull him closer as they tried to protect Max. "Help's coming!" he heard Jonas shout. "It *has* to be coming!"

Alex looked up and saw members of the opposing groups squaring off. Fortunately, other than the idiot with the baseball, no one seemed to have any weapons, but there was a lot of shoving and wrestling going on.

Alex sensed that he, Jonas, and Max were in the center of some fight-free zone. He could see that most of his teammates had surrounded them and that some of the King of Prussia players had joined them. He heard Coach Archer's voice above the din, yelling, "Clear a path, clear a path!"

He looked down at Max and saw that his eyes were open and blinking.

"You okay?" he shouted at Max, which was a ridiculous question. Clearly he wasn't.

Nonetheless, Max nodded—which was a relief.

Alex felt a hand on his shoulder and looked up to see a man dressed in some kind of firefighter's uniform.

"We need some room, son," the man said softly.

Alex stood up and backed away, and Jonas did the same. As he stood, Alex could now see that the area of the court where they were had been ringed by a mixture of security guards and police. It looked as if all the players and coaches from both teams were standing inside the protected area.

A woman made her way through security, waved in by Coach Archer: Max's mom. She knelt next to the man in the uniform and said, "This is my son." He nodded.

"He's conscious, which is good," Alex heard the man say. "But we need to get him out of here. You can ride with us in the ambulance."

More police and security were arriving, and the rest of the crowd was being pushed farther from the ring of players. He wasn't sure where the police had come from so fast, but he wasn't complaining. Several people were in handcuffs. The fighting had stopped. Order had been restored. He could also see a number of TV crews jockeying to get a better shot of what was going on. They were being held at bay by the police and security too.

"Is he conscious?"

Alex heard a familiar voice right behind him. He turned and saw Christine, who had somehow slipped inside the protected area.

"Yes," Alex answered. "He's talking too."

"Are *you* okay?"

"I'm fine."

She nodded, putting a protective arm around him anyway. Alex *was* fine, but he was still in a daze.

"Did you see what hit him?" Christine asked.

"I think it was a baseball."

"Yeah," she said. "They got the guy who threw it."

"Really? Who is he?"

"No idea. He was one of the crazies."

It suddenly occurred to Alex that he had no idea if they had actually won the game. The shot had been so close to the buzzer that it would normally have gone to automatic video review.

"Hey," he said. "I don't want to sound thoughtless, but did we win?"

"I have no idea," Christine said. "There was no chance for the refs to review it. But they called it good when it went in."

Alex nodded. He had a vague memory of seeing one of the officials with his arms raised as Max's shot was in the air.

The EMTs had gotten Max onto a stretcher and were gently putting him onto a gurney to take him out of the gym. Coach Archer, who had been standing right behind them while they spoke to Max, walked over and waved all his players toward him.

"He's talking, and he remembers everything," Coach Archer said. "The EMTs are encouraged, but they're going to take him to the hospital as a precaution. His mom and I are going to go with him."

He turned to a man in a suit who was holding a walkie-talkie. "This is Lieutenant Daniels. He and some other officers and security people are going to get you guys to the locker room and then to the bus and escort you out of here back to school. The gym is being cleared right now."

"Coach, did we win the game?"

It was Zane Wakefield. Alex wanted to be annoyed with him about it, but he had to admit he'd already asked Christine the same thing.

"Not sure," Coach Archer said. "One of the officials told me the video is going to be sent to the conference office, and they'll review it in the morning. But he told me they called the shot good."

He held up his hand as Patton Gormley started to say something. "Fellas, I gotta go. I'll text you when I know more." He turned and followed the gurney that the EMTs were starting to slowly push in the direction of the exit. Those who remained in the gym—some still in the stands, some on the court—clapped as the gurney began rolling. Alex noticed a lot of them were sitting on the King of Prussia side of the court.

Lieutenant Daniels moved into the circle of players. He was all business.

"Boys, I'm going to ask you to walk behind me and let my men fall in around you while we take you to the locker room," he said. "Don't talk to anyone. The sooner we get you to the locker room and out of here, the better everyone's going to feel. Once you're in the locker room, feel free to text or call your parents to let them know everything is okay. But don't take a lot of time down there. We want to get you all home quickly and safely."

Everyone complied. Alex did notice quite a few Chester Heights parents as they walked across the floor to the locker rooms—including his mom and Mrs. Ellington. The KOP players were also being led out at the other end of the gym.

When they got to the locker room, almost everyone grabbed their phones.

Coach Birdy stood at the front of the room. "Just want to check that you're all okay," he said. "Anyone need a trainer or a doctor?"

When no one responded, he went on. "Can I just tell you guys one thing before you shower and get dressed?" he said. "You should be really proud of what you did tonight. Even if Max's shot doesn't count—which I believe it will—that was a really gutsy game you played. I'm proud of you, and I know the whole school will be proud of you.

"Now let's get out of here."

Holder held his arm up, and they all fell into a circle around him. He said, simply, "Max."

Alex happened to see Zane Wakefield on the other side of the circle, who leaned in and shouted just as loudly as all the others: "Max!"

30

Alex heard his phone buzzing to let him know he had a text. He wasn't quite asleep or awake at that moment, so he rolled over and picked up the phone.

2:27 a.m.

The text was from Coach Archer.

Good news! it began. *Max is doing well. He took 12 stitches but apparently has a very hard head. The docs say he shows no signs of a concussion. Docs want to keep him overnight, but they think he could be in school Thursday. AND, if he has no post-concussion symptoms, he might be able to practice with us Thursday! Great job by all tonight! Coach A.*

Alex breathed a sigh of relief and read the text a second time. Assuming they had won the game, which they still didn't know, the Chester game on Friday would decide the conference championship. They had no chance without Max. But Coach Archer seemed to be saying he might be able to play.

Now Alex couldn't sleep for much better reasons.

When he went downstairs in the morning, he was surprised to find his mom sitting at the kitchen counter with her laptop. Normally she read the paper with her coffee.

"Well," she said. "You want the good news or the bad news?"

Alex wondered fleetingly if something had happened to Max since Coach Archer's text, but she didn't sound like it was that sort of news.

"Start with the good," he said.

"You won the game," she said. "I just checked the conference website. Apparently they reviewed the tape last night and ruled that Max's shot beat the buzzer."

Alex had expected that but was still relieved to hear it.

"So what's the bad news, then?" he said.

"Let me read it to you from the *Daily News* website," she said. "This story didn't make the print edition."

Alex sat down.

"This is a quote from Mr. White," she said. "Apparently they called him after the conference made it official that you guys won."

"Oh God, what in the world did he say?" Alex said.

She put up her hand to quiet him. "Let me read it: 'I'm very proud of our team for winning this game,' Chester Heights Principal Joseph A. White said. 'But what happened tonight can't be repeated. I was told by Principal Block that the antigay group in attendance has been planning this for the last several weeks and is planning a repeat performance in our gym on Friday. We cannot allow that to happen.'"

"Good for him!" Alex interrupted. "Finally showing some guts!"

"Not exactly. Let me finish."

She went on: "'I've already consulted with our conference commissioner, Alison Telco. She's in agreement that the best thing for everyone involved is for Mr. Bellotti to not play on Friday. This may be a moot point because of his injury, but, either way, we're in agreement that we can't risk another scene like the one that took place at King of Prussia. I feel bad for our players and our coaches, but my first duty as principal is to ensure the safety of *all* our students and staff along with the spectators at our games.'"

Alex was gaping at his mother. He thought she must be kidding, but clearly she wasn't. "So he's saying because these insane people might show up again on Friday that Max shouldn't play? That *he* should be penalized? That *we* should be penalized?"

"That appears to be what he's saying," his mom said. "I knew the man was spineless back in November when he couldn't even look me in the eye after your false-positive on that drug test. But I didn't think he was quite this much of a coward."

That's exactly what he was, Alex thought, a coward. No way would Coach Archer allow this to happen. The question was: could he stop it from happening?

■ ■ ■

Wired as he was, Alex almost fell asleep on the short car ride to school. Adrenaline was fighting with exhaustion. But he snapped awake when he got to the front door. It was blocked by both police officers and security guards.

"I need to see your student ID," one of the cops said to Alex. He noticed other kids showing their IDs too. He was glad he had arrived early and gladder that he actually had his ID card in his backpack. The cop looked at his photo, then at Alex, and smiled.

"Myers," he said. "You're the one who tipped the ball back to the gay kid for the winning shot." He shoved the ID back at Alex and added, "Congratulations."

"His name is Max," Alex said. "Max Bellotti."

"So?" the cop asked.

"So his name isn't 'the gay kid.' It's Max."

The cop's smile disappeared. "Whatever. Keep moving."

Alex found Jonas and Matt waiting inside the front doors. Matt didn't even say hello or comment on the security.

"Max *has* to play," Matt said. "White has to be the biggest idiot on earth. You can't give in to this kind of thing—"

He was about to go on when Christine rushed up, a little breathless. "You've all heard?" she said.

They nodded.

"Max *has* to play," she said. "The school can't just cave like that—"

She was cut off by the five-minute warning bell for first period.

"Let's talk at lunch," Christine said. "I can't believe I've got a math quiz right now!"

They all ran through the crowded hallways to their first-period classes.

■ ■ ■

"I just wish the *Roar* wasn't out today," Christine said when they were all in the cafeteria a few hours later. "If it were coming out tomorrow, we could embarrass Mr. White and the others by writing about what cowards they are."

"What about your friend Stevie Thomas?" Alex asked, suppressing a yawn. "You could contact the TV stations too. Remind them of how White was ready to let me get thrown under the bus in November. . . . Maybe you can stir up trouble for White that way."

"He'll have to back down before the game," Jonas said. "Right?"

"Don't be too sure," Matt said. "Remember, this is basketball, and football's his one true love. Plus, I'll bet there are some parents who would be just as happy if Max didn't play Friday."

"Still, we have to do something," Alex said.

"See what happens at practice today," Matt said. "Maybe Coach Archer has already told White this is unacceptable. We can decide what to do next when we know more."

Alex noticed that Matt was taking charge of the situation even though he wasn't even on the team, but he didn't mind. That was Matt. He was a natural leader.

Alex also thought he was right. They needed to see what Coach Archer had to say. They'd received another text from him after first period that said, *Heading home for some sleep. Max doing fine. No setbacks. Regular time for practice today . . .* But nothing since then.

Alex wondered if he even knew about what Mr. White had said yet. They would find out soon.

They were all dressed and ready to go when Coach Archer

walked in the locker room door just before three-thirty. Alex could tell something was wrong. Then a few seconds later, Mr. White walked in, and Alex knew exactly what was wrong.

"Fellas, grab your chairs and come on up here," Coach Archer said, sounding as if it were a game night—only in a much grimmer tone. They all picked up their chairs and moved to the front of the room. On the grease board Alex could still see the blue "2–0" that Coach Archer had scrawled just before they had left the previous afternoon for King of Prussia. That was the message: their season was down to going 2–0. Now all they needed was 1–0, but the man in the doorway might make that impossible.

"Okay, first things first," Coach Archer said. "That was a *great* win last night. You really pulled together when it counted. No matter what happens from here forward, I'm proud of all of you. I am proud to have coached you. I never could have dreamed a season like this."

His voice caught a little. "Also, Max is home, resting right now." Everyone in the locker room clapped on hearing that news. "He's got no post-concussion symptoms other than a pounding headache. And the guy who threw the baseball is still in jail. They're charging him with aggravated assault. Which is good news too."

Alex had seen that on Twitter earlier. He knew there was a bail hearing set for the next day and that the guy was apparently a member of an antigay group that thought homosexuality was a mortal sin. They'd been the ones who had organized the demonstration the night before. No one seemed to know why he had a baseball.

Coach Archer paused for a moment. "Okay, as you can see, the principal has something he wants to say to you. When he's finished, we'll talk about what comes next."

Alex couldn't help noticing that Coach Archer would only refer to Mr. White as "the principal."

Mr. White stepped forward.

"Let me add my congratulations to all of you," he said, forcing a smile. He looked over at Alex for a second, and Alex simply glared at him. "You've had a great season. We're all very proud of you."

He paused as if expecting applause or some kind of reaction. The room was dead silent.

"I'm afraid, though, that I have to be the bearer of bad news. I'm sure most of you have read about my conversations with Commissioner Telco. She and I have spoken again today, and we are in agreement that it would be dangerous for Mr. Bellotti to play Friday night. I thought you'd want to hear the news officially from your coach, but he seemed to think I should be the one to tell you."

"I wanted them to hear it from the one responsible for the decision," Coach Archer said, causing Mr. White to shoot him a very angry look.

"That's right, Coach. I am responsible. I am responsible for the welfare of this school and of its students. Of course I want to see the team win as much as anyone in this room."

Alex was tempted to shout "Liar!" but resisted.

Mr. White plowed on. "I consulted not only with the commissioner but also with my counterpart at Chester and with law-enforcement officials. Everyone was in agreement that it is simply too dangerous for Mr. Bellotti to play in to-morrow night's game."

He tried to plow on, but he was instantly drowned out by a dozen angry, disbelieving voices.

He held up a hand to ward them off. "Gentlemen, I understand how you feel. And I want you to know that I believe you can beat Chester without Mr. Bellotti, who I'm sure would want you to go out there and give one hundred percent—"

"He's not dead!" Alex yelled. He'd heard enough.

That set off another angry chorus.

"Of course he's not dead, Mr. Myers," White said, through what looked to Alex like gritted teeth. "But it isn't safe for him or for you or for anyone else attending the game for him to play. You saw what happened last night."

"We saw it," Coach Birdy said from the back of the room. "One nut lost his mind. So, make people go through a security check to get in the gym. Keep the nuts away from the game, not Max."

"It's not fair to Max," Jonas said, quickly backed up by other voices.

"You're right, Mr. Ellington," Mr. White said. "It's not fair. Sometimes life is unfair. But Mr. Bellotti made a decision to go public about his lifestyle. There are consequences that inevitably come with a decision like that."

"Like getting hit in the head with a baseball?" Tony Early said, causing everyone in the room to look at him in surprise. "*That's* a fair consequence? That's *inevitable?*"

"Of course not," Mr. White said. "That's not my point."

Steve Holder stood up and walked to the front of the room. At six six, Steve towered over Mr. White. He gave him a look of utter disgust, then turned his back on him to address his teammates. He started to say something, then looked at Coach Archer. "Coach, okay if I say something?"

"You're the captain, Steve," Coach Archer said. "The floor is yours."

Alex saw Mr. White start to say something, then hold it in.

"Guys, I can't speak for all of you, but as your captain, I can tell you what I think is right," Steve said. He turned to Mr. White.

"To me, Mr. White, this is simple," he said. "If Max *can't* play, I *won't* play. One of my teammates was attacked, and you want to toss him off the team because of it? Well, I won't do it."

There was a lot of murmuring then, which gave way to full-throated "That's right"s and "Me neither"s.

Steve nodded. "Okay, let's have a vote. All of those who will *not* play tomorrow without Max, raise your hand."

Every hand in the room went up. Even Wakefield and Early. Coach Archer raised his too. And Coach Birdy.

Coach Archer turned to Mr. White.

"It's unanimous. No Max, no game."

Mr. White glared at him. "I can fire you with cause for this," he said.

"Be my guest," Coach Archer said. "For the record, I think every kid in here will tell you I in no way influenced their decision. But until you *do* fire me, I've got a practice to run."

Mr. White had his arms folded as if he was deciding what to do or say next.

"Your move," Coach Archer said. "We'll be in the gym. Let's go, fellas."

They all followed him out the door.

31

Alex had grabbed his cell phone before walking out the door. As everyone walked or jogged in the direction of the court, he quickly tapped out the text he and Christine had decided would be her signal to swing into action if things weren't looking good: *Alert the media.*

Coach Archer called them together—without a whistle— at midcourt before they began warming up.

"I'm not even sure what to say to all of you about what's going on here," he said. "I love the way you all stood up for Max in there. That was brilliant, Steve. But I don't want it to come to that. I am going to fight to have Max play, assuming he's up to it. We've got two days to get this fixed, and I believe we will, so don't give up hope.

"Meantime, we have to focus on getting ready to play Chester, because if we don't—even with Max—we have no chance of winning the game. You all know how good they are."

They did their best to focus. But it was virtually impossible. Jameer Wilson was playing in Max's spot, and he wasn't close to being the same player. For one thing, even though Jameer was a smart, heady player, he couldn't shoot that well at all. The Lions' offense was predicated on having three players—Alex, Jonas, and Max—who could make outside shots. Taking away one-third of that perimeter offense made them a different team—even when playing against the less-than-great defense of the white team.

At one point, after three straight turnovers, Coach Archer blew his whistle and threw his hands up in frustration. "Fellas, you run the offense like that on Friday, we'll get shut out," he said. "You *must* concentrate right now on making plays. If the shots don't go in, that's fine. But we have to be sure we're going to get good shots against their defense. Remember how they attack the perimeter. We have to be prepared for that."

It got a little better after that—but not much.

Just before five o'clock, Alex noticed Christine walking into the gym accompanied by Stevie Thomas and a man he didn't recognize.

If Coach Archer noticed them, he said nothing. They sat in the bleachers and watched. A few minutes later the door opened again and Dei Lynam of Comcast SportsNet walked in, followed by a man carrying a camera. Dick Jerardi of the *Daily News* was with them. Then came another camera crew. And another.

By 5:20 the gym was filled with media, and almost no

one was paying attention to what they were doing on court. Coach Archer whistled them to the center-court jump circle.

"Someone has apparently let the media know that there's a story here," he said. He looked at Alex. "Any idea who it might be, Myers?"

He didn't wait for an answer, but there was the slightest trace of a smile on his face. "Since you guys aren't paying attention anyway, let's call it a day. I know we're all tired."

"Coach, what do you want us to do about all these media people?" Steve Holder asked.

"Talk to them," Coach Archer said. "Tell them the truth."

"Coach, if they're still saying Max can't play, do we practice tomorrow?"

The question came from Patton Gormley.

"If Max is healthy, he'll practice tomorrow," Coach Archer said. "No one said anything about him not practicing. We're going to prepare as if he, and we, will be playing on Friday, because I believe we will be. Let's get in."

They pulled into a tight huddle with their arms up in the air—Steve Holder, as always, in the middle.

"Max," he said simply. "On three."

Loudly, they counted to three and yelled, "MAX!"

If the assembled media members had any doubt about where the Lions stood on the issue of their absent teammate, it should have been dispelled at that moment.

■ ■ ■

Alex, Jonas, Matt, Christine, and Steve Holder were sitting at their usual table at lunch the next day when they heard a commotion at the door. They all looked up and saw Max

Bellotti—wearing a baseball cap, but still eminently recognizable with his long dirty-blond hair and bright blue eyes—walk into the cafeteria.

At first, as he went to pick up a tray, there were some pats on the back and offers of "Way to go, Max." Then, from somewhere in the room, came clapping. Then there was more of it. Then people began standing at their tables and clapping.

Alex saw a few pockets of kids—notably a table of his football teammates—sitting and staring at their food. By the time Max had walked to the pasta bar, just about everyone else in the room was on their feet.

At first Max tried to pretend not to notice, but it was completely impossible. He turned and waved a hand and kept saying "Thank you" over and over again.

Everyone in the school knew exactly what was going on. The story had been all over TV, the Internet, and the newspapers since the evening before. They had seen Mr. White and Conference Commissioner Alison Telco bleating about "student safety" and that this had nothing to do with Max's sexuality but with, as Telco called it, "our very real fear that another of our student-athletes might be injured the way Mr. Bellotti was on Tuesday. Our first responsibility lies with protecting our student-athletes."

They had been debating who was the bigger jerk—White or Telco—just before Max walked in.

"Anyone uses the term 'student-athlete,' hold on to your wallet," Matt had said. "And if anyone uses it twice, call a cop."

"You don't think she's trying to ensure the conference is

represented in the playoffs by a team that does *not* have a gay player in a key role, do you?" Christine said.

"Whoa," said Alex. "I hadn't thought of it like that."

"I don't know that I'd go that far," Matt said. "I think she's like White—a coward."

"Yeah, but what's White's motivation in all this?" Jonas asked.

Alex shrugged. "I think he just doesn't want a riot in his gym. And this seemed like the easiest way to avoid it."

"So maybe he's happy you're refusing to play without Max," Christine said. "Maybe no game at all is just fine with him."

"You're all being too kind," Holder put in. "I'm betting he's a closet homophobe."

"So, are you saying Mr. White is coming out as a homophobe?" Matt said, laughing.

It was at that moment that Max had walked in.

Now the applause had turned into a chant of "We want Max!" and it was clear it wasn't going to stop until he said something.

He finally put his hand up and asked for quiet. In an instant, the room was almost completely silent.

"I hope you can all hear me," he said. "First, I want to thank everyone for their support the last couple days. I'm not sure how everyone got my cell number, but thanks for all the texts and messages. It means a lot."

"We love you, Max!" someone yelled.

"I love all of you too," he said, blushing. "I want to thank my teammates for backing me. I know you all know what's going on, so I want to tell you—I plan to play tomorrow."

That set off another round of cheering and clapping and stamping of feet.

"But first I want to grab something to eat, because I don't want to be late for fifth period."

There was more applause and more shouts of "Go get 'em, Max!"

And finally, Max—after a couple dozen more pats on the back—was able to sit down.

"How are you feeling?" Christine asked.

"Exhausted—but better," Max said. "The headache's finally gone. I'm still a little sore where the stitches are, but nothing serious."

"Have you talked to Coach Archer?" Matt asked.

Max nodded. "Yeah, my mom and I met with him just now. He told me he and Coach Birdy are submitting a formal protest to the school board, saying that I've basically been suspended without any grounds for suspension."

"That should be a no-brainer, right?" Alex said. "White and Telco can't say that you *should* be suspended. What did you do wrong—get clocked by a baseball?"

"Can the school board overrule a suspension?" Christine asked.

"That's the question," Max said. "Jameer's dad is a lawyer, and he's advising Coach on this. He says the question won't be whether I've done anything to deserve being suspended, but whether the board has the authority to overrule a principal who says he is taking action to protect the school and students—not just me but anyone who comes to the game."

"That's bull," Jonas said.

"Of course it is," Christine said. "But does the school

board have people on it who will get that or who will be happy for an excuse to keep Max from playing?"

"Well, I wouldn't count on Wakefield's father," Alex said.

"He'll probably recuse himself since his son's team is involved," Matt said.

"That might or might not be a break for our side," Christine said. "There are nine people on the board. What happens in the case of a tie?"

"When do they vote?" Steve asked Max.

"Coach Archer isn't sure—about any of it," Max said. "There's no time to get all nine of them together, so they're trying to set up a conference call for tomorrow."

"That's cutting it close," Christine said.

"Very," Max said. He smiled. "But Coach said we're playing and that as far as he's concerned, they'll have to physically remove both of us from the court to keep me from playing."

"You okay with that?" Matt asked.

"Yup," Max answered.

"Well, if they take you off, we'll be leaving with you," Jonas said.

"Thanks, Jonas," Max said. "That means more than you can possibly know. I just hope it won't come to that."

■ ■ ■

Practice was completely closed to outsiders that afternoon. A couple of kids in the school had fathers who were Philadelphia city cops. They had rounded up a half dozen of their friends who were off duty to work the doors and keep media or onlookers out.

The empty gym, along with Max's presence, seemed to

energize the Lions. It occurred to Alex that this could be their last practice of the season. It might have been their best.

Max was as sharp as ever. The spot where his hair had been shaved for the stitches was highly visible, but it didn't seem to bother him. His shots were laser-like, and he didn't seem at all timid about mixing it up on defense or when re-bounding.

His enthusiasm fueled everyone else. There was even a funny moment when Max stole the ball cleanly from Wake-field and went in for a layup. As the ball went through the hoop, Wakefield yelled, "Dammit, Bellotti, can't you feel just a little bit worse?"

Everyone—including Wakefield—cracked up.

At 5:25 Coach Archer gathered his team at the jump circle.

"Okay, fellas, we treat tomorrow like a regular game day. Report here at five o'clock unless you hear different from me. I want you focused on one thing the next twenty-four hours: Chester. We *must* take care of the basketball and make them play half-court. We didn't do that last time.

"Don't worry about anything happening off court. Let me worry about that.

"Everybody understand?"

They did—or at least they said they did.

"What do you think?" Jonas asked Alex as they walked to the locker room.

"I think tomorrow's going to be a long day," Alex said. "A very long day."

32

Alex was out of bed before sunrise and came downstairs to find his mother already at the kitchen counter drinking her coffee.

"Trouble sleeping?" she asked as he poured some orange juice.

"Yeah," he said. "What about you?"

"A little," she admitted. "This is tearing Evan up, as you might imagine. He wants to win the game very badly, but he's also concerned about Max and about his job. No matter what happens today, he thinks Mr. White will fire him when the season's over."

Alex had thought about that. He had come a long way in his feelings about Coach Archer since the end of November. He and his mom hadn't talked much about their relationship the past few weeks, but he sensed it had become more serious. She had stopped asking if he was okay with it. It had just become a given.

He wished the same was true of his relationship with Christine. Things had been so hectic that they'd only been out once in February—another Saturday-afternoon movie, followed by another quick, but very encouraging, kiss on the lips. He guessed they were dating. She wasn't *not* his girlfriend. . . .

It was his dad he was really frustrated about. He had called a few times since the King of Prussia game and seemed genuinely concerned about what was going on. But he never even brought up the possibility of coming to the game, and Alex didn't ask him about it. There was no point. He and Molly were supposed to go back to Boston at spring break. Molly didn't want to go. Alex didn't blame her.

Alex never would have thought for a second that he'd end up having more faith in Coach Archer than he did in his dad, but at the moment it wasn't even close.

Coach Archer had proven to be a good basketball coach once he had gotten past his anti-football bias. And he had handled the situation with Max about as well as anyone could have asked. For him to be fired would be massively unfair. It would also probably mean he'd leave town in search of another job, which Alex knew would make his mom sad.

He sat down at the table and looked at his mother. "Remember what you told me when we were dealing with the switched blood samples back in the fall?" he said. "You said, 'Alex, it's going to work out because the truth is always an absolute defense.' Well, in this case it's going to work out because being *right* is an absolute defense. Coach Archer's doing the right thing."

His mom smiled. "Thanks. I hope that's true." She took

a long sip of her coffee, then asked, "What would you think about playing the game with no one in the gym? Just players, coaches, and officials?"

Alex made a face.

"Yeah," his mom sighed. "Evan didn't think it was a good idea either. He said it wasn't fair to either team, or to Max, really. He thinks the school board just needs to get this right and let Max play."

"He's right," Alex said.

"I know," she said. She stood up, kissed him on the forehead, and said, "I'll make some pancakes."

That sounded good to Alex.

■ ■ ■

In fact, the pancakes were the highlight of the morning. By noon, word had spread that the school board had scheduled a conference call for five o'clock. That was the earliest time all nine members were free. Some were traveling. Others had work commitments.

That meant the players would have to report to the gym and hope for good news before tip-off at seven.

According to the media, a number of Philadelphia's local gay and lesbian groups were planning to show up outside the gym to protest Max not being allowed to play. The antigay group from the last game hadn't said what their plans were, but everyone assumed they'd be at the school in force as well.

The man who had thrown the baseball, Glenn Greene, had been released on bond that morning after being formally charged with aggravated assault. His statement as he left the courthouse was up on YouTube by lunchtime: "First Jason

Collins. Then Michael Sam. After that, a college basketball player. Now a high school kid. Our society is in free fall. Someone has to stand up to the gay rights bullies."

It was such twisted logic that Alex found it hard to believe he was serious, but clearly he was—and he wasn't alone.

Greene had issued a nonapology apology for what had happened.

"I'm glad he wasn't hurt badly," Greene had said. "I thought his actions were obnoxious, just what you might expect from one of them. But if I had it to do over again, I would simply stand up and say, 'Sinner, repent.'"

"Unbelievable," Matt said at lunch.

"I guess we're lucky no one was carrying a gun," Christine said.

It was that specter that had caused both schools and the conference to agree to pay for full-on, airport-like security. Even the players had to have their bags checked when they arrived and had to be wanded.

Max had picked up Alex and Jonas at their houses, so the three of them walked in together. Alex couldn't help pointing out the irony that the security people were wanding the person who might be the target of the nuts they were supposed to be on the lookout for. The security person wasn't amused.

"Just doing what we were told to do," he said. "Don't need any lip from any of you."

Alex was about to respond when Jonas grabbed his arm and put a finger to his lips. Alex knew he was right. There were a lot more important things to worry about right now.

The locker room was quiet, none of the usual banter or

joking around. Alex asked Zane Wakefield if he had any idea about what his father was going to do. Wakefield groaned. "He thinks he has to recuse himself because I'm involved in the game," he said. "I told him he should do the right thing and let Max play.

"He said I was being selfish," Wakefield added, "that I just wanted to win the game. And I said . . ." He paused for a moment, taking a deep breath. "I said that of course I wanted to win the game, but that I cared more about being fair to a guy I've come to respect."

Alex patted him on the shoulder. Who would have thought there would come a time when he felt sorry for Zane Wakefield—let alone almost liked him.

Shortly before five-thirty Coach Archer walked in. They all looked up hopefully, but he had no news. Which was bad news.

"Apparently they're just now starting the call," he said. "Someone's plane was late. If I didn't know better, I'd think they were stalling."

"Now that they've got all this security, where's the danger in letting Max play?" Steve Holder asked.

"I asked Mr. White that a few minutes ago," Coach Archer said. "He said that just because someone doesn't have a weapon doesn't mean there won't be a riot. I pointed out that with five hundred people outside demanding that Max play, there might be a riot if he *doesn't*."

But Alex knew there were anti-Max people outside too. His mom had texted him as she was walking in.

"I know I'm asking the impossible," Coach Archer continued. "But let's try to go through our normal pregame. Get your ankles taped. Relax a few minutes; we'll go out at about 6:15 to warm up."

They did the best they could. When they came up the steps to the gym, they could see it was already almost full. There didn't appear to be any specific factions anywhere—signs had been banned, apparently—but there were very loud cheers when people spotted Max in uniform, and some loud boos.

There were security people posted all around the court and behind both benches. Alex was reminded of the movie *The Longest Yard*, about a football game between prison guards and convicts. The atmosphere felt a little like that. Except, as far as he knew, no one on either side had committed a crime.

It felt good to be moving—going through their usual warm-up drills. Alex noticed that several of the Chester players made a point of walking over to Max to shake hands and ask how he was feeling. Each time, the building rocked with cheers—and some boos.

At 6:45, as always, they headed back to the locker room to relax—ha!—and get their last-minute instructions.

Coach Archer was pacing—the way he always did—when they piled into the locker room. No one even had to ask the question.

"Still no word," he said.

He pointed at the grease board, where he always wrote down the starting lineups for both teams and then went over matchups. He always did the guards first, the center next, and the two forwards—Max and Patton Gormley—last.

When he got to Max, whose name was written in its usual spot, he said pointedly, "Waxman is their weakest defensive player, Max. We're going to come to you early, so be ready." He paused and smiled. "It also won't hurt with the crowd if you nail a shot or two right away. . . ."

He was about to go on when Alex heard Zane Wakefield swear very clearly and loudly. They all stared.

He held up his phone. "My dad just texted," he said. "He recused himself, and the vote was four to four. Which means they're not going to let Max play."

There was dead silence in the room. Coach Archer stared straight ahead for a moment, then turned back to the board.

"If they start to double you, Max, make sure you don't pick up your dribble too soon."

Alex knew what he was doing: sticking to his commitment to play Max until someone stopped him from doing it.

There was a knock on the door. Alex glanced at the digital clock in the corner that showed how much time was left until tip-off. It said 10:44. They always left the locker room with five minutes left. Coach Archer ignored the knock and was about to start talking again when the door swung open. Mr. White was standing there with Alison Telco and three security guards.

"The vote is in," White said. "Our ruling has been upheld. Mr. Bellotti, I'm here to inform you that you cannot play in this game. These gentlemen"—he nodded at the security guards—"will get you safely out of the building once you've changed into your street clothes."

He looked at the players. "Boys, I'm truly sorry about this."

"No you're not!" Alex blurted.

He stood up and took a step in White's direction, although he had no idea what he was going to do if he got to him. A security guard stepped in front of Mr. White.

"Alex," Coach Archer said. "Sit down. Let me handle this."

Steve Holder said, "No, Coach, let us." He looked around at his teammates. "Anyone in here going to take the court without Max?"

Dead silence.

"You might need more security guards, Mr. White," Steve said. "Because if Max has to leave, we're all leaving."

Mr. White's face turned an alarming shade of red. "Don't be ridiculous. The gym is full, your opponents are here, and your season's on the line. You *will* play."

He pointed at Coach Archer. "If your team isn't on the court before the anthem, you're fired."

"That's fine," Coach Archer said. "But this is still my locker room for, I'd say, seven more minutes. Leave now—all of you—and let me talk to my team."

When the door closed a moment later, Max stood up.

"Guys, listen," he said. "I appreciate all of you doing this for me—so much—but you gotta play the game. We can't let Coach Archer get fired over this. And I honestly believe you *can* win without me."

"Max, sit down," Steve Holder said, standing up. "We all know you're doing the honorable thing here. But we're *not* going out there without you. Not because we don't think we can win, but because it would feel unbelievably empty to win without you. Anyone disagree?"

Alex looked around. No one was saying a word, but every player was nodding. Except someone was missing. Zane Wakefield had disappeared. He must have slipped out when White and the guards had gone.

"Excuse me, Steve, Coach," Alex said. "Anyone know where Wakefield went?"

"I'm right here," Wakefield said, walking back toward them.

"Interesting time for a bathroom break, Wakefield," Coach Archer said, almost smiling.

Unbelievable, Alex thought. At the most critical moment of the season, perhaps of their lives—

"I didn't go to the bathroom, Coach," Wakefield said. "I went out the back door for a minute to call my father."

They all got very quiet very quickly.

"I told him if he didn't cast a vote, we were forfeiting the game.

"And then I asked him how he would feel if it was *me* they were doing this to. Would he tolerate that for even one second?"

They all stared at him, waiting for him to finish the story.

His phone buzzed. Wakefield looked down at the screen and smiled.

"They just recounted the votes," he said, his voice cracking. "It's five to four. Max plays."

They were all on their feet screaming. Half the guys were pounding Max, the other half Wakefield. Over the din, Alex finally heard Coach Archer's voice. They turned to him.

"Fellas," he said, a huge smile on his face. "We need to save some energy. We've got a game to play."

■ ■ ■

Two minutes later—with the clock under four minutes, not that anyone really cared—they charged out of the locker room. Word had clearly reached Mr. White and company, because no one got in their way as they surged up the steps to the gym. When they got to the top of the stairs, Steve Holder, who was normally the first one out on the court, stopped.

"Wait, wait," he said. "Max. How about you lead us onto the court?"

Max never had a chance to respond, because they were all pushing him to the front.

"Everyone ready?" Holder said. God, were they ready. "Go, Max!"

And so Max charged onto the court, followed by his teammates, as most of the building went crazy. Alex saw the Chester players, who were going through their final warm-ups, turn around when they heard the cheers. Almost all of them were smiling. Their coach, Robert Sprau, started yelling for them to turn around and focus on what they were doing.

Chester had dominated the first game, in part because Alex couldn't handle point guard Avery Jackson but also because Max had been way off his game. Now, just as Coach Archer had hoped, Max came out *flying*.

He made his first three shots—all from beyond the three-point line—and the Lions jumped to a quick 14–5 lead. Alex came in for Wakefield—they exchanged high fives for the first time all season—when it was already 8–3, and the lead kept building. By the end of the first quarter, it was 25–14, and Alex was starting to think all the pent-up emotions they'd had before the game were going to carry them to an easy win.

Of course it couldn't possibly be that easy. In the second quarter, Jackson began to use his strength to get inside on

Alex, and shooting guard Mike Tuller got hot too, just as Max was cooling off a bit. At halftime, it was 41–40, with Chester Heights clinging to a one-point lead.

"If I'd told you an hour ago we'd be in here leading by one at half, would you have been okay with that?" Coach Archer said. "This is just the kind of game we expected. You don't stumble into a championship—you have to go out and win it. You can see the game is there for you, right?"

They all nodded, sitting on the edge of their chairs, still pumping all sorts of adrenaline. "Okay, we're going to start the second half in zone, in part to give Alex some more help on Jackson but also because we've got some foul trouble. Max, Jonas, Steve, you've got two apiece. I may spell you here in the third quarter some to make sure you're fresh and okay with fouls for the fourth.

"Everybody okay?"

They all nodded, ready to run back to the court even though they still had ten minutes left before the second half started. Alex felt as if his heart were about to burst out of his chest.

The zone helped as the second half began. Playing a full step back from Jackson, daring him to shoot threes—not his strength—Alex was able to force him to give the ball up sooner than he would have wanted. But Jackson was smart, and found Tuller in the creases for open shots. What's more, as often happened when a defense played zone, the Clippers began to get offensive rebounds.

The lead seesawed. Chester Heights still led by one, 60–59 after three quarters, and neither team was able to build more than a three-point lead at any time. As promised, Coach Archer had used the bench in the third quarter, getting minutes for Jameer Wilson and Cory McAndrews and even for Wakefield and Early. Even so, Alex could feel himself flagging as the game wound down, still running on adrenaline but tired by the pace and intensity of the evening.

With 1:09 left, Tuller shot-faked Jonas, got him in the air, and jumped into him, creating contact. It didn't matter who had created the contact—since Jonas had been faked off his feet, the foul was on him. The crowd groaned. It was Jonas's fifth, meaning that Wilson had to come in for him. Tuller, who already had twenty-seven points, added two more from the line, and Chester led, 79–76.

Things were getting desperate. Coach Archer called time.

"Jameer, we need you to be a screener—a solid one," he said, looking at Wilson. "Max, you gotta be a decoy here; they're going to load the defense to your side because they know Jameer's not a shooter." Max and Jameer both nodded.

"Alex, you have to make this play happen. If Jackson plays off you and you feel it, you can take a three. My guess is, up three, they're going to attack the line. You need to get in the lane and find Steve or Patton. One of them's going to be open." He looked at Gormley. "Patton, if it were me on defense, being honest, I'd guard Steve like crazy and see if you can make a shot. You ready?"

Gormley looked him right in the eye. "You bet, Coach," he said.

They came out of the huddle with everyone in the place on their feet. If they didn't score on this possession, they would be forced to foul right away, and Chester was the best foul-shooting team in the conference. Alex couldn't remember anyone missing for them all night.

He took a deep breath and looked over to the bench at Jonas, who was on his feet trying to encourage everyone. The regular bench guys—McAndrews, Wakefield, Early, Taylor, Ceplair, and Bogus—were on their feet too. They'd come so far, Alex thought. Did it really end here?

He took the inbounds and came upcourt, trying to appear calm even though he was anything but. Jackson was up on him as soon as he crossed midcourt, daring him to drive. There would be no open three here. He paused, backed up his dribble to reset himself, and checked his teammates. Sure enough, one of the Chester forwards was hedging toward Max to double if Alex even thought about going to him.

Wilson came up to the right of the key and set a hard screen to give Alex some space. He cut around it and, as he got into the lane, saw Anton Bennett, one of the Clippers' forwards, coming at him. He took a hard dribble right at Bennett, then flipped the ball to Gormley, who was wide open on the baseline, about eight feet from the basket. Gormley caught the ball, took one dribble, and went in for a layup— daring someone to risk a foul trying to stop him. No one did. The ball banked home with forty-eight seconds to play. Chester's lead was 79–78.

The Lions only had one time-out left, and Coach Archer didn't want to use it. Coach Sprau didn't want to call time to let Chester Heights set up its press, so he didn't call time either. The ball came in quickly to Jackson, and he charged across midcourt, then backed up and held up a fist. Alex was pretty sure that was the signal for their delay game. There was no shot clock. They would need a steal, or they would have to foul.

"Patience!" he heard Coach Archer yell. "Trap under 30—under 30!"

That meant they were about to double-team every pass, going for a steal. If the clock got to ten seconds, they would foul whoever had the ball. Jackson dribbled forward, and Wilson jumped out to trap. Jackson quickly flicked the ball to Tuller. Now it was Max and Patton trying to trap. Tuller quickly found Bennett wide open inside. But with twenty seconds left, Bennett passed up the layup and flipped the ball back outside to Jackson. The clock ticked under fifteen.

Alex had an idea. It was clear to him that Bennett wasn't going to shoot even if everyone left the gym, meaning there was no reason to even guard him. So as soon as he and Wilson started to trap Jackson again, Alex turned and—hoping he was guessing right—lunged in Tuller's direction. Sure enough, he saw the ball reaching Tuller just as he, Max, and Patton got there. Tuller was triple-teamed. He started to pick the ball up to pass it, but Max slapped at it and got the ball cleanly. It was on the floor with at least six bodies diving at it.

Alex knew the possession arrow favored Chester. A tie-up would just give them the ball back. That wasn't good enough. He saw the ball in front of him in the scrum and pushed at it, trying to make sure it stayed alive. Alex saw Max dive on it and he instantly screamed, "TIME-OUT!"

At the same moment that he heard the official call, "Time-out, white!" he heard Max let out a scream too. He looked and saw Max writhing on the floor, holding his right ankle with one hand, still clutching the ball with the other, but clearly in pain. He went to see what was wrong. J. J. Crowder, the trainer, was right behind him, growling, "Myers, get out of the way!"

"What happened?" J. J. asked Max.

"Someone stepped on my ankle," Max said.

"It was me," Gormley said, standing right behind them. "I felt it. God, Max, I'm sorry."

Max waved him off, his face a little bit white. "Accident, don't worry."

Jackson and Tuller were both standing there.

"He okay?" Jackson asked.

Before Alex could answer, he heard Coach Sprau's voice: "Jackson, Tuller, over here—*now!*"

They both turned and jogged to their bench.

Coach Archer was on the floor too, kneeling over Max. He looked down at him.

"I think he just rolled it," J. J. said, still applying pressure to different spots on Max's ankle. "He'll be fine in a couple days, but now . . ." He shook his head.

"Let me try it," Max said. "You gotta let me try."

Taylor and Ceplair came out to help Max up. As soon as he tried to put weight on the ankle, he screamed in pain. Coach Archer put a hand gently on his shoulder. "Max, you've done everything you can."

Max looked like he might cry, but there was no arguing.

The referee came over. "Coach, I'm starting the time-out

clock as soon as your injured player's off the court. You've got the usual sixty seconds."

Coach Archer nodded. He turned to the bench and pointed at Zane Wakefield, who looked more scared than a deer caught in headlights.

"Zane, go for Max," he said.

For a split second Alex thought Wakefield might try to talk Coach Archer out of it. But he nodded and reported to the scorer's table. He came back to the huddle, still looking terrified. Coach Archer's voice, even shouting over the noise, was completely calm.

"Okay, fellas, this is what we practice all the time, right? We've got nine seconds—almost exactly the same time as the King of Prussia game. We don't have Max to make the shot, though, do we? It's okay, though, because we've got a point guard who is going to do what he just did a minute ago—get in the lane and create. Alex, Jackson will be on you again because you're the only outside shooter we've got in the game right now. Understand?"

Alex nodded.

"No one's a screener on this play," he continued. "Let Alex get in the lane, and all of you look for open space. Steve, get near the basket for a rebound. Patton, you too. Jameer, Zane, if the ball comes to you, make a quick decision. If someone's coming at you, find one of your teammates. If not . . ."—he stopped for a second and then smiled—"make the shot."

He looked around the huddle. "Any questions?"

It didn't matter if there were any, because the horn had sounded and the referee was herding them back onto the court.

As Alex walked away, Coach Archer said, "Alex, don't be afraid to take it yourself if it's there."

Alex nodded and waited for Holder to inbound to him. He caught the ball at the top of his own key and quickly came upcourt. Jackson was giving him a little space to make it tough for him to drive. Alex saw him glance over his shoulder, looking for a screener.

As he neared the top of the key, Alex hesitated, as if waiting for a screener. He saw the clock tick to five seconds and knew he had to make a move. He drove the ball straight at Jackson, who backpedaled to stay in front of him. He saw Tuller, who was guarding Wakefield, coming to double him. Holder and Gormley, both inside the key, and Wilson in the corner were all guarded.

Alex had two choices. He could go all the way to the basket, knowing he almost certainly wouldn't get a good shot but might get fouled . . . or he could flick the ball to his left, where Wakefield was wide open at the three-point line left of the key. Something in the back of his mind was telling him he had to make the play himself. But there was another voice back there saying they'd never call a foul in this situation.

Just as Tuller reached him, he took one last dribble into traffic, then flicked the ball to Wakefield. For a split second it looked as if Wakefield wasn't even going to catch the ball, but it hit him right in his hands.

"SHOOT!" Alex screamed, because he knew there couldn't be more than a second left.

Wakefield went up to shoot, and no one from Chester even moved in his direction. Wakefield always shot the ball high, and now the ball hung in the air as if it were going to bring rain.

But then, just when he thought it would never come down, Alex saw it splash through the basket—not even touching the rim. The buzzer went off, and Alex could see Wakefield standing there, staring in disbelief at what he'd done.

They all charged Wakefield, mobbing him, while the referees went to make it official that the shot had counted. There was no doubt that it was good. Coach Sprau, Alex could see, was already walking toward Coach Archer, hand out, offering congratulations. The Chester players were in a state of shock.

They all waited for a moment until they saw the official's arms go up in the touchdown signal, indicating the shot had counted. Chester Heights had won the game, 81–79, and had also won the conference title. Wakefield was engulfed again.

"Max!" he screamed as they tried to pick him up on their shoulders. "Not me—Max!"

They all headed for Max, who looked absolutely terrified.

"No," he said, laughing and crying at once. "It was Zane who saved the day—twice!"

Alex felt Wakefield push his way past him to get to Max.

"No, Max, you saved the season," he said, throwing his arms around him, while J. J. tried to make sure his injured player didn't lose his balance.

Alex could see that Max had tears in his eyes. So did Zane.

Then the rest of the team picked them both up on their shoulders for a victory ride around the gym.

■ ■ ■

Just as they put Max and Zane down, Alex saw Christine pushing through the crowd to reach him. So he picked *her* up, whirling her around in a circle, kissing her without even thinking about it. Then he thought about it and kissed her again—and she kissed him back!

Alex put her down and spotted his mom over her shoulder. She was standing arm in arm with Coach Archer, and they were both beaming with joy and pride.

His mom pointed at Christine and gave him a thumbs-up, which made him blush and grin and roll his eyes, all at the same time.

He took Christine's hand, and they plunged back into the crowd, searching for Max and Jonas and anyone else they should hug.

This, Alex thought, is about as good as life gets.